"Gosh, you're so easy to talk to," she said. "Why are you so easy to talk to? It's probably because you're a temp."

He snorted a laugh as he headed for the loaded rack. "A temp?" *Really?*

"Yeah. You're only here till the wedding, right?" Her eyes sparkled with amusement...and something else. Maybe a question? "And then you'll hop on that Harley and off you'll go. North to Alaska. Right?"

He shoved his hands in his front pockets and shrugged. "That's the plan." At least, it had been. He was starting to rethink it.

"So maybe that's why—"

She paused so long, he glanced at her and said, "What?"

"I don't know. I just feel...free with you now. No expectations. No worries about the future. Just two people hanging out together, enjoying each other's company for a moment, just..." She trailed off and something in her expression shifted. It was a softness, a wanting, a hunger in her eyes that something inside him recognized, because he'd been aching for it too. The energy in the small fragrant room changed, warmed, sending a sizzle through him. The hairs on his neck prickled...

Dear Reader,

One of my favorite things as an author is doing research for my books. I'm a nerd like that. Years ago, while researching for a book I was writing about navy SEALs, I read about another elite military force: the Air Force Pararescue jumpers, or PJs. These incredibly brave and talented folks literally leap into the jaws of danger... *That Others May Live*. Their exploits include parachuting into active combat zones, water rescues, advanced life-saving medical intervention and so much more.

What a great idea for a hero! I thought, and I filed the idea away, as I often do.

It wasn't until I was writing the proposal for The Tuttle Sisters of Coho Cove that the idea resurfaced. At the time, I was thinking about Amy—a military widow with two small boys. I knew she would need someone really special to help her heal from a tragic loss that had caused her to isolate herself behind nearly insurmountable emotional walls. But who?

While I was cogitating on this, I met a woman at a dog park and we started to chat. She told me her husband was a former PJ and I lit up like a Christmas tree, wanting to know more. Her husband had actually written a book about his adventures, so naturally (research nerd!), I got the book for myself (and a copy for my dad). *Never Quit* by Jimmy Settle and Don Reardon was a fascinating read, during which I decided that Amy's hero had to be a PJ.

While I knew PJ Noah would be a perfect match for Amy, I didn't realize, until I was deep into the narration of the book, that Amy and her two fatherless boys would be able to save and heal Noah as well. But that's what love does, I suppose. It fills in all the little nooks and crannies of our sou̶l̶s̶ ̶t̶h̶at feel empty and heals the wounds of the past.

̶ ̶l̶ love saves us all, if we let it.

The Airman's Homecoming

SABRINA YORK

HARLEQUIN®

SPECIAL EDITION™

ISBN-13: 978-1-335-59445-7

The Airman's Homecoming

For questions and comments about the quality of this book, pleas~ contact us at CustomerService@Harlequin.com.

Recycling programs for this product may not exist in your area.

Enterprises ULC
St. West, 41st Floor
~io M5H 4E3, Canada
~com

Sabrina York is the *New York Times* and *USA TODAY* bestselling author of hot, humorous romance. She loves to explore contemporary, historical and paranormal genres, and her books range from sweet and sexy to scorching romance. Her awards include the 2018 HOLT Medallion and the National Excellence in Romantic Fiction Award, and she was also a 2017 RITA® Award nominee for Historical Romance. She lives in the Pacific Northwest with her husband of thirty-plus years and a very drooly rottweiler.

Visit her website at sabrinayork.com to check out her books, excerpts and contests.

Books by Sabrina York

Harlequin Special Edition

The Tuttle Sisters of Coho Cove
The Soldier's Refuge

The Stirling Ranch

Accidental Homecoming
Recipe for a Homecoming
The Marine's Reluctant Return

Visit the Author Profile page
at Harlequin.com for more titles.

This book is dedicated to Gaele Hi,
reader, reviewer, friend and more.
Darling, you are indeed, and you will be missed.

Well, it just wasn't how she'd thought her life would play out.

No. George had factored into all her dreams back then, but now in his place was a dark and gaping hole she had no idea how to fill. She was living their dream... without him.

Maybe that old grief was the cause of this melancholy. It rose up sometimes, even now, years after—

Her heart hitched as she realized, remembered that the anniversary of her husband's death was looming, yet again. This one would be four years. Four years as a widow and single mother. Four years alone. Longer than they'd been married. The thought was a gut punch.

Well, Amy Tuttle Tolliver was a survivor and melancholy didn't suit her, so she straightened her spine and sucked in a deep breath and blew it out, trying to get the wayward bangs out of her face in a loud sigh that sometimes amused her two little boys. She smiled as the thought of their giggles and mimicry of her heavy sighs brought a bit of lightness to her heart.

Yeah, losing the love of your life at the tender age of twenty-one was the worst, but George had left her with a treasure in the form of his namesake, George Patton Tolliver II—Georgie for short—and his younger brother, John J. So, as lonely as she felt sometimes, there were gifts for which she could be grateful.

Her own mother had dedicated herself to her children, and all Amy wanted was to do the same. But sometimes, all that responsibility was simply...well, exhausting.

The deep bass thrum of an engine—unmistakably a Harley—resonated from the road and snatched her from

Chapter One

It was almost closing time.

Amy Tolliver gusted a sigh of relief, followed quickly by a slither of unease. Was it a terrible thing that her glorious dream of owning her own bakery was sometimes...boring?

Monotony wasn't all that terrible. It meant, at the very least, that terrible things weren't happening.

She sighed again, but this one was more a sigh of resignation. Things were good. Not exciting, certainly not exhilarating—the way life had been when she and George had been young and in love and planning their future—but good. The bakery was a grind—no pun intended—but a success. Amy was able to take care of her sons and put food on the table. She had friends and family nearby and lived in a beautiful coastal town with fantastic pine forests and hiking trails you could lose yourself on (although thankfully, she never had). It just...

her reverie. She glanced up from her cleaning, perhaps a little wistfully, to catch a glimpse of freedom and adventure. Ah. It was a beautiful touring bike, splattered with mud from other places, driven by a large, muscular man in full leathers. And…it zoomed right by. It was a little sad hearing the roar of that powerful engine peter away to nothing.

It was summer now, and the little coastal town of Coho Cove was bursting at the seams with tourists. It was great for business—Amy made the lion's share of her profits during the summer months. And while it brought in interesting new faces—and their money—occasionally there was this longing too. The tourists came and went, and Amy stayed.

She glanced at the clock again and made a face. It was two minutes to three. Not time yet to flip the sign and lock the door. She'd already finished today's cleaning—even the bag of flour her assistant had spilled before Amy had sent her home early. Lately, Eloise had been all thumbs and highly distracted, but with Eloise out of the way, Amy had already finished tomorrow's prep and the end of day cleaning as well. She was itching to get out of here and go pick up the boys from the sitter, but the sign on the door said they closed at three, and she refused to flip the sign a second earlier.

Her heart lifted when she caught the sound of the Harley again. She didn't know why, and she didn't care. It was a tiny thing to get excited about, but when your life was small, tiny things became that much larger. So, when the bike slowed and pulled into a parking spot in front of her store, a little thrill shot through her.

Steelhead Drive was Coho Cove's answer to Rodeo

Drive in Beverly Hills, just without all the swagger. There were lots of trendy shops and restaurants in what the town council and chamber of commerce had designed into something of a retail district, mostly to attract tourists. It was likely that this adventurer from parts unknown had something a little more sophisticated than baked goods on his mind this late in the afternoon. A fine whiskey at Bootleggers, perhaps, or maybe a visit to Angel's art gallery a few doors down. So, she was well and truly stunned when he took off his helmet, levered his long body from the saddle of his ride and sauntered toward her door. There was confidence in his stride, despite that hint of a limp.

Indeed, her breath caught at the sight of him; some unfamiliar energy swirled in her belly.

He made a fine figure, dressed in black, all muscled and tight, Oakley glasses and heavy boots. He was tall—very tall—and broad and powerful. The military élan, surrounding him like a cloud, was palpable. As an Army brat and former military wife, she could smell it on him. This man was a warrior, plain and simple.

Also, he was hot.

Any woman would notice. Of course she would. Any woman would feel this rush of blood and heat in her veins. And Amy wasn't immune.

Her pulse thudded as he came through the door and smiled, a crooked lift of his lips. And goodness gracious, they were beautiful lips. Well-formed and full. They looked soft and inviting. She nearly swooned—and she was hardly the swooning type. His smile widened a little, and a dimple winked, causing a sizzle to dance through her. She'd always been a sucker for a dimple.

"Afternoon." His voice was low timbered and velvety; it made her shiver.

"Hey." Yeah. Pretty much all she could manage. He kind of stole her ability to think.

"You still open?"

"Uh-huh."

She couldn't see all of his face—because of the glasses—but what she could see was unadulterated male beauty. His neck was muscled and tanned and braided with veins. The amber spatter of day beard on his hard-cut chin made her mouth water. Above the V of his black T-shirt, the hint of a tattoo peeped out. The tip of a tiger's tail, perhaps?

Oh, but all that was nothing compared to the impact his pale blue eyes had on her when he pulled off those glasses and her gaze met his. It crashed into her like a rogue wave, sending her spinning.

Lord have mercy.

He chuckled, as though something had amused him. She had no idea what it was—because as hot as he was, he was probably used to women drooling and stuttering around him—but it irritated her enough, his amusement, to snap her out of the hot-guy stupor.

She'd seen hot guys before. Hell, she'd married one.

"'Cause it's almost three." He thrust a thumb at the door. "Sign says you close at three."

She tipped up her chin and cleared her throat. "Well, it's your lucky day. What would you like?"

Oh, hell. Wrong question.

His expression shifted into something sultry, something naughty. His smile widened. A glint in his eye danced.

A warm slurry swirled in her gut. What was he thinking? Surely not something sexual. Surely not. She was sweaty and work worn and probably looked like a wet dishrag after a long day in a hot kitchen.

Unfortunately, her thoughts about his thoughts ignited a fire in her bloodstream, and heat rose within her, crawling all the way up to her cheeks. She'd always hated that she flushed so easily, but never more so than now.

Thankfully, he didn't comment on her blush, other than a ghost of a smile. He glanced at the near-empty pastry cases, and his smile dimmed. For some reason, she felt it to her core, like the dimming of the sun. He put out a lip; it should be illegal for a man that gorgeous to pout. "Shoot," he said. "I was kind of hoping for an apple fritter."

She nodded. "Let me check in the back." She knew perfectly well she had two fritters left. She'd already bagged them up, along with a leftover croissant and a maple bear claw to give to her friend Jax because he would eat anything she offered, even leftovers. Aside from that, Amy didn't like serving day-olds and she deplored waste.

When she came back into the shop with the bagged fritters, the hottie was studying the pictures on her walls, all neatly framed shots she'd taken of celebrated European tourist destinations. She'd wanted her bakery to have a Continental elegance, and when she'd been decorating, she'd thought the black and white pictures from France and Italy and Germany carried the kind of cache she wanted for an upscale patisserie. Well, as upscale as things got in Coho Cove at least. They marched along the walls above the white wainscoting in color-matched frames, and every time she looked at them, she got a warm sense of satisfaction with a whiff of nostalgia. From the scrollwork on the parlor tables to the bright pink striping on the walls, she loved the way her bakery had turned out.

The tall, dark and handsome stranger—with the very fine butt, by the way—shot her a grin. Did he have any idea how lethal that grin was? "These shots are really stunning," he said.

"Thanks. I used to be a photographer." Used to be a lot of things, really.

His eyes widened. "You took them?"

"Mmm-hmm." She glanced at the collection of memories. Munich's Marienplatz, the Trocadéro in Paris, the Florentine boar… She flashed him something akin to a smile. "I was in junior high school when I took these."

He arched a brow. "That's a lot of travel for a teenager."

She tipped her head to the side and studied him. He was so stunning physically, it was hard to see past that, but it seemed as though he was sincerely interested, so she said the one thing that she knew would explain it all to him. "Army brat."

His expression changed, just ever so. Softened a little, maybe, because they had something in common now. Other than a deep love for apple fritters.

"When my dad was stationed in Pattonville," she added, "we did a lot of traveling."

"Ah." He nodded. "Stuttgart."

Yeah. If she hadn't already known he was military, that sealed it. A civilian probably wouldn't know the name of that small station on the outskirts of the city; it wasn't a commonly recognized base. She eyed him up and down and then asked, "Navy?" He looked like a SEAL. He just had that Special Forces, elite-warrior vibe.

"Air Force." And yeah, he said it with pride. They all did.

She made a little bow. "Thank you for your service." It was a playful offering, in a way. But also, not so playful. She knew the sacrifices military men and women—and their families—made for their country. She'd lived it. She'd lost a husband to it. It deserved acknowledgment.

"Thank you." He put his palm on his chest in a gesture of appreciation, but all it did was make her notice how long and slender and perfect his fingers were. Which made the sizzle start again. Which made her start feeling awkward again. She wasn't used to feeling tongue-tied and shy around men, and she didn't like it.

So, she held the two pastry bags aloft and waggled them as totally confident women of the world did. "I found *two* fritters." She handed them over and totally ignored it when their skin brushed, even though electricity shot through her. "No charge. Closing-time special." Not because he was super cute and imbued with that military vibe she found so attractive, but for Dad and George and all the other soldiers who never came back to eat apple fritters and hug their sons and daughters again.

"Are you sure?" The gratitude in his gaze made her feel all warm and squishy. "That's awfully generous."

She forced a grin. "It's after three. I'm allowed to be generous."

"Well, much appreciated." He chuckled, and she tried to ignore his irritating dimple.

"Sure thing."

And then he turned to leave. She had no idea why panic flared in her, why she wanted so desperately to say something to make him stay. Pity she couldn't think of a damn thing. Even though it had been a little awkward and very short, she'd enjoyed chatting with him. Not just because he was beautiful to look at, but because, for the first time since George, she'd *felt* something for a man. Felt something like *that*.

Excitement, attraction, interest. Desire.

How sad to be reminded that such feelings existed, especially by a tourist…who would walk away.

But he didn't walk away. He paused at the door, and her mouth went dry. When he turned back, her heart kicked up and started thudding. She knew she was mooning, and worse, she figured he probably did too, but she didn't care. All she wanted was a little bit more of him. Just a little bit more.

"Say, would you be able to recommend a good restaurant around here?"

Her pulse surged. Was he trying to draw out this interaction too? Or was he just hungry?

Did it matter?

"Depends," she said in what she hoped wasn't a too-flirty tone. "What do you like?"

Ohh. *That* expression again. Sexy and amused and a little lurid. They were talking about food, right?

"I mean, Smokey's has great ribs but no ambiance unless you really like sticky tables. Bootleggers is more high end. Kind of a steak-frites-and-whiskey vibe. They're both that way, just down the street." She waved in that direction. "Then the other way, down by the marina, there's the Salmon Shack and a fish-and-chips place on the dock... Lots of options. Where are you staying?"

Well, crap. She hadn't meant to ask that. Not out loud.

His grin widened. "Not sure yet. I just got into town."

"Oh. Yeah. Well, the B and B on Main is nice. How long are you planning to stay?"

Stop! Just stop!

And yeah. The dimple popped. Goodness, he was hot. Way too hot. "Not sure yet," he said. Then he stepped closer. Her stupid heart kicked into gear. Her lungs locked, but not before she caught a tantalizing whiff of his breath. "But hey," he said. "Do you, ah, have plans tonight?"

For a second, a blinding excitement scudded through her. Just a second, though, before reality, like a dash of cold water, brought her back to the here and now. She did have plans tonight, and they included chicken and dumplings and footed pajamas and cuddles and story time with her two young sons.

Probably definitely not what he had in mind.

But it was fun to think about for that flash of a second—hopping onto the back of that beast of a machine behind that beast of a man and taking off for parts unknown... and sex. With an actual person.

Gosh, she missed sex.

Her expression, or the inelegant pause, must have

alerted him to the fact he'd lost the fish because his jaw tightened and he nodded and said, "Ah. Well." And then, "Thanks for the fritters."

And, because she was socially awkward around hot men and always would be, she responded with "Y'all come back now, ya hear?" like a complete doofus—as the sexiest man who'd ever almost propositioned her left her shop, closed the door gently behind him and sketched her a wave before leaving her life forever.

So yeah. A pretty exciting afternoon in the scheme of things. At least for her life as it was.

If nothing else, she'd learned that she could have feelings like that again. That the sexual part of her had not completely atrophied. It was nice to know. Aside from that, tonight she had something interesting to think about in her lonely, lonely bed.

Noah Crocker shook his head as he slipped the fritters into his saddlebags and fitted his helmet back onto his head. He tried not to look back at the bakery as he started his bike, but he couldn't help it. She was there, watching him. Or maybe just locking the door.

He'd met a lot of women in his life—a lot—but he'd never felt electricity like *that* before. He'd certainly never experienced that kind of savage attraction at first glance. It had been like magnets snapping into place. *Click* and *click*. He'd thought for sure that she'd felt it too, but maybe she hadn't.

The first thing he'd noticed about her was how cute she was, with a splotch of flour on the tip of her slightly crooked nose. She probably hadn't been aware of the flour, but that had made her even cuter. But if he was being honest with himself, everything about her had called to him. The curly hair, pixyish features…that smile. Those eyes. And her curves… Yikes.

He'd been congratulating himself for yielding to the desire to go back for a doughnut after he'd initially passed the shop…right up until he had, like an idiot, asked her out. Her reaction had nearly gutted him. Had he really hoped that hard that she'd say yes?

A pretty woman—whose name he didn't even know— shouldn't have the power to slay him like that. Should she?

But her smile, her laugh, that sparkle in her eyes… everything about her was a lure.

She hadn't been wearing a ring. He'd checked her finger. Like, first thing. But that didn't mean she wasn't in a relationship. Of course it didn't. He chuckled to himself and reset his GPS for the address his buddy Jax had given him, started up the Harley and headed out for Razor Clam Way.

A woman like that couldn't possibly be single. Who wouldn't want to claim her as a partner?

What a shame. What a damn shame.

It had been a while for him since he'd been with a woman, mostly because he didn't care for one-night stands and, since his discharge from the Air Force, he'd been a nomad, on the road traveling the highways and backroads of the country, too restless to stay put for long. If anyone had asked, he'd have said he was on a quest for adventure…but the truth was he was desperately seeking a place to call his forever home.

So no wild one-night stands. He would have made an exception, though, for *her*.

Although he doubted a one-night stand would be enough with a woman like that.

It had always been his dream—since he'd been a boy—to travel the country, to see the sights and soak up the flavors the United States had to offer. So, for the last year and a half he'd been doing just that. Exploring the country and visiting friends from sea to shining sea. After visiting Jax and a few Air Force buddies who were stationed at McChord Air Force Base here in Washington State, he'd be heading up to Alaska, the last state on his list.

Hard to believe his grand adventure was almost over. His bucket list was almost complete. His time was almost up. Soon, he had to make one of the biggest decisions of his life. The trouble was—even though he'd been looking, and he'd experienced some wonderful things—he hadn't found a place that truly felt like home to him. At least, not yet.

He ignored the little niggle at the back of his brain whispering that maybe there was no place for him to call home. Maybe because there was something lacking in him. That his rough childhood had broken the part of him that felt like it belonged anywhere. As a foster kid, shuttled from house to house, he'd never felt as though he'd belonged anywhere. He'd certainly never had time to put down roots. Even in the military—where he had felt a blessed sense of belonging—nothing had ever been permanent.

And now even the Air Force didn't want him anymore.

He hated these thoughts when they floated up from the depths from time to time. Again, as always, he pushed them back down and focused on the drive. It was beautiful here. Lots of tall, majestic trees, fat white clouds, and the taste of the ocean in the air.

He headed west along Silver Salmon Drive to Razor Clam Way, then followed the bumpy track into the woods, toward his buddy's place. Jax had known he'd been planning to head up to Washington when he was done exploring California and Oregon, but Noah hadn't called to say he was on his way, so he was prepared to be fluid. If Jax wasn't home, he'd probably head back into town and see if the B and B had a vacancy.

When he pulled through the old-growth woods and into the drive, Jax's yard surprised him. First of all, it wasn't much of a yard. More of a garden…of statuary. Lions and tigers and bears, and all kinds of creatures, all crafted from wood, speckled the sprawling front lawn leading down to the shoreline. Jax had mentioned that after leaving the service he'd gotten into wood-working, but Noah had pictured something very different. Maybe he'd been thinking rocking chairs and baby cradles rather than art. The whimsical creatures Jax had crafted made him smile.

It was intriguing to discover a side of a friend you weren't aware existed. But then, when you met a man in a war zone, there were lots of parts of him he kept to himself. Noah had experienced this kind of discovery in his recent travels again and again. It was half the fun, discovering who your friends really were when they weren't wearing their armor.

He and Jax had met by chance on a transport to

Bagram, and they'd hit it off, chatting through the entire flight; for both of them, it had been their first deployment to Afghanistan. It so happened—as it happened sometimes, when you met people you were supposed to know—they kept running into each other on base. Considering how many troops were stationed there and the fact that Noah's tours were short four-month spurts and the fact that their Military Occupational Specialties, or MOSs, were so different, it was quite the coincidence… if you happened to believe in coincidence. Noah did not.

He hadn't had a lot of friends growing up—at least none who had stuck through all the chaos—and his adult life had been nomadic, following the pipeline for acceptance into the Pararescue Jumpers through multiple specialty schools and trainings all over the country. So, when he'd met a real friend, someone like Jax, he'd learned to appreciate the gift.

The last time they'd met by chance had been when Noah's Pararescue team had responded to an Army patrol that had been ambushed during a routine recon and taken heavy casualties. Noah hadn't realized the soldier he was patching up for exfiltration was his friend—the man's face had been covered in blood and mud—until Jax had barked a laugh and muttered, "Crocker. I should've known." They'd had a hell of a laugh over that. Shortly after that, Jax had taken an honorable discharge and come back to the States. They'd stayed in touch but hadn't actually seen each other since.

Honestly, Noah couldn't wait to see him again—

"So…how was it—"

Noah whirled to see a woman coming out of the front door of Jax's place with a warm smile, wiping her hands on a rag spattered with a kaleidoscope of colorful paint splotches. She wore a pair of ratty jeans and an old T-shirt covered by an equally spattered apron. She stopped short, and her mouth made an O.

After a second, she recovered herself and said, "Hello. Sorry. I heard the Harley, and I thought it was Jax. Can I help you?" She was really pretty, with a bright smile and a smear of orange on her cheek. She kind of reminded him of the cute baker. Maybe all the women around here were perky and bright. Maybe something in the water here?

"Hey." Noah lifted a hand. "Sorry. I'm Jax's friend, Noah Crocker, and—"

"Oh, my goodness. Noah?" she broke in. Her face lit up even more. "He said you might be coming. He'll be so excited you're here. Come on in. I'm Natalie." She put out a hand. He stepped forward, taking it, and she looked up at him and said, "My, you're tall."

He grinned because she was tiny. "Yes, ma'am."

She made a face. "*Ma'am* makes me feel old."

His grin widened, and because he had the suspicion she had a sense of humor, he said, "Yes, ma'am."

She grinned back and thwacked him with her rag. He liked her immediately. "Come in. Let me get you something to drink, and I'll call Jax. He's just out giving his bike a test ride." She chuckled. "That's why I thought it was him."

"Jax has a hog now?" he asked as he stepped inside the long low building. And then he stopped short. Because there were more wood statues inside—a lot more—along with a couple of easels, a ratty sofa, card table and kitchenette. And still, more racks of wood along the wall. "Wow."

Natalie laughed. "Right?"

"I knew he worked with wood, but…"

"Yeah. He's pretty into it. Can I get you a beer? Soda? Water?" She dropped her rag onto the stool by the easel and headed for the fridge.

"Water is fine." He might be driving to the B and B yet tonight, so he didn't want alcohol. He peeked over at the painting she'd been working on and blinked. "You're a painter?" he asked, even though it was a stupid question to ask someone wearing a spattered apron with an orange splotch on their cheek. Also, because she was good. Like, really good. It was a seascape at sunset, and it was stunning.

"Mmm-hmm. Come on over and sit. Relax. Are you hungry?" She handed him a bottled water. He took a swig and moaned. It was cool and refreshing and washed the dust from his throat.

"No, thanks. I'm good. I don't want to put you out."

She laughed at that. "Jax is going to be thrilled you're here. He's been telling me all about you."

"Yikes."

"Aww." She shook her head. "It's all good. Is it true you saved his life over there?" She took a sip from her soda.

Noah shrugged. "I patched him up. I'm pretty sure the doctors back at the base did all the saving."

"I'd never heard of Pararescue jumpers before Jax told me about you. It sounds like a very exciting job."

He nodded. "Yeah. There were definitely some heart-pounders out there."

"I mean, being a medic in a war zone alone would be something, but to parachute in?"

He had to grin. *"Hooah."* The PJ battle cry. "Yeah, we'll jump out of almost anything."

"So exciting."

"You don't have to be crazy, but it helps."

She nodded. "Still. It's a very elite group. Is it true most applicants don't make the cut?"

"A lot don't. Yeah, it's a tough process, but it's a tough job."

"Did you like it?"

He leaned back and grinned. "Loved it." He had. It had been hard and grueling and interesting and rewarding. He'd probably still be suiting up if he hadn't torn up his knee. But for Noah, becoming a PJ had also been a means to an end. Carving a place in the world where he belonged.

Until he didn't.

"And now you're traveling the States. Tell me—where have you been?"

They talked about that for a while, all the places he'd been since his discharge. It was clear from Natalie's responses that she'd traveled around the States a lot herself before she'd landed here in Coho Cove. They were discussing their favorite beignet place in New Orleans when they heard Jax's Harley rumble echoing in the woods and Natalie leaped to her feet.

"Oh. He's here. He's going to be so excited." She ran to the door, and of course, Noah followed. He stood there in the doorway and watched as Jax parked his bike and removed his helmet. Their eyes locked, and something rose in his chest. Damn, he'd missed Jax. They'd devel-

oped a deep friendship over their time in Afghanistan—
one hewn of heartbreak, loss and laughter. He really
shouldn't had waited so long to come.

"Crocker." Jax strode forward, a grin splitting his face.

"Stringfellow." Wow. It was good to see him. They
met each other halfway and slammed into a manly hug.
"I've missed you, you son of a bitch."

"Same, you bastard. Why didn't you call?"

Noah shrugged. "You know me. Footloose and fancy
free."

"Still?" They turned in unison and headed back to
the shop. "I thought this trip was all about finding a
place to settle."

"Yeah." Easier said than done. "I'm working on it."

"Damn, it's good to see you."

"It's pretty damn good to see you too."

Jax put his arm around Natalie's shoulders and held
her close. "Have you met Nat? Natalie Tuttle."

Natalie smiled. "We've met."

"Nat's my girl," Jax said. But by the look on his face,
Noah already knew.

Jax had found his soul mate, that rarer than rare miracle that made a man whole after the world had chewed
him up and spit him out. And while Noah could not
have been happier—Natalie really was a gem—he had
to admit, he was also a little jealous.

Because that was what he wanted more than anything. To find *that* woman. The woman who could fill
the gaping hole in his soul. Trouble was he was begin-
ning to doubt she existed at all.

Or worse…that she did, and he simply wasn't worthy
of her.

* * *

Amy was still thinking about the hottie on the Harley when she pulled into her friend Kim's driveway to pick up the boys. It bothered her that she couldn't stop thinking about him—his smile, that flash of a dimple, the scent of his leathers. She kept circling back to the conversation where he'd asked her out—he had asked her out, right? She wished she'd said yes, even though she knew she never would. A date with a random stranger? *Ha!* Not with the boys to think about and a business to run and a mortgage…and everything.

As she headed up the driveway to Kim's house, she shook her head, as though she could loosen thoughts of him. Still, he hovered.

When the bakery had first opened, the boys had stayed at Momma's while Amy was at work, but this year things had changed. Momma's housekeeper had broken her hip, and when Momma suffered her stroke, Amy had no choice but to find a sitter. Things were even more complicated by the early hour at which she needed to drop the boys off. Since the bakery opened at seven, prep work—from proofing the dough, forming, baking and filling the pastries as well as decorating— all needed to happen prior to opening. That meant she needed to drop the boys off by five, at the latest. Dylan's mom, Kim, had been the best option she could find, and she hadn't had a problem with the early hours. She and Kim had been mom friends going all the way back to Georgie and Dylan's first Mommy and Me classes.

The boys, of course, had been delighted to spend more time with their friend—who had a Nintendo. Amy, however, was still on the fence about the arrangement.

She much preferred that the boys spend their days engaged in some kind of intellectual enrichment rather than playing video games and watching movies all day long. But Coho Cove was a small town and there weren't a lot of day care options. Beggars couldn't be choosers, could they?

Kim greeted her at the door with a big smile. "Hey, Amy. Come on in. Coffee?"

"Ah, no thanks. We should scoot…"

"Sure. They're down in the basement playing video games. *Boys, your mom is here!*" Kim shouted down the stairs. Then, to Amy, in a non-yelly voice, "How was your day?" Amy appreciated her asking because there was no one else to do it.

"Well…" She waggled her brows. "A hot tourist came into the bakery today."

"Ooh. Fun. Must be nice to be single."

"I think he asked me out to dinner."

Kim's eyes boggled. "You think? You don't know?"

"I'm pretty sure?"

"Why aren't you having dinner with a hot tourist, then?"

Amy made a snort noise. "I'm the mother of two young boys. I can't go to dinner with a rando."

"A *hot* rando."

"Come on. I don't know him from Adam. He could be a serial killer."

"Did he strike you as a serial killer?"

"Do they ever?"

"Hmm." Kim thought about it for a minute, then got a look on her face, one Amy knew well and dreaded. "Are you sure you're not just scared to start dating again?"

"Scared? Me? I'm not scared of anything." Okay. Maybe a little. He was one intimidating package, her sexy tourist. But she wasn't going to admit it to Kim. It hardly mattered though, did it? Tourists were tourists. They always left. "Oh, is Dylan coming to John J.'s birthday party?" A lame segue, but a necessary one.

"Of course. He wouldn't miss it."

"Good. John J. is worried no one will come."

Kim chuckled. "What a funny thing. Everyone's coming."

"You know him. He's sensitive."

"Yeah, but it's a *pool* party...at the *Sherrod*." She said it like that—the *Sherrod*. Granted, it was the fancy new resort on the point. "And how, may I ask, did you manage to book that?"

Amy shrugged. "Ben Sherrod is a friend."

"Is he?" Kim's brow arched. "Now there's a guy you should date."

Amy barely kept another snort-laugh from exploding from her face. "Right."

"He's handsome, successful...rich."

"He's a nice guy, and John J. is close with his daughter, Quinn—"

"All the more reason! Ready-made family. *Brady Bunch*. Oh." Kim was easily distracted. "Do you want to stay for dinner?"

"No. I have chicken and dumplings in the slow cooker, thanks. Look, Ben and I have been friends for years. We are both very firmly friend-zoned with each other. We're comfortable there. Besides, I don't have those kinds of feelings for him."

Her mind flickered back to another man, another

dimple, a whole slew of scorching feelings that had hit her like a Mack Truck, unexpected and devastating. What would it be like to *be* with a man like that? Even now the thought of him made her a little weak at the knees. And she wasn't a weak-at-the-knees kind of gal. She'd never felt that way for Ben, not even remotely. Call it chemistry, call it lust, call it whatever you wanted, it wasn't there with Ben, no matter how perfect the matchup might've looked on paper.

But *him*? Whatever his name was?

It was silly to think about because she'd never see him again, but at the same time, the thrill she'd felt when he'd looked into her eyes, when he'd come close— well, that gave her hope, somehow. Hope that it wasn't all over for her—the love and romance and all that nonsense that now felt so far away.

Kim shrugged. "You could fake it. Lots of women would fake passion for a catch like that."

Amy swallowed the bitterness in her mouth at the suggestion. Though she and Kim had a lot in common, their values didn't always align. "Ben deserves better. He really is a great guy. And honestly… I deserve better too." Sure, she'd had her one great love—many people never got that, not even for three short years—but she still wasn't inclined to settle for less than that, should a chance ever drift her way again.

As. If.

She huffed out a breath and leaned into the basement doorway and bellowed, "Boys! Let's go." Because, all of a sudden, she wasn't in the mood to talk about it anymore. Not really. Not at all.

Chapter Two

As usual, getting two rambunctious boys and all their gear into the car was a circus. As was listening to them tell her about their day—and talk over each other—on the drive home. But Amy enjoyed every moment. This was what she lived for. This was what mattered to her.

Sure, it was exciting to fantasize about hot guys and adventure, but chicken and dumplings and funny conversations with the two most precious people on the planet was real and soothing and not a bad way to spend an evening. Or a lifetime.

After dinner that night, Amy put John J. to bed first, as she always did, tucking him in and reading a chapter from a copy of *Mrs. Piggle-Wiggle* she'd had since her childhood. After she kissed him goodnight, she headed to Georgie's room.

He was nearly seven now and old enough to put

himself to bed, but he still liked the cuddle time, even though he'd never admit it.

"Momma," he said after she'd finished the chapter from an old Hardy Boys mystery she'd found in the library. He'd just had a bath and smelled of soap and freshly laundered pajamas.

"Yes, hon?"

"Do you ever think about Daddy?"

"Oh, honey." Her heart hiccupped. She kissed his brow. Inhaled his little-boy scent. "I think about him every day."

He nodded. His throat worked. "Do you... Do you think he would be mad if I...missed a day?" His tortured expression sliced through her mother's heart like a knife.

"What?"

He looked up at her, his eyes pooling. A lone tear spilled out and tracked down his cheek. "I forgot yesterday. I forgot to think about him." And then Georgie, her darling brave boy, launched himself into her arms and wept. Hard, jagged sobs.

She held him tight and patted his back and stroked his hair and whispered, "It's okay, baby. It's okay," even though she was bawling herself. After a while—quite a while actually—he calmed himself and snuffled and pulled away. Still, she met his eye.

"You know what I think?" she asked.

"What?"

"I think what your dad wants is for you to live your life and grow up to be the best man you can be. That's all."

He snuffled again, and she grabbed him a tissue. He blew. "I miss him."

"Me too, honey. Me too." She hugged him a little

closer. "But he left me something, something very special to remember him by."

He looked up at her, eyes wide, hopeful. "What was that?"

She kissed his forehead. "You, honey. You are part of him, you know. Both you boys are. The part of him he left for me, so I wouldn't be so alone."

It was the best gift ever.

Noah never made it to the B and B that night. He ended up having a nice dinner at Nat and Jax's place—talking about old times—and then staying the night in Jax's studio, which had a bed tucked in a back room. Jax had used to live in the studio—that was why Noah'd had the address—but he'd recently moved. Now he and Natalie lived in a charming cottage, outside of town, on a hill overlooking the crashing ocean. They'd just moved in and were in the middle of renovations, so they didn't have a spare bed there. Natalie had been mortified to offer Noah the studio, but he didn't mind. It suited him better than sleeping on their couch. He could come and go as he wished without interfering with their lifestyle. Or them interfering with his.

That was the hard part of being a lone wolf—balancing between too much company and too little. Not everyone understood his need for space. Fortunately, Jax did.

The back room of the studio wasn't the fanciest place he'd ever slept in but certainly not the worst. It took him a while to fall asleep though, but mostly because that cute baker kept popping into his head. He tried not to think about the fact that if she had said yes to his invitation, she might've been here with him right now and the bed wouldn't have been so lonely.

It probably only haunted him like that because it was rare for him to feel an immediate connection with someone—it usually took him a while to warm up to people, something he attributed to growing up in foster care. He'd learned early that people shouldn't be trusted until they earned trust. He didn't know why, but something about her called to him, like a siren. He wished he could figure out what it was and maybe block it.

Even though she kept him awake way too long, he still woke up early enough the next morning to watch the sun rise over a cup of coffee and an apple fritter, and then he wandered down the hill to watch the waves crash on the shore. A short hike from the studio, he found a spot where Jax had built a firepit, and with a couple of Adirondack chairs, it was, possibly, one of the best views on the planet. The gulls flirted with updrafts and called to each other in the cloud-speckled sky. The early morning breeze was cool and salty and brisk. He even saw an eagle perched in one of the old-growth trees in the woods, scrutinizing its dominion for a hapless meal.

As a kid, he'd read about the Pacific Northwest. Seen pictures. To his young mind, it had always seemed like kind of a fairy-tale place with tall trees and mystical beauty. Now, sitting here, it was all that and more. Unrelenting rugged coasts littered with long, savage, boulder-strewn beaches. Wildlife. The vast expanse of the sea. It really was a beautiful place, and it gave him a warm feeling, the kind he imagined was like being home.

Growing up, he'd never really known that feeling in

any of the houses he'd bunked in, but it was something he'd looked for his whole life.

And he felt it here.

"There you are!" Jax's call broke through his reverie—a welcome intrusion—as he made his way toward the firepit. "I see you found my meditation spot."

Noah chuckled. "Man, this is beautiful. I can't believe you decided to live somewhere else."

Jax dropped into the other chair and spread out his long legs before him. "Well, I couldn't ask Natalie to live in the studio. I was happy here when I was living out here on my own, but honestly, I'm getting used to the luxury of living in a *real house*." He barked a laugh. "That's what my sister used to say whenever she visited. *You need to live in a real house*." He shrugged. "Nat and I still spend a lot of time here, working—her with her painting and me with my sculpture. But it's really nice to go home at the end of the day. You don't get that when you live where you work."

"Well, I appreciate you sharing this with me."

"You are welcome. I'm so glad you came to visit. It's…been a long time."

Noah nodded. It had been nearly six years since they'd been stationed together in Afghanistan. "I'm glad we stayed in touch." Guys always said they would when they rotated out. Sometimes it happened and sometimes it didn't, but he and Jax had always had a strong bond.

"How long do you think you'll be staying?" Jax asked, and then he quickly followed with, "You're welcome to stay as long as you want, of course. I'm excited you're here. In fact, we'd love it if you'd stay for the wedding, if you can."

Something warmed in Noah's heart. It was nice to know he was wanted. "Well, I don't have firm plans before heading up to Alaska, other than to visit Al Ricter and Jake Tommins at McChord. Did you ever meet them?"

Jax grinned. "I think I remember Tommins. Wasn't he the guy who dressed up as Santa at the holiday party?"

"And got falling-down drunk? Yeah." They both chuckled a little because, at the time, it had been pretty funny.

"Well, Joint Base Lewis-McChord isn't far. Two, maybe three hours, depending on traffic. A day trip, easy. But there are some nice hotels near base, if you want to stay longer." Jax paused and cleared his throat. "I wouldn't mind going with you, if you'd like the company."

Noah nodded. It had been a long time since anyone had offered him company. It felt nice. "I'd like that. Do you think your old hog can make it that far?" he jibed because last night at dinner, Jax had told him he was rebuilding the junker.

"One way to find out."

"Sounds good to me. Um, would Natalie be okay with that?" In his experience, some women weren't comfortable with their men taking off on road trips with old service buddies. And the last thing he wanted to do was irritate Natalie. He liked her.

Jax laughed. "Nat brought it up. She thinks I need more of a social life. And she likes you."

"I like her too."

"Good." Jax blew out a deep breath and turned to pin Noah with a somber expression. "Because you've been invited to Sunday dinner tonight with the Tuttles. It's kind of a family tradition. They all get together once a week to catch up."

"Oh, I wouldn't want to intrude on a family supper." How awkward would that be?

"I don't think it would be an intrusion. It's just Nat's mom, her sisters and her nephews. Sometimes my sister or my dad comes too." He shrugged. "Besides, Natalie has already mentioned you to her mother, and the second Pearl heard you're former military, she insisted you come. So yeah, you can consider the invitation pretty much a command." He grinned, and Noah had to follow suit.

"I would like that very much, then. Thank you."

"Great. Nat and I will pick you up around five, if that works?"

"Perfect." It was. And, damn, it felt good to be wanted.

"Good glory." Amy huffed a sigh as the last customer of the morning left. She turned to Eloise and made a face. "That was a lot."

Eloise nodded. "Is it me, or was today even busier than last week?"

Usually Amy had to close the till before she knew how the sales had gone, but today the crumbs in the pastry case—and her aching feet—told her it had gone well. Sundays at the bakery were busy, especially in the summer because there were so many tourists in town, but since she was only open until noon, it was a short day.

Her sister Celeste, who lived with Momma, didn't work on Sundays, so Amy had taken the boys over to their house so they could spend the morning with their grandmother and aunt while she worked. It was a solution that worked because Kim needed a day off and Momma and Celeste loved having time with the boys. Amy had tried bringing them along to the bakery once or twice, but the boys were far too rambunctious to play quietly for hours, so Amy was thankful for the option.

"Let's go ahead and start closing," she said, even though it wasn't noon yet, because she knew Eloise had plans for the afternoon with her boyfriend, Ethan. It didn't take long to close, as the two of them had the routine down pat by now. Besides, Amy liked to keep on top of the cleaning throughout the day. When everything was pristine, Amy sent Eloise home and sat down to run today's numbers. The results were pleasing. Sunday mornings were always profitable, but things were just getting better and better. It was satisfying that her business was thriving, yes, but there was also an element of relief as well.

Early on the bakery had struggled to gain traction, and there had been times when she hadn't been sure it would make it. After George's death, she'd used a lot of the insurance money to start her business and if the bakery had failed, she and the boys would have been in a world of hurt. Those had been very difficult and scary times.

Sometimes when she looked back, she wondered how she'd survived it. Missing George, raising two babies, taking online classes to get her business degree and running a business...

No. She knew how she'd survived.

She'd had her family. Momma and Celeste especially.

She and the boys had lived with them, in Grandma and Grandpa's old house, until she'd been able to put money down on their own place. No, it hadn't been easy, but at least she'd had them.

Amy was about to wrap up and head for Momma's house to pick up the boys when her cell phone rang. It was an unknown number. Usually Amy let calls like this go to voice mail, since most of them were spam, but for some reason she answered.

"Hello?"

"Hi." A chirpy female voice. Amy lifted her finger to disconnect—chirpy was usually spam—but the caller continued. "I'm trying to reach Amy Tolliver."

"And who's calling?" Hmm. This didn't sound like a spam call, but still, she was cautious.

"Oh, hi. This is Dani Mitterand. I'm a segment producer for *Best of the Northwest Weekend*. You know, the show on channel 11?"

Amy's eyes widened. Her heart squeezed. She dropped into her office chair. She knew the show. They traveled around the region highlighting restaurants and bars and all kinds of eateries. She watched it every Friday night. "Uh, hello, Dani. Yes. This is Amy."

"Oh, Amy, I'm so glad I caught you. I just wanted to let you know that we've selected your bakery for a profile piece." She paused, as though expecting an excited squeal, which Amy would have happily provided if she could have made a peep. But no sound would come out because her throat had closed up with shock. A profile with them could bring customers from all over. This could be huge.

"I, ah, I'm honored." She couldn't manage more. Her brain was all atwitter.

"Yeah. Someone emailed us a tip about your bakery, and we sent one of our secret shoppers out to visit and, well, they loved it. Your bakery was selected for this year's Best of Bakeries award."

Wow. "Thank you. That is fantastic."

Dani chuckled. "I'm calling to see if we can set up a time to send over a crew and do the taping for the feature."

"Oh, my goodness. Yes. Of course." It was all she could do to keep herself from dancing.

"We can have a film crew there on the twelfth of next month. Would that work for you?"

The twelfth? She flipped madly through her planner for the calendar. The twelfth was just six weeks away. *Six weeks!*

"That sounds perfect." She quickly scribbled it into the box and then added a smiley face.

"Last year our Best of Bakeries award went to a place in Butterscotch Ridge, over in Eastern Washington. I'm sending a link to the email on your website so you can watch the profile. That will give you an idea of what to expect. But if you have any questions, feel free to call me. Let me give you my number."

Dani continued on, giving Amy all the details of the coming profile, what was required and recommended, and Amy madly scratched out notes. Somehow she was able to ask the questions that needed to be asked and sound cogent, but she didn't know how she did it. It was, simply put, the most exciting thing to happen to her in a long, long time. It was also a wonderful validation of all her hard work.

By the time the call ended, Amy was emotionally drained—and still madly excited at the same time. She wanted, very desperately, to have someone to share this with. So, when her phone rang a few minutes later, she was thrilled to see her friend Candace's face pop up on the screen.

Though Amy and Candace had gone to high school together, they hadn't been friends back then. It hadn't been until they'd both been pregnant and alone that they'd found each other in a Lamaze class. Amy's husband had been on a tour overseas, and Candace's had always been on business trips. They'd bonded and had been fast friends ever since.

"Hey, Candace," she said with a grin.

"Hey, Ames. How's it going?"

"Candace, you're not going to believe this. I just got a call from *Best of the Northwest Weekend*. They want to do a profile on the bakery!"

"Sounds like you're excited. Is this a good thing?"

Amy's excitement dimmed, but only a little. Not everyone would understand the implications here, and the bakery was hardly a passion of Candace's on account of the fact that she never ate carbs. It was silly to be disappointed by her lack of enthusiasm. At least her family would be excited when she told them. "It's fantastic. Basically, my bakery will be featured on TV."

"Oooh!" Yeah. Candace understood the power of media platforms. She was an Instagram influencer after all. "Ames. That's great." And then, "So…are you done for the day?"

"Yep. Just finishing up. Dang, I'm tired."

"Oh." It was something of a pout. "I was going to ask if you were going to take the boys to the carnival today." The carnival was a summer tradition in Coho Cove, and today was the opening day. "Maya wants to go, and I thought if you were going, maybe you could take her along as well?"

Amy made a face. "I'd love that." The boys had been nagging at her to go ever since they'd seen the rides going up. "But we have a family thing tonight." Sunday supper at Momma's was something of a tradition as well. Candace knew Amy and the boys spent Sundays at Momma's, but she'd probably forgotten.

"Bummer." Candace wasn't one to pout for long. "I could really use some me time. Maybe later in the week?"

"We'll see." Amy was still too overwhelmed with the news about the TV show and her racing thoughts to make plans to take Candace's daughter to the carnival for her.

"So," Candace gusted a sigh. "What else is going on?"

"Well…a hot customer came into the store yesterday."

Candace squealed so loudly Amy had to take the phone away from her ear. "Oooh. Lucky you."

"He, ah, kind of asked me out."

Silence crackled. Then Candace murmured, "Wow. Really?"

"I told him no."

"What?" Another howl. "Why?"

"Um, total stranger?"

"But he's hot."

"He's a tourist, Candace. Just passing through."

"Amy, go get some."

Amy laughed and rolled her eyes. She wasn't that kind of woman, and she never would be…no matter how much she might want to. If she ever did *date* again—and how lame was *that* word?—it wouldn't be a one-night stand. Or ever a two-nighter. And it wasn't even about the boys, though they factored into everything. She simply wasn't interested in a shallow, temporary fling. When she thought about what she wanted, what she yearned for, it wasn't that.

No matter how good a man smelled or how sexy he looked in leathers.

And he had looked good. Smelled even better. She'd always been a sucker for good clean sweat…and leathers.

Still, she shook her head. *Go get some?* "No thanks."

"Come on, Amy. You deserve to be happy."

"I can be happy without having *everything* I want. Can't I?"

Candace snorted. "Can you?"

Amy sighed. Candace was so beautiful and sophisticated and svelte and stylish and utterly put together. It was hard to believe her life wasn't perfect. She had a beautiful house—that was always spotless—a handsome husband who made money and kept her well. It all seemed perfect. And yet… "I mean, no one has everything they want, right?"

Candace snorted again. "I mean, what is 'everything' anyway?"

"Right?" But really, a supportive partner to share life

with was a pretty big chunk of everything, and Candace had that. Amy didn't.

There was still joy to be found in her work and the boys. With her family and friends. But while she hated the construct that a woman was an incomplete entity without a man, she missed having a partner in her life. She missed that a lot.

She wasn't really unhappy so much as…alone.

"Listen, Candace. I gotta scoot, but let's plan to get together for dinner sometime soon, okay?"

"Absolutely, hon. Call me."

Amy sighed as she ended the call. Then she turned her attention back to the notes she'd written, and her heart lifted again.

She was getting a *Best of the Northwest Weekend* profile! This was amazing. Things were really changing for the better. She could feel it in her bones.

All of her hard work was paying off.

Finally, things were starting to go her way.

Noah felt welcome the second he stepped into Pearl Tuttle's house. Even though it was clearly a challenge for Natalie's mother to do so, she rose to her feet and came to greet him when he entered her sitting room. He noticed the walker by her chair and the slackness on one side of her face, which made the gesture even more meaningful because Jax had mentioned she'd recently had a stroke.

It strummed at his heartstrings because after Ma had had her first stroke, she'd struggled with simple things like standing and walking as well. Her real name had been Gloria, the foster mother he'd had in high school.

Of all of his foster mothers, she'd been the only one he'd called Ma because she was the only one who'd felt anything like a mom. Funny thing, she'd been a baker too...

That Pearl Tuttle reminded him of Ma only made him feel more at home. While Nat went into the kitchen to rustle up some drinks with her sister Celeste, he and Jax chatted with Pearl. Or, more to the point, she grilled Noah, wanting to know everything about his tours overseas.

He didn't tell her everything—there were just some things a man didn't bring home from a war zone—but she seemed to realize and understand. When Jax's dad, Alexander, arrived, the topic shifted from PJ adventures to rockhound adventures. As much as Jax loved woodcarving, his dad, it seemed, was equally enamored of his rocks. He collected them, polished them and made jewelry, which he sold at a couple local stores. It was fun listening to Jax and his dad razz each other about their passions. When Jax teased his dad about having mountains of rocks all over his little house, Noah had to laugh because Jax's studio was exactly the same.

The table in the dining room was laid out as though it was a formal dinner, with crystal glasses and linen napkins and everything. Noah counted nine place settings, so he wasn't surprised when more family showed up.

The door blew open, and a young voice bellowed from the foyer, "We're here!"

Based on the reaction from everyone in the room, this was a very anticipated arrival. Pearl was especially excited. "My boys," she whispered to Noah. "My boys are here." It was sweet the way her eyes glistened.

And then a second later, two little boys came racing

around the corner into the room, jostling for position all the way. One of them managed to step on the cat's tail. The yowl surprised Noah because he hadn't realized there was a cat.

"Boys, come meet Noah Crocker," Pearl said in a very proper tone. It was a very particular tone that the boys, apparently, knew. Their roughhousing stopped abruptly, and they both straightened up and put their shoulders back and wiped the grins from their faces. "Noah is a friend of Jax's who is visiting. They served together in Afghanistan."

The boys sobered even more. The little one even raked back his hair. "How do you do, sir," he said, holding out a hand. "I am John J. Pershing Tolliver."

A long name for such a small critter. Noah grinned and took the offered hand. "Pleasure." It took a second for the name to ring a bell. "John J. Pershing? You wouldn't happen to be named for the famous general, would you?"

Clearly he'd hit the nail on the head. The boy's face flooded with a grin. "I am! Gosh, hardly anyone knows that!"

"We're both named after important generals," the older boy said, nudging his brother out of the way with an elbow. He thrust out a confident hand as well. "I am George Patton Tolliver the Second. It is very nice to meet you, Mr. Crocker." He glanced back at his brother, probably to make the point that *this* was the proper way to meet a stranger, but Noah was focused on something else. Something gut wrenching.

Oh, sure, he recognized the general this boy was

named after—who didn't? But a more visceral realization gutted him.

He'd had a friend named George Tolliver.

He'd lost a friend named George Tolliver.

George Tolliver, in fact, had died in his arms.

Oh, the name triggered a memory—a horrific memory. It threw him back into a war zone. Into a helicopter bathed in blood, suffused with the scent of ozone and gunpowder. The sounds of explosions, flack whizzing by as Noah worked madly to stabilize a sucking chest wound as they made their retreat from the heat of the battle. The feel of the rotors whomping like a heartbeat, and the tilt of the bird as it turned sharply back to base, hoping against hope that they'd make it in time...

It had been one of the worst nights in his life.

He had a thousand such memories, but this one was particularly sharp. Because his patient had been George. His buddy. He'd taken a bullet in the chest during an ambush. He'd had tension pneumothorax, dropping blood pressure and another bleed in his leg from where a second bullet had nicked his femoral artery.

Noah pushed the memory away. The boy was waiting for a response. He forced himself to move, taking that wavering outthrust hand and shaking it heartily. He even managed to smile, although he had no idea how he did it.

Because the boy had George's eyes.

That was probably the worst part. His eyes and his nose too. Even the grin was similar.

In that split second, the realization hit him like a freight train.

The boy was George Tolliver's *son*. Damn.

He was so stunned that he barely even heard a some-what familiar voice call from the foyer, "Sorry we're late. It's been a day—"

He looked up then at the woman following the boys into the house. Their gazes clashed and locked. And they stared at each other across the length of the room for a moment. Or an eternity.

Something stirred in his heart. Compassion and maybe a little bit of heartbreak. Because there she was, the bright, beautiful baker who'd made him feel so alive just the day before. The one he couldn't stop thinking about.

And she was George Tolliver's widow.

Chapter Three

Amy had not expected this. She'd been totally unprepared to see her sexy stranger again. (Wait. He wasn't hers! He was just a guy who'd taken some day-old fritters off her hands, damn it.) Most especially, here, in her mom's house, for Sunday dinner.

And good glory, he was taller than she'd remembered, broader. It was as though her mind, in resistance to that unexpected attraction, had tried to diminish him. She nearly laughed because that was ridiculous. This man had a presence. Something magnetic that drew her, made her want to be close. He could not be diminished.

He wore a simple, spotless black T-shirt and jeans, yet somehow he was even hotter than he'd been in his leathers. How was that even possible? Amy found it hard to keep her gaze from clinging to him.

"Oh, here's Amy," Celeste chirped, but Amy barely heard. It was as though all the other sounds dimmed or wafted away. All she was really conscious of was the thud of her pulse in her ears. It irritated her because she prided herself on being sensible and cautious and a good mother. But he made her want to…well, be very un-sensible.

She turned her attention to Celeste and thrust out the sheet cake she'd brought, like an automaton. "I brought dessert," she said inanely. She always brought dessert to Sunday supper. She usually didn't make an announcement, but she needed something to say other than *Who's the hot guy?* Which was what wanted to come out of her mouth.

"Ohh, German chocolate!" Natalie gushed. "Momma, that's your favorite!"

Momma smiled and nodded and then turned to the hot behemoth standing in the living room with the boys staring up at him in awe and said to him, "I love German chocolate cake. Do you like German chocolate cake, Noah?"

Noah.

His name was Noah. Something suffused her, something warm. Yeah. He looked like a Noah.

Why did learning his name feel like an uncomfortable intimacy?

Well, she supposed, because it was.

It was one thing to see a random hottie and fantasize about him in the darkness of her lonely bed. It was another thing entirely to know his name and personify her dreams even more.

That felt so…specific. Especially since he was now standing in front of her. In her mom's living room. Surrounded by her family and her kids. That was about as real as it got.

He smiled at her then, a small quirk of his lips that seemed to note the secret irony of this meeting. "Yes, ma'am," he said to Momma, even though his gaze never left Amy.

It was hard to not smile back. She didn't know why.

"Amy," Natalie said, sidling up and pushing the two of them closer together. "This is Noah Crocker. He's here to visit Jax. Noah, this is my sister Amy." To Amy's horror, or delight, he thrust out a large, tanned hand and she knew she had to juggle the cake and take it. You know. To be polite.

What she didn't expect was the sizzle of heat that shot through her at his touch, or the disinclination to let him go. Though neither of them said anything, with words at least, there was an unspoken understanding, something visceral between them. Amy felt disinclined to say, *"Yes, we've already met,"* because somewhere, deep inside, she wanted to keep that meeting, hold that moment, private. And she sensed he felt the same. Was it the look in his eyes or the quirk of his smile or something more? She wasn't sure. But she did know she didn't want to have to explain things to her family. Simple things became exhausting, sometimes, when you tried to explain them to family.

"Well, don't just stand there." Momma shattered the moment with an impatient snort. "Put the cake on the sideboard. And now that everyone is here, let's eat."

"Woo-hoo!" the boys crowed, capturing Noah's attention for a second, just long enough for Amy to break from his spell and carry the cake into the dining room. She sat it on the breakfront, then headed straight into the kitchen—to catch her breath, to regain her equilibrium. And, by the way, a glass of wine sounded pretty good at the moment.

She was just taking her first sip when Celeste and Natalie followed her in. "Mmm. Smells good," Nat said, sniffing the roast resting on the butcher's block.

"Mmm," Amy parroted. Not that it didn't smell delicious, she just hadn't noticed. Her brain was still in a froth.

Together, the three sisters carried out the roast and sides, along with serving implements, while the others found their places at the table. Amy dawdled with the corn casserole—she just wanted a moment more to prepare. She realized her strategic mistake the second she pushed through the kitchen door. The only seat left was next to Momma at the head of the table, directly across from Noah. She'd have to look at him throughout the entire meal. Yikes.

The thought sent her heart to thumping again.

It could have been worse, though, because in their family, especially at Sunday supper, they held hands for grace. So, during the long prayer, in which Momma thanked God for just about everything, Amy would have had to touch him again. The thought gave her shivers. He had warm hands. And they were...*large.*

Though she tried not to look at him, she gave in and peeped at him just before Momma said, "Amen." That sent shivers through her as well because he was gazing at her, with that ever-so-slight smile on his gorgeous lips.

And then, at the end of the prayer—as they did every Sunday—the boys responded with a raucous, *"dig in!"* and everyone laughed and did just that. A cacophony of laughter and passed dishes ensued.

Amy took a sip of her wine, just for something to do, but when she realized she was nearly halfway through her glass she reminded herself to slow down. She didn't drink much, and she most certainly didn't want to get tipsy in front of *him*. Aside from that, she still had to drive home, and while it wasn't far, she never drove under the influence.

"So, Noah," Alexander, Jax's dad, spoke up from the other end of the table. "I know you and Jax met in the service, but where are you from originally?"

She had to look at him then—it was expected—and the expression that flickered over his face caught her heart in a vise. It vanished in a flash, replaced with a polite smile, but Amy knew she hadn't imagined it. She recognized it because she had a similar reaction whenever someone asked where she was from—because as an Army brat, she hadn't really been *from* anywhere. He'd had that same lost look in his eyes.

But he set down his fork, cleared his throat and said, "Well, sir, I was born in Virginia." He cracked a practiced smile. "Joined the Air Force the day I turned eighteen."

Alexander nodded. "Good for you."

"Why the Air Force?" Momma asked. She was of the persuasion that everyone would prefer the Army. Or should. Both her father and her husband had been Army soldiers. It was the only life she'd known until Dad had died unexpectedly.

Noah's grin widened at the question. It made Amy's heart go pitter-pat, which, all things considered, was annoying. Why should his delight make her happy? "I wanted to be a Pararescue jumper," he said, so simply, but his tone said so much more. The way he said the word, he might as well have said, *I wanted to be Superman.*

"What's a Pararescue jumper?" John J., sitting at his side, asked.

"John J.," she said—totally without thinking, certainly not to bring Noah's attention to her. "Don't talk with your mouth full."

Noah grinned at her, even as he responded to her son. "You've heard of a medic, right?"

Both the boys nodded.

"Well, a Pararescue jumper is a medic who jumps into places that are hard to get to."

John J. knitted his brow and shook his head. "What do you mean, jumps in?"

"You know. Out of airplanes," Jax offered.

The boys' jaws dropped, and in unison they both bleated, "Cool!"

"And helicopters," Noah added solemnly. "It sounded exciting to me, so I wanted to do it."

"Was it fun?" Georgie asked.

"Was it scary?" This from John J. before Noah had a chance to answer.

"Both." He leaned toward the boys. "It's a very important job. People's lives depend on you, and that's the most important thing to remember, not whether it's scary or fun."

"Is it hard work?" Georgie asked with a fascinated glint in his eye, and a little chill slithered through Amy's heart. She tried hard not to influence her sons either way when it came to the military because it had provided her with a good life—until it hadn't. It was a noble and important profession. At the same time, the thought of either one of her boys putting themselves in danger—the way her husband had, the way her father had—terrified her. But, she supposed, it was probably just a reflection of motherhood—especially single motherhood—and the responsibilities and fears that entailed. Heck, the first time she'd seen Georgie tumble from his bike her heart had stopped a little. You can't protect your children from everything, after all, and when they grew up, they would be making their own choices. Still, the thought scared her.

Noah nodded. "Oh yes. It's very hard work. You have to be in top physical condition…" *Oh, he was.* "And you have to be able to remember a thousand details about how to treat wounded soldiers. And we did rescues too, so we had to learn how to get in and out of tough places as well. That's a lot of stuff to know." He paused for a second, then added, "But hard work is nothing to be afraid of."

"See?" Alexander nudged Jax with an elbow. "That's my mantra." Which launched another conversation between father and son that Amy didn't listen to because she was still watching Noah.

She liked the way he talked to the boys. Some people were patronizing and treated the boys like stupid adults. Noah talked to them as though they were intelligent, curious people…which they were. She wasn't sure why it irritated her that he was so good with the boys. Or so charming with Momma—who he had eating out of his hand.

She wasn't sure about anything when it came to Noah. In fact—

"So, Noah," she said before she even realized she'd opened her mouth, "how long are you staying in town?" Heat rushed up her face the second the words came out. She hadn't intended to ask. She'd asked him before, at the bakery, hadn't she? And he'd been noncommittal then. The second query probably made her look thirsty beyond words. How awkward. But it was too late. The question was out.

Indeed, his gaze hit her like a laser, holding her in its thrall. His lips quirked, as though her question had pleased him, and again, heat crawled through her belly. He toyed with the stem of his wine glass. "Well…"

"We've asked him to stay for the wedding," Natalie said, staring at him challengingly. That Nat stole his attention sent a slash of annoyance thorough Amy, which was ridiculous, but it happened.

Jax chuckled. "We did. He hasn't answered yet."

The wedding was two months away. All Amy could think was, *He could be here for two months*. And at the same time, she was swamped with relief and panic. How aggravating. She'd never met a man who made her feel so off balance. She had no idea why he had that effect on her, but she was not inclined to explore it. So, she put back her shoulders and said, quite clearly, "He probably has other plans."

She wasn't prepared when he caught her gaze again, grinned again—*Will you stop grinning?*—and said, "I don't have plans. Other than visiting some friends who are stationed in Washington and, eventually, getting up to Alaska."

"So, stay for the wedding." Natalie should just shut it.

"What's in Alaska?" Georgie asked.

Again, Noah turned to him, giving him his full attention. "It's the only state left on my list."

John J. gaped at him. "You've been to *all* the states?"

"Yep. Except Alaska."

"Wow." Both the boys were impressed. Amy should have been amused by that, but she wasn't. She didn't know why.

Noah grinned at their awe. "I remember, as a kid, learning about the gold rush up there, and I read they have actual places where you can pan for gold. They also have amazing wildlife and glaciers. Gorgeous scenery." He shrugged. "It seems like it'd be a cool place."

"Noah's been traveling the US looking for a place to settle," Natalie said with a smug smile. Okay, maybe it wasn't a smug smile, but it irritated Amy that Natalie knew so much about him. Not that it mattered to her. Not at all.

"Why not Virginia, then?" she asked, again without thinking. Virginia was, after all, where he was from. And, it should be mentioned, on the other side of the continent. Maybe then she could go back to the business of not thinking about him.

This time, when his gaze clashed with hers, there was a hint of pain; she nearly winced at it. Yes, his presence irritated her a little, but she hadn't intended to hurt him.

He gave a little shrug. "There's no one there," he said simply.

And yeah, she felt like a total jerk for asking. Her "Sorry" was hardly adequate, but he nodded all the same.

"What about your family?" John J. asked him— which made Amy's gut turn in knots. There were lots of reasons people left their family and never looked back. It was an uncomfortable question. Her sons were very good at asking uncomfortable questions.

But Noah, to his credit, was gracious and answered the intrusive query very simply and matter-of-factly. "I don't have a family." He flashed that grin again, but this time it had a completely different aspect. It made something in her chest ache. Her family was everything to her. She couldn't imagine not having them around.

John J., who was notoriously sensitive, teared up. "No mom?"

"Nope." Noah shook his head. "I never met either of my parents."

John J. looked at Amy, then back to Noah again. "But who tucked you in and told you bedtime stories?"

"Who cooked your dinner?" Georgie asked.

Noah chuckled. Actually chuckled. "I had foster parents." When the boys still looked puzzled, he added, "Those are people who take care of kids who don't have parents."

Even though his smile was gentle and reassuring, Amy knew he was softening his story for her boys, and she appreciated it. Foster care failed often. And even if it didn't, it was a tough life for a kid. The thought of Noah as a little boy, all alone in the world, nearly broke her heart. She had to look away.

"Well," Alexander lifted his glass. "Here's a toast to foster parents who open their homes and their hearts to all those kids." Everyone lifted their glasses and said, "Hear, hear," so Amy did too, even though her head was abuzz.

"You turned out pretty good," Jax said when the

cheers had faded. "I mean, world traveler, decorated veteran, paramedic—"

"Paramedic?" Celeste's eyes brightened. "Are you still licensed as a paramedic?" Amy nearly rolled her eyes. Celeste was a nurse. Of course she would find that a topic of interest. Noah wiped his mouth on his napkin and nodded, but before he could say anything, she continued. "Because I was at the last town council meeting, and they're actively looking for a new paramedic since Ray Stahl retired."

Jax nodded. "I forgot about that, yeah." He grinned at his buddy. "You'd be a great addition to the VFF as well."

Natalie snorted. "All the volunteer firefighters do in Coho Cove is meet up twice a month to train and drink beer."

Jax grinned. "Right?"

Noah laughed. "Sounds awesome."

"Closest thing we have to a country club," Jax joshed.

Momma snorted. "We're lucky there aren't many fires."

"But if we ever have them, we'll be ready," Jax said. And then he added, batting his lashes at his buddy, "We could use a paramedic though." Coho Cove was a small town—too small for its own fire department, though they did contract with the county for some services, including police and ambulance.

Noah was diplomatic. He merely smiled and said, "I will keep that in mind."

The conversation moved on with Alexander sharing stories of his recent sojourn to Arizona and Natalie sharing the news that several of her paintings had sold, but when the conversation lagged for a moment, Amy decided to share her news as well.

"I got an interesting call this afternoon," she said, glancing around the table. "My bakery has been selected for a profile on *Best of the Northwest Weekend.*"

"What is that, honey?" Momma asked.

Nat jumped in to answer. "It's that TV show, Momma. The one on channel 11 where they talk about fun things to do on the weekend in the region."

"That's very exciting, Amy." Celeste lifted her glass. "Congratulations."

Alexander nodded. "So great." He leaned over toward Noah. "She makes the best bear claws I've ever tasted."

"Thank you, Alexander." Gosh, it was nice to have their support, even though they probably didn't understand the full implications of the news and what it meant for her future. But that was okay.

What really shocked her was Noah's response. He said, "That kind of exposure could bring in a lot of new business." Their gazes tangled, but only until she looked away.

"Yes. That's the hope. The show has a following of people who enjoy gastro-tourism."

Momma shook her head. "Gastro-tourism? I've never heard of that."

To Amy's surprise, Noah chuckled. "Oh, it's a thing."

"People travel to places just to try food, Momma," she explained. "Mostly locally, but some people plan their vacations around specific bars and restaurants… and bakeries."

"Well, that sounds silly."

Alexander grinned. "I don't know. I would travel pretty far for Amy's bear claws."

"Thank you," Amy said with a smile. Jax's dad was one of her best customers. "The bottom line is it's going to be even busier at the bakery after that story comes out. At least. That's my hope."

"Well," Nat said, "if there's anything we can do to help, just holler, okay?"

Jax nodded. "Absolutely. I mean, you know I can't bake to save my life, but I'm happy to help out if things get crazy."

"Thanks, you guys." Gosh, it was nice to have their support. "Eloise is doing a great job, but it's hard to prepare, not knowing how many new customers we may attract."

Momma made a little snort noise—she was replete with snort noises. "If you're happy, then I'm happy for you."

A warmth rose in Amy's chest. "Thank you, Momma." Honestly, what else could she ask from her family?

After dinner was finished and dishes were done and Alexander left, Jax suggested they all take a walk to the park. Because it was midsummer it was still sunny outside and would be until late in the evening. The boys, who'd been bouncing off the walls since dessert, cheered.

Momma demurred because she was tired and Celeste wanted to stay home as well, so in the end, it was Jax and Nat, Amy and Noah and, of course, the boys who headed out. The boys ran ahead, followed by Jax and

Nat holding hands. Amy and Noah brought up the rear of the phalanx. Which wasn't awkward at all.

Amy glanced at him as they headed toward Main Street. She felt there should be a conversation but was unsure what to say. Oh, there were a lot of things she wanted to say. She'd never been a timid conversationalist, but something about Noah tipped her off her axis. Made her question every potential topic before it came out of her mouth.

It bothered her, certainly it did. She'd always prided herself on being confident, but something about him... well, scared her. She wasn't sure what it was.

Then again, maybe it wasn't him. Maybe it was *her*. Yes, he was attractive, exceedingly so, but she'd met lots of attractive men and she'd never had a problem talking to them. But when she thought about it, her circumstances had been very different back then. She'd been with George. She'd always been with George. Or grieving George. Up until now, her whole life had been George.

She wasn't sure what had changed, but she couldn't deny that something had. Noah made her look at the world through different eyes. He made her think about things she'd thought long dead. He made her *want*.

That was probably what was scaring her.

She sucked in a deep breath and resolved to force herself to face her inner fear and talk to him like the confident woman she was.

"So...you and Jax were stationed together at Bagram?"

"Sure is pretty here."

They both spoke at the same time.

He chuckled and nodded. "Small world, right?" Her

comment was meant to be a conversation starter, but he didn't pick up the thread or elaborate. Was it her imagination, or was he as nervous as she was? Or was she boring him? No. It couldn't be that. Not with the way he looked at her, matched her step, allowed Jax and Nat to get further and further ahead.

They walked a little while longer, side by side, just taking in the sun and the breeze and the hint of salt in the air. It was a peaceful silence, but she broke it anyway. "Was it my imagination, or did you almost ask me out yesterday?" she softened the gauche question with a smile.

He gored her with an amused glance. "Was it my imagination, or did you turn me down?"

They both chuckled, then she shrugged. "I'm a single mom. I don't date strange men."

"I'm not all that strange." His teeth flashed, and she had to laugh. And then he said, "So you don't date at all?"

She shook her head.

"May I ask why?"

It was a friendly question asked in a friendly manner. And despite the inelegance she felt because of her attraction to him, she liked him and felt comfortable talking to him. "There were—well, there are—so many reasons. Mostly I'm busy."

"And a mom."

She grinned as they turned a corner, and the park came into view. She could see the boys racing for the slide, Georgie in the lead, as usual. "It does complicate things. Besides, I live in a really small town. There's not a lot of single men I want to date." A lie. There were none. "Besides, I don't know. It feels like I'm being unfaithful to my husband even thinking about it." Gosh. She hadn't told anyone that. She was surprised it slipped out. When he shot her a sharp glance, she clarified. "My husband…died." It always felt so raw, so fresh when she said it out loud. Probably why she tried to avoid it. "He was killed in action in Afghanistan."

He stopped, and she did as well because his expression had gone serious, and his throat worked a little. It seemed as though he wanted to say something but, for some reason, was hesitating. But then, before she could ask, he said, out of the blue, "I knew your husband."

Amy's heart lurched. Her lungs failed. She gaped at him. "I beg your pardon?"

"George Tolliver. I knew him. He was a good man. I'm…sorry for your loss."

"You… You…" She wasn't sure why the revelation had flustered her so much. It had been nearly four years. She was used to the idea that George was gone. She was used to people bringing him up with no warning.

But this was different somehow. *Noah* was different.

Or maybe it was the other way around. Maybe the situation was different because it was Noah. Lusting after a random stranger was one thing, but lusting after a man who knew and respected George, well, it just felt wrong somehow.

"Are you okay?" he asked. His tone was low, concerned. She could hardly blame him. No doubt she appeared to be in shock. And, in truth, she kind of was.

"Sorry," she mumbled. "I don't mean to be melodramatic. I just needed a minute."

"Not at all. I understand. I'm sorry it came out like that. I just…felt you should know."

"I... Thank you." What else was there to say?

He cleared his throat with a concerning *ahem*. "I, ah... There's more."

More? Great! "Just tell me." Rip off all the Band-Aids.

He blew out a breath and scrubbed his face with a palm, then straightened his spine and looked her straight in the eye. "I, ah... Well, I was with him when he died, Amy."

Oh, God. Something cold and hard gushed through her. Her skin prickled. Her mouth went dry. She stared at him silently, unable to muster a response.

"Are you okay?"

She shook her head. No. Not really.

It happened like that sometimes, with the waves of grief when they came. Sometimes they brought pain as sharp as the first time. Sometimes they knocked her off her feet.

But this time, she wasn't alone. He was there—Noah, big and strong. When she wobbled, he steadied her; his hand on her arm was warm, a comfort. "I'm so sorry," he said.

She had no idea why she turned to him, into him, as the emotion pummeled her. But there was one thing she knew for certain: How safe she felt when his arms came around her and held her. That he rocked her a little, back and forth as he murmured, "It's okay, it's gonna be okay," into her ear as she sobbed.

She didn't know how long they stood there like that, how long it took her to gather herself again and regain her balance and gently push away. All she knew for sure was that he never wavered. He never pulled away.

"Are you okay?"

"Yeah." She sniffed, then rummaged in her pocket for a tissue, then honked her nose. "Sorry. I, well, I wasn't prepared."

"Nothing to be sorry for." He raked his hair back. "I didn't mean to upset you. I just thought, well, I thought you should know. And…"

She glanced at him when he trailed off.

"Well, if you ever wanted to know anything about… it, you can ask me."

If she wanted to know anything? Her pulse pounded in her ears. She had thousands of questions. They'd haunted her for years. What she didn't have—at least at the moment—was the courage to ask. So, she simply said, "Well, thank you for that."

He studied her for a moment, then nodded. "Sure thing. I'll be here."

It was a simple thing to say, but it enveloped her in something of a hug, nearly as warm as the one they'd just shared. She swallowed and, somehow, managed a smile. "Thanks for letting me know."

"Sure thing," he repeated. And then, "I wasn't sure if I should say anything or not…but it seemed wrong not to." They shared a glance, something warm and deep, as though truly seeing each other for the first time.

"Mom!" John J.'s bellow echoed from the swings, shattering the mood and stealing her attention. He was swinging high and pumping his little legs madly. It made her a little dizzy. "Watch me! Watch!"

"I'm watching," she called. And then, to her horror, at the highest point in the arc, he released the chain and went flying through the air.

* * *

Noah heard Amy's gasp and turned his attention to the playground in time to see John J. fly through the air and land with a thud on the hard ground. They both took off at a run, covering the distance in record time.

She fell to her knees at his side. "John J. Are you okay?" she asked as the others came to stand around.

In response, John J. held his ankle and wailed.

"Let Noah look at it," Jax said, urging him forward.

Noah hunkered down next to Amy. The first thing he needed to do was calm the boy because he was close to hyperventilating. He made eye contact and said in a measured voice, "Okay, John J. I need you to take a deep breath. Can you do that for me?"

The boy sniffled but nodded. "Uh-huh."

"Great job. Now another, but blow it out slowly."

Noah waited until he'd taken enough breaths to interrupt his crying, then said, "Okay, let's give this a look." Gently, he palpated the bones in the boy's foot and ankle, searching for a break but, more importantly, watching John J.s response. That would tell him more than anything about the injury. "How old are you again?" he asked. Not because he didn't remember, but to shift the boy's raptor-like attention from his pain to something else. It worked.

"I'm five. Almost six."

"Wow." No obvious breaks. Good. "That's pretty old."

"I know. My birthday party is coming up pretty soon."

"So, I'm going to slip off your shoe. Okay?"

A sniff and a nod.

"You just stop me if anything hurts. Okay?"

Another nod.

"So, what are the plans for your birthday?"

Oh, that perked him up. John J. chattered about a swimming party and a cake with a velociraptor on it and someone named Dylan as Noah unlaced and worked off his shoe and sock, checking for signs of swelling or bruising. Thankfully, he didn't find anything. He glanced at Amy, who'd been watching on tenterhooks, and nodded.

"Well, young man. It looks like it's nothing serious, but let's take it easy for a while, just in case, okay?" He looked at Amy. "You're going to want to ice it when you get home. Keep down the swelling."

"Of course."

"Do you want to try to stand up?" That was the next test. There was still the chance of a non-displaced fracture. If the ankle couldn't bear weight or if it was too painful to stand, it could be a break rather than a sprain, and he'd have to tell Amy to take the boy for an X-ray.

John J. stood—albeit cautiously. He even took a few tentative steps. Then, when that didn't hurt, he hopped a little. Right on the injured foot. Noah nearly swallowed his tongue.

"Easy," Amy barked. "He said take it easy!"

"Yeah," Noah had to say. "Maybe don't hop for a while, okay?"

John J. blew out a breath and rolled his eyes, probably at his mother. "All right," he muttered.

His response made Noah want to laugh, but he bit his lip to stave it off. "How about a piggyback ride to the house?"

"Yahoo!" John J. cried, then clambered onto Noah's back.

"I want a piggyback ride too," Georgie complained.

Noah chuckled. "I can only handle one customer at a time." He sent a sneaking glance to Jax who made a face but then bent down to let Georgie climb on as well.

Amy collected John J.'s shoe and sock, and then they all walked back to the house, Noah carrying John J. on his back and Amy by his side. Nat and Jax followed behind with Georgie.

"Thank you," she said softly. Her smile made something warm in his belly. Hell, her smile made his entire day.

That night, as he lay in his bed trying to sleep, Noah struggled. It was funny how learning one small fact about another person could shift a man's perspective completely. When he'd met Amy, his first reaction had been a deep, visceral attraction, so much so that he'd asked her out without any compunction. He usually moved more slowly when it came to dating, but there had been something there, some vibrant attraction. He could feel it in his bones.

He'd been shocked when she'd walked through the door at Pearl's house…with her boys.

Yeah, he'd wanted to ask her out the moment he'd seen her, but now he knew he would not be having a fling with her. She had two kids, for pity's sake. Was it wrong that learning she was a mom to two small boys had taken him aback? Granted, he liked Amy's boys. They were both clever and funny, and, well, they reminded him of his friend George.

But that was another barrier, wasn't it?

She was George's widow. That alone gave him pause because it set her apart from other women. The tenor of any interaction with her was and always would be colored by that filter.

That didn't mean he magically stopped being attracted to her. It just…complicated things.

Most certainly, it slowed things down in terms of his pursuit of her.

He made a face. He didn't even like that word when it came to Amy Tolliver. She wasn't prey. But she definitely didn't need some random horndog popping into her life and then skating away when he'd had his fun. She wasn't that woman.

Aside from all that, he was only here for a short while. Getting entangled with a woman—who had a family—was not in the plans. But when you tossed the fact that she was George's widow into the mix, the thought of a fling was simply untenable. He just couldn't do it.

Trouble was, while his mind was clear on that point, there was something else, deep inside him, that wanted something different. A little voice whispering that she was something special and he shouldn't let her go. That he should explore whatever this was with her.

So, yeah. It would suck to hang around with her for the next couple months—which would happen, considering how close Jax was with Natalie's family—all the while trying to ignore his attraction to her. A second option would be to make a point to avoid her and the boys while he was here, but he really didn't want to do that either.

The final option—the nuclear option—would be to make some excuse and continue his journey to Alaska and avoid the problem all together. But that was the coward's choice, wasn't it?

Aside from the fact that he did not identify as a coward, the thought of leaving turned his stomach. Oh, missing Jax's wedding was in the mix, but the main point of resistance—if he was being true and honest with himself—was that he didn't want to leave *her*. This woman he'd just met did something magical to his soul. She made him feel…good.

Good was a stupid word, and he knew it, but he wasn't really ready to explore what that feeling really meant, that warmth, that comfort, that rightness… Not yet at least.

Yeah. He wasn't going to precipitously leave. All in all, the best option would be to suck it up, keep his feelings to himself and simply enjoy the time he had here. He and Amy Tolliver could be—would be—friends and nothing more. It was as simple as that.

Chapter Four

Amy's phone woke her up early the next morning, which was really annoying because it was her morning to sleep in as Eloise was opening the bakery. She cracked open one eye and glared at the phone. When that didn't stop the ringing, she groaned and reached out for the beast and checked the screen.

She groaned again when she saw it was Kim calling. It was never good when the sitter called this early. She sucked in a deep breath and answered with a too-chirpy "Morning!"

Kim didn't even bother with the niceties. "Amy, I'm so sorry. I'm not going to be able to watch the boys today—Dylan's sick."

Amy flopped down onto the pillow and stared at the ceiling. Yeah. She'd expected as much. It wasn't the first time Kim had canceled, but today her sister Celeste wasn't available to cover for her, and Amy didn't have a lot of other options. It was aggravating, but she couldn't take it out on Kim, so she merely said something inane like, "No problem. Thanks for letting me know," and ended the call.

But it was a problem. It was a huge problem.

She groaned and forced herself out of bed and into the bathroom for a shower. It was easier to think, sometimes, in water.

By the time she was dressed and pouring her coffee, she'd made a decision. She hated to do it, but she had to call Nat.

She and her sister hadn't always gotten along, but lately, since Nat had come back home and gotten together with Jax, their relationship had gotten better. They were almost…friends. It was an astounding thought, given their past history, but at the moment, it was a huge relief that she had someone to turn too. *If* Nat was available.

It was a big if.

Amy sat at the table, fortified with a huge mug of wake-up juice, and dialed her sister—hoping to God she wasn't waking her up or, worse, interrupting any early morning romps with Jax.

Nat picked up right away. "Hey, Amy. What's up?"

"You're awake? Thank goodness. Nat, Kim can't sit today. Can you watch the boys? I hate to ask, but I really need your help."

Silence crackled on the line, and Amy panicked, just a little. Yeah, they were getting along better, but their relationship was still rocky. Amy never knew what might set off a rift.

But, when she responded, Natalie's tone was one of delight. "Yes. Oh, yes!" she said. "I would love that."

"Are you sure? You…hesitated."

Nat let out a laugh. "I'm thrilled, just a little surprised is all. You've never asked me to watch the boys by myself before."

"Haven't I?" *Um, you never* lived here *before.* Thought but not said. In the interest of keeping the fragile peace and all. Amy had leaned heavily on Momma and Celeste before she'd found a permanent sitter. Heck, even Jax had been a tremendous support in the past years on account of his friendship with George and his affection for the boys. But Nat had lived in LA until recently.

"I… I guess I thought you didn't trust me with them."

While Nat's words made the little hairs on her nape prickle, Amy ignored the looming trigger. It bothered her that Nat would be thinking something like that without giving voice to it, but considering that they'd been trying to work on their relationship, they'd both been cautiously dancing around issues. "Of course I trust you! The boys love you, and you're so good with them."

"Well, I'm honored. I'd love to watch them. Anytime. Truly."

"Great. Thanks, Nat. We'll be over in about an hour."

"I'll be at the studio."

Amy shook her head as she disconnected the call. Relationships could be a challenge sometimes—especially with sisters—but it was wonderful to have people there for you when you needed them. That made all the work worth it. Of course, it was just as wonderful if you could be there for them when they needed it too.

* * *

Noah woke up with a start. He wasn't sure what woke him until he heard it again. A whoop. Then a laugh. Footsteps heading for his door, and Natalie calling out, "Wait. Stop!"

He barely had time to jerk up and rearrange his covers—yeah, he was used to sleeping in the buff—before the bedroom door banged open and Georgie and John J. piled into the room with Natalie on their tail.

She stopped short when she saw his naked chest, then slapped her hand over her eyes and spun around, but the boys just stood there and stared.

"I'm so sorry," Natalie said. "I couldn't stop them."

"Wow," John J. took a step closer. "Is that a tiger?"

Noah glanced down, although he already knew there was a tiger on his chest. "Uh, yep."

"Boys. Please." Natalie tried to corral them back into the studio without glancing in Noah's direction, but it didn't work. "Come on. Give Noah some privacy, please?"

"How are your muscles so big?" Georgie asked.

"Boys. Outside. Now." There was a hint of panic in Natalie's tone or something…something that got through to them. Because they, though grumbling, turned and shuffled from the room. "I'm so sorry," Nat said again before she dipped out as well and closed the door behind her.

Noah was out of bed and dressed like a shot; he didn't suppose the boys would stay out for long. Indeed, when he stepped into the studio they swarmed him immediately, peppering him with questions as he poured a cup of coffee from the old pot and made himself something to eat. Jax, Natalie explained, had gone over to help his dad with a project, so it was just the four of them. And the boys were relentless.

"Please," Natalie said after a bit. "Give Noah a little space, won't you? Would you like me to set up easels so you can paint too?"

The boys cried *hurrah* and ran over to help her, and that activity gave Noah at least a moment to eat in peace, but it wasn't long before they got bored of painting and headed over to the table where he was scrolling through his phone, catching up on emails and news. They were like little magnets, as if they couldn't stay away. They pummeled him with questions and stories and brags.

Though Natalie was deep into her work, Noah could tell she had an ear on what was happening and was ready to leap in if he needed a break from their chatter, but Noah found he really didn't mind. Granted, the incessant attention might have annoyed a man like him, a man who'd had no exposure to children and no inclination to have said exposure, but these were *Amy's* boys. Somehow that made it different. Rather than being irritating, as he suspected might have been the case, they amused him. Their innocence and trust was charming.

For example, when, out of the blue, John J. announced, with a hint of pride in his voice, "I passed kindergarten this year, you know."

Noah couldn't help but smile. "Really?"

The boy nodded. "Straight stars."

"Pretty impressive."

Georgie, sitting across from Noah, rolled his eyes. "Everyone gets straight stars in kindergarten."

John J. turned on his brother. "Nuh-uh. Dylan got a frowny face when he hit Sylvia!"

"Dylan hit Sylvia?" Noah had no idea who either of them were, but John J.'s outrage at this atrocity made him want to respond.

The younger boy nodded and blew out a sigh. "Sometimes Dylan hits people."

"You should just hit him back," Georgie suggested.

"He's bigger than me. He pushes too."

"Well..." Noah hadn't spent much time with children, but he figured he should probably step in and say something. "Seems to me there may be better ways to deal with problems than hitting."

"Tell that to Dylan," John J. huffed.

"Kindergarten is for babies," Georgie put in. "*I* finished first grade and can even read." This in a tone of supreme superiority.

Noah's heart ached when he saw the hurt on John J.'s little face. He really didn't know why he wanted to fix that, but he said, "That's an exciting thing to look forward to, John. Learning to read this year."

The younger boy sniffed and put out a lip. "John *J.*"

"I beg your pardon?"

"My name is John J. Not just plain John."

"Of course. Sorry. Are you looking forward to learning how to read?"

"I suppose." He shrugged. "But I like that Mom reads to me to sleep every night."

Noah was unprepared for the gut punch. He hadn't even been aware of his own lingering wound until this moment. No one had ever read to him before bed. He'd never thought he'd missed it. But maybe he had. "What kind of books does she read?" he asked, not because it mattered, but because he needed a moment to process the swirling emotions.

Maybe that was why he'd never been anxious to be around kids, because they were a reminder of how many tiny cuts there had been in his childhood, cuts he preferred to ignore. But the boys took the bait and ran with it, both of them chattering on about the books they were reading—with their mom—right now, as well as probably every book she'd ever read them all the way back to *Goodnight Moon*.

Yeah. This was the way childhood should be. The way he'd always wished it could be. With love and care and, simply, time together. To him, it seemed like the perfect expression of love to cuddle up under the covers and go on an adventure together through the pages of a book—to share that experience with someone you loved and who loved you back.

"Did anyone ever read to you?" John J. asked out of the blue.

A lot of their questions and observations were from out of the blue, he noticed. A lot of them were tough. That was the thing about children—they hadn't developed filters yet. While Noah had to admit it made him a little uncomfortable, never knowing what they were going to say, he also appreciated a straightforward question. Adults were terrible at straightforward questions. And straightforward questions deserved straightforward answers. "I read to myself," he said.

"Oh." The boys exchanged a glance. There might have been sympathy in it.

"Why didn't you have parents?" Georgie asked.

"Well, they died when I was a baby." At least, that was what he'd been told.

"We had an uncle who died," John J. piped up.

Georgie nodded. "And a dad that died." This softly, solemnly.

Noah swallowed heavily as memories of George whipped through his mind. It was a bald reminder that while these boys had a seemingly idyllic childhood— one he envied—they'd had tough losses too. "It's hard when people die, isn't it?"

John J. frowned. "Why didn't your grandmother take care of you when your parents died? Our grandmother used to take care of us before she got a stroke."

Fun question. Noah had to shrug. "I don't know. I was a baby back then." But since he'd ended up in foster care, it was a good probability that his parents' parents hadn't been able to take care of him either.

"Don't you know anything?" It wasn't a rude question, even though it sounded that way. Georgie was a pragmatist, Noah could tell.

"I know that sometimes we have people to count on and sometimes we have to take care of ourselves. I know it's important to figure out what you want in life and to try for it and be strong. And that it's important to know what's right and wrong—and to choose right." Not what the boy was asking, but it was an apt answer, nonetheless. What he also knew, but didn't share with these tender minds, was that sometimes there were no answers to the questions haunting you, and you had to find a way to move on without knowing. You had to carve out a life that pleased you, because no one else could do it for you.

But he also knew that having the answers to your burning questions wasn't always a good thing. Sometimes it was better not to know. Sometimes it was better to be free of the weight of the past.

The third degree about his parentage was interrupted when Natalie got a call and then, when she hung up, made her way over to the table and sighed. "Noah, I need to run into town for about a half an hour to deal with a problem at the gallery. Would you mind staying with the boys for a bit?"

A trickle of panic swirled in his gut. He wasn't good with kids. At least, not that he knew. Granted, he'd never really spent much time alone with them. Still, he forced a smile and said, "Sure. Not at all."

He regretted it as soon as she drove off because the boys turned at stared at him like meerkats on the Serengeti. Then John J. said, "I'm hungry. I like grilled cheese."

"Uh… I can probably make that."

Turned out with small boys, as with grown soldiers, food was always an excellent time filler. The boys helped him hunt down the large frying pan and spatula in a drawer beneath the stove—the ones that Jax used when he cooked for them, then they watched him like hawks as he cooked. They chatted a bit, but it was mostly a commentary on how his grilled cheese making style differed from their mom's.

"Be careful," John J. warned him as he prepared to make the flip. "Pans are hot."

Noah bit back a grin. "Yes," he said. "They are."

When sandwiches were melty and golden, and he

transferred them onto plates and set them on the table before the boys, Georgie shot him a—disappointed?—look.

"What is it?" Noah asked.

"Mom always cuts them in triangles," he said.

"Triangles? Okay." He went into the drawer and pulled out a butter knife and sliced each sandwich into four triangles. "Better?"

John J. shook his head. "It needs a ketchup bloop in the middle."

"A ketchup...bloop?"

"I'll show you." Georgie marched to the fridge and found the bottle and squirted a generous blob of ketchup on each sandwich. "See?"

"Ah." Again, Noah had to hold back a smile. "Okay. So this is how Mom makes them?"

John J. surveyed the offering from several angles and then nodded. "Yeah."

"Pretty much," Georgie added.

"Great," Noah said with a huge sigh of faux relief. "Shall we eat?"

The only response to that was chewing.

After they ate, Noah and Georgie were in the middle of a conversation about the relative superiority of Batman or Superman when Noah felt a poke on his bicep. He glanced down to see John J. staring at his arm. "What is it, buddy?" he asked.

The boy looked up at him. "How do you make it like that?" he asked.

"Like what?"

John J. poked him again. "So big?"

"My muscles, you mean?"

"Yeah. Mine don't do that thing." He made a muscle—
or tried to, gritting his teeth and everything.

It took an effort, but Noah held back a chuckle.
"Well, first you have to build muscle through exercise.
And then you have to use it to keep it."

They spent the next while outside with Noah showing
the boys the kinds of exercises they could do to make
their muscles stronger. And though he was teaching
them, he learned something too.

The secret of handling high-energy children was
wearing them down. It wasn't long before he had the
boys running sprints. And then they built an obstacle
course in Jax's yard and he had them run that.

Most importantly, when they were exhausted, there
were a lot fewer questions.

By the time Amy had dropped off the boys off with
Natalie and gotten to work that morning, Eloise had already finished the morning baking and had opened the
shop. When Amy walked through the door, there was
a line, so she dropped her purse in the office, quickly
donned her apron, and helped clear the customers.

Her plan was to sit Eloise down—once they had a
minute of peace—and tell her about the coming TV profile and the plans she had to prepare for it, which she'd
worked out yesterday, long into the night.

It was a great feeling, having a plan. It freed her from
stress, gave her a path forward and made her excited
about the truckload of work that was coming.

She'd hired Eloise straight out of a culinary school in
Seattle and had spent the past few months training her
on the specifics of working in a real bakery. Training

was critical and a firm education was important, but there was nothing like doing the work in an actual bakery. To Amy's delight, Eloise was coming along nicely.

The only fly in the ointment was that Eloise had met Ethan and once the two of them started dating, well, problems started to crop up. Early on, Amy had had to ask that he not visit when Eloise was on shift because the work just didn't get done when he was around. Aside from that, a couple times, Eloise had been late for work.

In some businesses, being late for work wasn't that big of a deal, but for Amy's business, it was critical. Many of her items were freshly baked, which meant starting hours before the doors opened. Aside from that, if Eloise didn't show up on time for some shifts, Amy didn't get any breaks, and that was grueling.

But lately they'd gotten into a groove, Eloise had been on point and everything was fine. It was a huge relief.

Unfortunately—or not—there was a steady flow of customers for most of the day. It was nearly closing when they finally had a moment to talk. How aggravating was it, then, that just as she was about to lay out the opportunity-slash-plan, Ethan walked in.

Amy huffed a sigh. Yes, okay, it was almost closing time. That wasn't a direct defiance of the boundaries she'd set for the two of them, but it was pretty close to annoying. Before she could say anything or decide if this breach of the rules was worth making a stink over, Ethan said, "Have you told her yet?"

Eloise flushed, which made something in Amy's gut churn.

"Told me what?"

"It was busy all day," Eloise said, heading over to give Ethan a kiss. It was a long kiss. Way too PDA for work, but Amy held her tongue because she suspected something else was coming. Something worse. She recognized the vibe. She'd been quit on before.

When Pierre left her in the lurch, it had been devastating, but now, with the TV show coming… She just couldn't think of it!

"Just tell me," she said. She tried not to snap but probably failed.

Eloise looked at Ethan and grinned. "We're getting married."

Oh. Okay. Not quitting? "That's wonderful." She gushed out a breath and went to hug them both. "Congratulations."

"See," Ethan said. "I told you she wouldn't be mad."

Amy chuckled. "Why would I be mad? I think it's great. I'm sure you'll be happy." They were really cute together, when he wasn't distracting her from work. Also, it meant she'd be less likely to move back to Seattle like Pierre.

"We're getting married *today*," Eloise clarified.

Amy gaped at them. Literally gaped. With her jaw slack and everything. "Today?"

Ethan grinned. "We're heading to Reno to elope."

"Today?!"

"Yes. Ethan proposed last night, and we decided to leave right away—" Eloise began.

"But she wanted to come in and tell you today, so you had time to get someone else to, you know, help out." Ethan finished for her. His grin was brilliant.

"Time?" It was the only word Amy could manage

because a cold snowy avalanche of stress had started the slow tumble over her head and catching her breath was hard. "Time?"

"We have to go, babe," Ethan said. "We don't want to miss our flight."

"Wait, wait, wait, wait." They both seemed surprised that she stopped them from leaving. "When will you be back?"

The two of them, so young, so clueless, exchanged a glance, and then Eloise shrugged. "A week?"

Ethan shook his head. "Maybe two?" Another brilliant grin. "Honeymoon—you know."

"Wait." The only word she could remember apparently. She turned to Eloise. "Are you quitting your job?" She was a businesswoman. She knew it was important to clarify. It had taken her a while to replace her last pâtissier on account of the fact that very few people were willing to move to a small town way out on the coast to work.

Eloise stared at her like a deer in the headlights. "Well, I don't want to quit." No. Of course she didn't. She wanted to have her cake and eat it too. Who didn't? "Can't you hold the job for me?"

"If you leave, you must realize I have to replace you." Amy was stunned her voice was so calm because inside she was screaming. Her mind was numb, and her gut was like an active volcano. She simply refused to think about the summer crowds and the coming interview and Coho Days, and John J.'s birthday cake— which Eloise had promised to decorate—and all the other things barreling her way…because she might have snapped. She could save that for tonight, her sleepless, stressed-out night.

Eloise's eyes went wide. "But I love this job."

Amy turned away and scrubbed at her face. "Look," she said after a long moment. "I love the work you do, Eloise, and the customers adore you, but you're leaving me in the lurch right in the middle of the busiest time of year. As valuable as you are, I can't hold your job open indefinitely. And I cannot run this bakery all by myself. I'm going to have to look for help. Bottom line, I would love to hold the job for you, but I can't make any promises."

"Dude," Ethan said. "That's totally unfair."

Unfair? Amy said nothing, just stared at him. *Unfair?* He didn't know the meaning of the word. But there was no point trying to explain, was there? They had made up their minds. She could see in their eyes— they were going to elope today and let the chips fall where they may.

As Amy watched them make their way to Ethan's van, packed with luggage, she couldn't help remembering another young and impulsive couple who'd been madly in love and who'd decided to run off and elope— come what may. No one and nothing could have deterred her and George back then.

And look how that had turned out for them.

Something was wrong. Noah could tell the second Amy stepped into the studio that afternoon. Her expression was tight, a far cry from her usual, energetic appearance. Jax and Natalie had taken the boys down to the pier for ice cream, and Noah had elected to stay behind because, frankly, he was pooped. Though he'd figured out how to engage with the boys and they'd had a lot of fun together, it had been a long day. Clearly he wasn't as fit as he'd thought he was. It had been a shock because, as a PJ, he'd been in top physical condition. He hadn't realized how much stamina he'd lost during the last year and a half. Granted, riding a Harley was hardly a hard-core workout. Somewhere during the day, he'd made a resolution to get back to a regular training schedule, whether he was on the road or not.

"Hey, you," he said as she came in and dropped onto the chair by the sofa, where he'd been lounging. And then, when she blew out a sigh in response, he added, "Tough day?" He was horrified when tears pooled in her eyes in response.

"The worst."

"I'm sorry." He wished he knew what to say or do to comfort her, but all he could think of was to say, "What happened?"

And then he wished he hadn't said anything because Amy burst into tears. Well, damn. He couldn't just sit there and watch. He stood and moved toward her, and next thing he knew, she was in his arms, sobbing her heart out. Again. Noah held her, rocked her a little, hoping it soothed her, but really, he felt helpless and frustrated. There wasn't anything he could do but this, and that sucked.

After a while, Amy pulled back and dried her eyes and sniffled. "Thanks, Noah. No. I'm okay. I…" And then, to his dismay, she dissolved again.

"It's okay," he said, pulling her back into a hug. "Just get it out."

And she did. She seemed to cry forever there in his arms, and while it was hard to hear, he was glad he'd been able to be there for her. That someone had been around to comfort her.

Then, all at once, she dried up and pushed away. She mopped at her cheeks and sniffled and made a growling sound.

"That bad?"

Somehow, she pushed out a laugh. He liked that she was resilient, that her humor was still within reach. "The absolute worst."

"Come and tell me." He led her to the table, and after she sat, he went to the fridge and grabbed her a beer, even though she hadn't asked for one. He popped the top and handed it to her, and she took a long draw, then gusted a huge, heart-wrenching sigh. "Thanks," she said. "I needed that."

"Sure." He didn't ask her again what had happened, rather sat and waited. He knew some things took time to process. Besides, he had all day, and he liked being with her. He liked being able to comfort her. He really liked it when she looked up at him and there was fire back in her eyes.

"Eloise quit."

"Wow."

"I mean, I think she quit. She and Ethan announced that they're eloping to Reno. Tonight!"

The intensity in her expression elicited another "Wow."

"Right? They're on their way to the airport."

"And Eloise is…?"

She made a face at him. He wasn't sure why—probably because he'd just exposed that he didn't have a clue what the problem really was—but he didn't mind. He didn't mind as long as he could distract her from this disaster, at least a little. "She's my assistant. I'm training her to be a pâtissier. I have been for the last four months."

"Oh. Wow." This time he meant it. He'd been bailed on before, and it straight up sucked. Also, he'd learned, from Ma, how much a bakery on a shoestring needed each and every person.

"Now I have the busy summer season, and the TV show to prepare for, and Coho Days, and John J.'s birthday party, and a bunch of huge projects coming up, and I'll be all on my own."

"That's a lot."

She pulled a tissue from her pocket and blew her nose. "Right?"

"Can you hire another person?"

Wrong thing to say. She glared at him. "It took three months to get her. I mean, I can't just hire anyone, you know. I need someone who knows how to bake." She blew out a wet sigh.

"Right."

"Oh, I just don't know what I'm going to do."

He hated the hint of a panicked wail in her tone. He hated that the tears threatened again. That was probably why he said, "I'm more than happy to help out if you need a body." He wasn't sure where the offer had sprung from, other than the fact that he really wanted to help her. That and the undeniable truth that he wouldn't mind spending more time with her as well. She was a bright and bold presence. And damn cute.

Especially when her eyes boggled and her nostrils flared like that. She gaped at him. "I need a *baker*."

He shrugged. "I can bake."

Her smile was sweet and only a little condescending. "I'm not talking about a pan of chocolate chip cookies, Noah. I need someone who has at least a basic understanding of how a commercial bakery works. There are all kinds of safety issues and health codes and…"

He nodded. "Uh-huh."

She gaped at him. "Wait. You bake?"

"I'm…adept." And then when her gape became even gapier. "Why are you so incredulous?"

She waved at his person. "You don't exactly look like a baker."

"Ha." He waggled a finger at her. "Exactly why you should not judge the proverbial book by its cover." He waggled his brows as well, just for good measure. "I have hidden skills."

She wet-snorted a laugh. He loved when she did that. "I have no doubts about that at all. But you absolutely do not look like a baker."

"And yet here I am. Utterly adept."

"Okay." She crossed her arms and took on something of a businesslike demeanor. "Tell me about your experience in a kitchen, then."

Great. She was taking him seriously. At least he hoped so. "Well, when I was in high school, my foster mother had a bakery and gave me a job. It was my first real job. Granted, I started off washing pans and cleaning the kitchen after school—"

She gusted a sigh. "A man who can clean." He was pretty sure she was teasing, but there might have been some honestly in her sarcasm because the back end of baking—the mess—was a lot of work.

"But it wasn't long before I was pounding butter." Ma had done a lot of French pastries, so there has been a lot of pounding butter.

Amy huffed a laugh. "Okay. You know your lamination."

He knew a hell of a lot more than that. "And then when I showed the inclination and the ability, she started teaching me more. I mean, I'm not a professional pâtissier or anything like that, but I know my way around an éclair. At least enough to help here and there."

Her smile dimmed, her amusement replaced with something akin to consideration. "Would you be willing…" She trailed off, and he frowned.

"What?"

"Would you be willing to do a test bake for me? I mean…" A rosy hue flushed her cheeks. "I don't mean to be rude, since you're offering to help out, but it is my *business*, you know? It's my livelihood."

"I'd be more than happy to." In fact, the idea kind of excited him. Baking again? It had been a really long time since those days, but that time had been filled with good memories. He'd loved that bakery. Loved all the smells. Loved the flavors. He'd really loved Ma. She'd been the closest thing to a real parent that he could remember, and she'd come into his life at just the right time. His childhood had been filled with uncertainty— being shuttled from home to home, often with no notice, constantly recreating himself and, occasionally, finding himself in hostile environs. But when he was fifteen— a really troubled kid headed for disaster—he'd been moved from a group home to live with Ma, and everything had changed. She'd given him the stability he'd been craving, and guidance and warmth. She'd been the one to support his interest in the Air Force. She'd been the one who'd encouraged him to get his grades up so he'd be accepted. She'd been the one to drive him to the recruitment office. In his estimation, he was the man he was because of her. She'd saved him.

Amy tipped her head to the side. "I need someone right away."

He shrugged. "I'm just hanging out until the wedding." In fact, he'd been thinking about how he could spend the time here before then. Jax and Nat both worked pretty much all day, though they were both artists and therefore not locked to a schedule. Jax had suggested a fishing trip with his friend Ben, and they planned to head over to visit Noah's friends at Joint Base Lewis-McChord, but other than those plans, he was wide open.

"Well…" He could tell she was really taking him seriously now. "If you're sure you wouldn't mind helping out, you can come home with us tonight and show me your stuff."

He had no idea why a niggle of excitement shot through him at that. She was talking about his baking skills and nothing else. And he didn't want anything else. Did he? At least that was what he'd been telling himself. She was George's widow and the mother of his two sons. She was the kind of woman a man didn't toy with. She was the kind of woman a man took seriously.

He didn't know if he was ready for something serious…but he just couldn't deny the feeling that this was an opportunity for him, for them, to get to know each other better and maybe, just maybe, find something special.

And he also couldn't deny the sudden gush of heady anticipation surging through his veins to get his hands in a wad of dough once again.

Noah was fabulous.

There was no denying it.

He'd followed Amy and the boys home on his Harley and then, while she was making dinner, he'd whipped up the most amazing cream puffs with a light pastry cream and chocolate drizzle, all made from scratch. She'd watched him like a hawk, and he hadn't made a single mistake. She was, in a word, flabbergasted.

And incredibly thankful.

She'd thought her world was crashing in around her, and he had—so easily, so simply—propped it all back up.

Sure, she still needed to think about finding a permanent replacement for Eloise, but she knew, with Noah's help, she could at least make it through the next few weeks without falling flat on her face. Most importantly, she wouldn't have to do it all on her own.

After supper, after they'd put the boys to bed, they sat at the table and talked, mostly because she wanted to get a better idea of where his skill base was, and explain the basics of how she ran the bakery—the nitty-gritty of the daily and weekly schedule, what the priorities were, her business philosophy and so on—but also, well, she enjoyed talking to him. He was entertaining, intelligent and funny.

She'd forgotten how much she enjoyed conversations like this.

"So," she said, after assessing what he could do and outlining for him the kind of tasks she needed help with, "Let's talk wages."

Noah made a snort. "You don't have to pay me. It'll be fun."

She made a face. "It'll be fun for a little while, maybe." It had been for her. "But it's hard work too. I wouldn't be comfortable not paying you." Besides, it was important to have clear parameters when working with a friend, and a paycheck was one of the definitive reminders.

After they settled on a number, they talked a little about the items on offer at the bakery, and the ones he was comfortable helping out with. "I'm going to need some time to get back in the flow," he warned. "I'm a little rusty. But I'd love to learn new things too." Gosh, she loved the twinkle of enthusiasm in his eye.

"Anything in particular?"

"I mean, I can laminate dough, but I'd love to learn more about working with pastry."

She smiled at him. "I'd be more than happy to show you what I know…if there's time."

"Great."

"In the meantime, let me grab a copy of my recipes for the things you'll be helping with."

"That would be great."

She left him with a cup of decaf and what was left of the cream puffs he'd made and went into her office to print out copies of the recipes. While she was there, she grabbed one of her old course books on pastry so he could bone up.

He was excited to see it and flipped through the pages with interest. "This is great," he said. "Thanks."

His enthusiasm made her feel a lot better about the situation, because somehow it felt like she was taking advantage of him, or intruding on his visit with Jax. But his eagerness belayed all her fears.

As she started to wrap up the orientation—which was the way she was thinking of it in her mind, as difficult as that was sitting there with this gorgeous fragrant man across the table from her in a cozy room—there was one more thing on her mind. One very awkward thing.

She gusted a breath and steeled her spine and then blurted, "There is something else I want to bring up before we start working together tomorrow."

"Mmm-hmm." He glanced at her curiously.

"I…ah… Oh, how do I say this?"

"It's okay. Just say it."

"Are you sure?"

"I'm a big boy." He chuckled. "I can take it."

"Okay. Well, Noah, this bakery is my business. It's, well, other than my family, it's everything to me."

"I get it."

"And, well, you did ask me out. You remember?"

He chuckled. "Yeah. I remember." He leaned closer.

She held up a hand. "I just want to clarify that this is…"

"Ah." He stared at her. His full lower lip kicked up. There might have been a hint of regret in that smile. "A business arrangement?"

"Yes." She gusted a relieved sigh. Thank God. He got it. "Yes. So absolutely no hanky-panky." When his eyes gleamed at that, she added, "No flirting." It was just too easy to get swept away. At least, she might if he batted those lashes at her.

"So...just friends?"

"Yes." Definitely that.

"Okay." Was he hiding a smile? "But since we're clarifying things?"

"Yes?"

"Just because I'm not flirting with you doesn't mean I don't find you attractive." His expression made her shiver a little. "Because I do."

Her jaw dropped. Oh, good glory. That was unexpected. Both his straightforward comment and the slurry of heat it sent through her. "Um, I see."

"I just wanted to clarify that."

"Well..." She shuffled her papers and tried to look all professional and whatnot, but her blush probably ruined the effect. "I appreciate that, but..."

"But this is business, right?"

"Yes, please."

He slapped his palm over his heart. "I hereby promise while we are at the bakery it'll be all business. You don't need to worry about that."

"Thank you." Gosh, she appreciated his directness.

It wasn't until he had gathered up the recipes and left that she realized he hadn't made any promises about their time *outside* the bakery. And she hadn't asked for one.

Chapter Five

After Noah left—to head back to the studio for a good night's sleep because they both had an early morning the next day—Amy headed to bed with her heart full.

It had been a horrible day, the worst since she'd received the news about George, but it had ended on such a high note that all the stress and anxiety she'd felt pressing down on her after Eloise's announcement had been wiped away.

She awoke the next morning before her alarm, filled with an elation she hadn't known in a long while. Everything seemed easy—even getting the boys up and dressed and out the door, which sometimes was a chore. She dropped them off at Kim's—because she'd called to say Dylan was feeling better—and headed to the bakery in the predawn darkness. Noah was already there waiting for her, leaning against his Harley, looking too hot for words.

"Morning," he called with a wave as she got out of her car.

She grinned. "You're early." Gosh, he looked sharp. Freshly shaven and sexy in his black T-shirt. And his aftershave… Yummy.

He grinned back. "I'm looking forward to baking again."

"I'm looking forward to seeing you in action." Then she gave an evil cackle. "Just wait until you see how much work there is." She was joking, but deep inside there was a harbored fear that after he saw just how much there was to do each morning, before the bakery even opened, he might decide he'd made a mistake. And though she knew he would give this his all—he just seemed like that kind of guy—it was a possibility.

So, there was a hint of trepidation in her soul as she opened the door and turned on the lights. They headed straight for the kitchen. It was a smallish kitchen, so the tour didn't take long—the fridge, the freezer, proofers, fryers, ovens… The storeroom in the back was much more complicated. She gave him a quick tour of where she kept everything then pointed out the office to the right and, of course, the toilet in the back.

Once she'd shown him everything they got right to work. During the next few hours, they shaped the pre-laminated dough for the croissants, mixed up doughs for fritters and bear claws and did last-minute finishes on the cakes that would go into the pastry case today. Amy was impressed with Noah's decorating skills, especially his dexterity with an icing bag. It was kind of funny watching this hulking, muscled warrior—wearing a

pink apron because that was the only color she had—
doing fine and delicate swirls with a thin line of icing.

Yes, he messed up a few times, but she appreciated
how he chuckled, scraped off the error and patiently
tried it again. It wasn't long before his work was practically flawless.

They didn't talk much, other than when Noah needed
clarification or had a question—but Amy didn't mind
the quiet. Neither did Noah. The kitchen was warm and
fragrant, and they were both up to their elbows in dough
creating delicious treats…together. It was like heaven.

Once or twice, when she glanced over to check on
him, she caught him with a smile on his face.

"Having fun?" she had to ask at one point.

He nodded. "I forgot how much I love doing this.
It's been a while."

"Could have fooled me." He went at it like a pro—
and he'd never even been to a class. "Your foster mother
trained you well."

She didn't expect him to pause and look at her the
way he did, with a hint of pride in his eyes. "Thanks."

"She must have been a wonderful person."

"Yeah. I thought so."

Amy's heart thudded at his expression. How wonderful to know that, somewhere in his difficult youth,
he met someone like the woman he called Ma. It was
nice to know he hadn't been all alone. He deserved as
much, she felt.

Once the bakery opened, they switched gears to sell-
ing. Whenever the flow of customers slowed down,
Amy headed back into the kitchen to prep for the next
day and also to get started on a cake one of her custom-

ers had ordered. Cakes for events such as weddings or birthdays weren't her favorites to handle—she usually handed them off to Eloise, who loved decorating—but it was a profitable arm of her business because she could charge more for special orders.

She kept an ear out as she worked though, monitoring Noah's interactions with the customers, and damn if he wasn't good at that too. The bell over the door dinged just as Amy was taking some cakes from the oven to cool. She nearly dropped the pan when the customer in the other room spoke.

"Ohh, you're new." Something of a sultry squeal. Amy's gut clenched as she recognized the voice. Sherrill Scanlon. Ugh. Usually when Sherrill or Lola or one of the other holy terrors from her high school days came to the bakery, she let Eloise serve them, but the thought of leaving Noah out there all alone, on his first day, didn't sit well with her. In town, Sherrill was known as the Barracuda because when she set her sights on a man, she usually got him—with the possible exception of Jax, but only because Jax hadn't been interested.

And now, judging from her lurid tone, she'd set her sights on Noah. Who wouldn't? He was hot. Even in a pink apron. Maybe even more so because of it. Amy quickly overturned the cakes onto the cooling trays, wiped her hands and headed out to provide protection.

"Hey, Sherrill," she said in a cheery voice.

Sherrill's lusty smile faded. *Good.*

"What can we get for you this morning?" She emphasized the *we*.

"Amy. You're here."

She smiled bigger. "It's my bakery."

"And who are you?" Sherrill asked Noah, practically batting her lashes.

"This is Noah." Was it wrong that Amy answered for him? Probably not. He wasn't aware of the danger he was in. Not at all, poor soul. Noah glanced at her quizzically but didn't say anything. "He'll be helping out for a while."

Sherrill smiled at him as though Amy wasn't there at all. "You don't look like a baker," she said.

"And yet he is fabulous." Amy reached out and put her hand on his arm. Yeah, it was a possessive action— both Sherrill and Noah recognized it as such. But only Noah grinned.

Amy frowned at him in response, a little glower that said *I'll tell you later.* A trickle of relief ran through her when he gave her a nearly imperceptible nod.

"Oh, Noah, can you go check on the cookies?" She had a batch in the oven. They weren't near done yet and he probably knew it, but he nodded, sketched Sherrill a wave and headed back to safety.

Sherrill wasn't happy as she tracked his departure with her lizard-like stare. Once he was out of sight, she turned on Amy. "Who was that?"

"That was Noah. What can I get you?"

It was clear Sherrill didn't want to order or leave, at least not until she got another look at Noah's pecs in that black T-shirt, but Amy wasn't planning to budge. It seemed to take forever for Sherrill to pick out half a dozen pastries. Amy boxed them up as fast as she could. Anything to get Sherrill, and her suffocating cloud of perfume, out of the store. When the door closed behind her, Amy blew a sigh of relief.

"What was that?"

She turned to see Noah leaning against the doorjamb, and even though she tried not to, she couldn't help noticing how fine a figure he cut in that black shirt and hot pink apron. It was wrong for a man to be that hot, wasn't it?

"That," she gusted, "was Sherrill Scanlon." She waggled a finger at him. "Do not touch."

He barked a laugh. "That bad?"

"She gobbles up men like Ms. Pac Man. We call her the Barracuda."

"Ah. Good to know. The, ah, cookies are done now."

Yeah. That had been a lame excuse to get him out of the room, and they both knew it. Amy couldn't help her flush. It walked up her cheeks. He grinned when he noticed. "Sorry about that. But trust me, you'll thank me later."

He chuckled. "No worries. You can always send me into the kitchen when a Barracuda swims in." And then, he winked. "Thanks for looking out for me."

"You are welcome."

The grin they shared was probably one of the best moments of her day, which was saying something, because it had been a rare delight sharing the day with him. She'd enjoyed every minute.

Noah loved his first day at the bakery—mostly because he got to spend so much time with Amy. And he learned from her too. Though he had most of the basics down, she had some tricks she'd developed over the years to streamline the process and keep ahead of demand. It hadn't taken too long for his skills and muscle memory to come back either. The bakery was busy most of the day, but there were some quieter times where the two of them had time to chat about the boys, the bakery and some of their traveling adventures.

All in all, it had been a really great experience and a good reminder of how much he'd loved working with Ma. When they'd talked, the day before, and Amy had insisted that they keep things on a friendly basis, he'd been a little disappointed. Yeah, he found her attractive, but he'd really enjoyed their interactions as friends too. She was the kind of person he could be friends with. Heck, she was the kind of person he wanted to be friends with.

By the end of the day, he was tired, but he wasn't too tired to say yes when she invited him to come over for supper. He probably should have turned her down though because the boys were bursting with energy, and they strafed him with questions all the way through the meal. What blew him away was that Amy had experienced the same day he had, she had to be as tired as he was, but she still seemed to have energy to spare.

She laughed when he mentioned it to her as she walked him to the door. "Don't worry," she said. "You'll get used to it." Then she paused and waited until he caught her gaze. "You did really great today, you know?"

"Thanks."

"No. Really." She looked down at her feet for a second, and then when she looked back up, her eyes were a little damp. "I really appreciate your help, Noah. I don't think I can say that enough."

Her sincerity, her gratitude hit him hard somewhere

in the region of his chest. He shook his head. "My pleasure. Really."

She cocked her head to the side. "So, you'll be there tomorrow?"

Was she really asking? Was she really unsure? "Bright and early."

"Awesome." And yeah, her relief was real. "Hey, do you want me to swing by and pick you up? It's on my way."

It wasn't, not really, but he nodded. "That would be great."

"Well, okay. Good night. And…thanks again, Noah." He didn't expect a hug, but he sure appreciated it. The feel of her body—her warmth, her scent—just felt… right. Although, overall, the hug was far too short.

He thought about it long into the night—how it felt, holding her close. He thought about her. And yeah, he'd enjoyed the work—it had been a revelation of nostalgia, good times he'd forgotten to remember. But beyond that, when he was with Amy, he felt…at home. And it was a feeling he wanted to explore for as long as he could.

The next morning, with the boys in the back of her car, Amy drove over to Jax's studio to pick up Noah. Even though he was a little sleepy eyed, he was very patient with the boys, who were excited to see him and chattered at him all the way to the sitter's. After they got to the bakery, they went right to work.

Amy was surprised at how much she liked working with Noah. The help was nice, that was for certain, but it was more than just that. His company was soothing and entertaining and energizing—all at the same time. It was fun having someone like him to talk to. A grown-up. The fact that he was an attractive man didn't hurt, but he was also charming, funny and humble. He didn't have a snit if she corrected his work, as Pierre had, and he was careful not to make mistakes, unlike Eloise. And if he did make a mistake, he owned it. And fixed it.

Granted, he wasn't a trained and certified pâtissier—no doubt that lack of training led to an openness to improvement—but Amy suspected his military training also played a large part in his approach to work. He understood how important it was to operate as a team, and he didn't mind when she asked him to do something differently.

And together, they were a well-oiled crew, even after only one day. It was amazing.

It was a good thing too because that day was busier than usual, certainly much busier than a Wednesday should've been—midweek there was always a slump in business. It wasn't lost on Amy that the majority of the customers were locals.

And female.

They had come to gawk at—or drool over—Noah. It amused her at first when she realized what was happening, but that didn't last long. It soon became irritating.

She didn't mind when her friend Susan stopped by, or Lynne or Clara or Angel or Gwen—because they were all people she was delighted to see. She wasn't even irritated when old Mrs. T., who'd been the high school librarian way back when, came sniffing around. It was actually cute the way she waited until Noah went back to the kitchen before she leaned in and waggled her brows at Amy and said, "Hubba-hubba."

No, the irritation arrived in a flash when Lola Cheswick waltzed into the shop. Lola, like her BFF, Sherrill, had been a terror in high school to anyone who hadn't been gorgeous and cool—which had included Amy and her sisters and most of her friends. Like Candace, Lola rarely ate carbs, so it was weird to see her walk through the doors. She stopped short when she caught sight of Noah, who was helping another customer at the time. She gave him a look—up and down, all assessing and predatory. It made Amy's gut clench. Then Lola made a noise deep in her throat that sounded a little bestial.

Gross.

She managed to wait patiently until the customer Noah was serving left, then she stepped up to the counter and gave him—yet another—smarmy once-over. "So, it's true," she said in a deep sultry Southern drawl. Amy nearly rolled her eyes out of her head. Where had that accent come from? Lola had never been farther south than Portland.

Noah was equally befuddled. He blinked. "I beg your pardon?"

Amy frowned at her. "Is what true?"

Lola sniffed and tossed her hair at Amy—just like she always had in high school—then turned her attention back to Noah. She batted her lashes at him. Actually batted her lashes. At him. "A little birdie told me there was fresh meat in town."

Ugh. Was it wrong to gag in your own bakery?

Even as her stomach churned, Amy's ire rose. Noah wasn't "fresh meat." He was a real human person, and he was doing her a favor. He didn't deserve to be treated like this by every woman in town, especially Lola.

She was about to lose her cool—which she tried not

to do at work—and read Lola the riot act, but before she could form a response, Noah handled it.

Very cordially, he said, "Well, ma'am, if it's fresh meat you're looking for, you're in the wrong place." He turned to Amy with an adorably innocent expression on his face. "Is there a butcher's shop in town, or should she go to the grocery store?"

Amy blinked. "Ah… Yeah. Grocery store for sure." She flashed Lola an enormous, very helpful smile.

"Yeah." Noah was *sooo* cute when he played dumb bunny. "We have some pastries and stuff though, if you're interested."

Lola stared at him as though trying to figure out if he was joking or not. Finally she shook her head and gave up on trying to hit on him. She blew out a breath, ordered a baguette and an éclair and departed. Thank God.

When the door closed on her, Noah chuckled.

Amy frowned at him. "What's so funny?"

He cocked his head to the side. "Why are you mad? That was funny."

"I'm not mad."

"You look mad."

"I'm *irritated*." She put her hands on her hips to illustrate. "She was rude to you."

His shoulders lifted. "I don't care."

"I do. You're not here to be treated like an object."

He arched a brow. "Thank you?"

"If you're here, in my place of business, I am not going to allow you to be disrespected or…harassed. Certainly not by the likes of Lola Cheswick."

"Her name was Lola?" His eyes danced. She should have been warned. "Was she a showgirl?"

She sent him one of her best Disappointed Mom looks at his attempt at a joke. "I'm serious. And don't joke about one of my favorite Barry Manilow songs."

He wasn't. She could tell by the way he was trying to hide his smile. But he made an attempt to sober. "Thank you, Amy," he said. "I appreciate your concern. But I, ah, think I can take care of myself."

"I'm certain you can. But I won't accept any kind of harassment in my business." She waited until he nodded before she broke. "But did you see her expression when you called her *ma'am*?" It had been hysterical.

He grinned. "Did you like that?"

She couldn't hold back her smile. "I did. I think it was my favorite thing all day." And it had been a pretty darn good day.

After they closed up on his second day, Noah folded himself into the front seat of Amy's car and they headed to the sitter to pick up the boys. It had been dark when they'd dropped them off, but now the summer sun was shining bright. Yeah. He remembered that part from when he was a kid, the early mornings. Not that he'd minded—then or now. The butt crack of dawn was one of the most peaceful times of the day.

It was funny, though, how fast he'd slipped into the routine of bakery life again, in just a couple days. It wasn't his favorite kind of work—when you considered jumping out of airplanes—but it was familiar and brought back good memories. And of course, Amy was there.

If he was being honest with himself, the only reason he'd agreed to help out was because of her. The attraction he felt compelled him to explore, the friendship they were slowly developing. He wasn't so sure why she fascinated him like that or why he wanted to get to know her better to the extent that he'd take a job at a bakery again just to be around her, but he also couldn't deny how right it had felt when he'd made the decision.

When he'd first clapped eyes on her, he'd had one singular thought, and that had been getting her in bed. It wasn't a typical thought for him. Unlike a lot of his friends growing up, and his buddies in the service, who'd always been on the hunt, Noah had always been reserved with women, especially when it came to sexual relationships. He'd never been the kind of guy to just leap into bed with someone. He figured it came from his unsettled childhood. That maybe it took him longer to trust.

Now that he knew her a little better, that desire hadn't waned a bit. Not even when she'd made it clear that bakery time was strictly for business. Heck, that made him respect her more. That and the way she tried to protect him from any Barracudas. The thought made him grin because while he could handle himself with a predatory woman—and often had—he liked that she was willing, and inclined, to shield his tender sensibilities.

"Why are you grinning?" she asked as she turned into a modest neighborhood on the south end of town.

He shrugged. "I had fun today."

She shot him a look. "Fun?"

"Yeah." He'd never served customers at Ma's—he'd usually worked in the kitchen before and after school—but he'd liked that today too. He'd always found tremendous satisfaction in serving others as a PJ. It was kind of refreshing to be able to do so when they weren't in crisis. A lot more smiles, for sure.

"Well, I'm glad you're enjoying it." She pulled into a driveway, parked and glanced at him again. "Have I mentioned how much I appreciate your help?" she asked.

He had to chuckle because she'd been saying it for two days now. "Yup."

"Well, I do."

"I'm glad to help." He didn't say more, didn't mention he wanted more or that he was thinking about her constantly or how much he wanted to kiss her—just once—because he knew, instinctively, that the time wasn't right. They were building trust with each other now, and he suspected she needed that strong foundation, if there was to be more, just as much as he did.

Also, the boys were coming, plodding out of the sitter's house with their backpacks slung over their shoulders, and there wasn't time for the conversation those revelations would require.

"Hey, guys," he said in a chipper tone as John J. and Georgie piled into the back seat of the car.

"How was your day?" Amy asked. In response, they both put out a lip in twin pouts and crossed their arms. Her brow furrowed. "What's wrong?"

"Dylan wasn't sick."

Amy glanced at Georgie. "What?"

He lifted a slender shoulder. "His mom told you he was sick the day you took us to Aunt Nat's, but he wasn't sick. They went to the water park in Auburn. Dylan wasn't supposed to say anything, but he told us."

"They didn't want us to come," John J. wailed.

Damn. The expression on Amy's face made something in Noah's gut wrench. It sucked when people lied. Trust was fragile and just that easily crushed.

Amy glanced at the house and then back at the boys. She swallowed heavily but said only, "That's disappointing."

"It sucks!" Georgie yelled.

"Yeah," John J. rejoined. "It sucks."

Their mother blew out a breath. "Okay, guys. I know you're upset, but let's remember our language."

In response, Georgie threw his hands up in the air and snapped, "Why?"

Amy turned back to the wheel so the boys couldn't see her face, but Noah could. He could see the dampness in her eyes and the tightness of her jaw. She was trying to hold in her anger as well. He had a sudden swell of empathy for her as the true tests of single parenting peeked out from under the veil of perfection she was so good at arranging.

"Hey," he said, stepping in, just to give her a moment to pull herself together. "Sometimes people let you down. The real question is how do you handle it? That's what defines you."

This earned him a frown from Georgie. "What do you mean?"

"Well, you can feel left out that you didn't get to go." He glanced at Amy. "Or upset that someone wasn't honest. But, hey. Sometimes people let you down. You can't let those feelings influence the way you feel about yourself. You know?"

"But they did something fun and didn't take us along." John J. reminded him of the salient facts.

"That's okay. Why don't *we* do something fun? We

deserve it." He looked over at Amy with a gamine grin. "We've been working hard, haven't we?"

She stared at him for a bit, and then her eyes crinkled and she smiled. "Right!" And then, to the boys, "What should we do?"

The boys looked at each other and then, in tandem, chanted, "Carnival! Carnival!"

Amy shot Noah a look. "You up for it?"

"Carnival?" He made a pained face, but only because he was teasing them. "What is there to do at a carnival?" He knew, of course—about the rides and the food. He hadn't grown up under a rock. He just hadn't ever actually been to one. There hadn't been money for it, or the opportunity, when he'd been a kid, and as an adult, well, there'd never been time.

"There's a Ferris wheel," Georgie wheedled.

"And cotton candy!" John J. crowed.

"And games!"

"And pizza!"

"And you can win an enormous stuffed toy!"

"And," Amy added softly with a wink, "they have a beer tent."

He grinned at her. "Sold!"

And, of course, the boys cheered.

As Amy backed out of the driveway and headed off for the fairgrounds, Noah settled back into his seat and listened to the boys chatter happily away. He couldn't help feeling very satisfied with himself at the way he'd helped them work through that disappointment. And Amy.

Oh, and he was going to a carnival. He was a little excited about that too, mostly because the boys' excitement was a little contagious. Granted, he was a grown man. Probably too old to enjoy such frenetic mayhem, but it would be fun to experience it through young eyes. Wouldn't it?

Amy laughed as she watched Noah and the boys ride on the Tilt-a-Whirl. Heck, Noah was screaming and laughing harder than the kids. She hadn't expected this side of him. She liked it. He'd been the one to buy a handful of ride tickets—ostensibly for the boys—but after they'd talked him into joining them on the first ride, he hadn't missed a one. They'd all cajoled her to join them too, but she'd demurred because the wild rides always made her woozy. She had promised to go on the Ferris wheel though. Because yeah, that was more her speed.

And watching them? That was her speed too. Seeing Noah giggle—actually giggle—was revealing. And sweet. It was like catching a glimpse of him as a boy.

She shook her head. He'd been so solemn and practical in the car when the boys had shared the news about Kim's lie. And oh, she'd been furious about that lie. Not for herself as much as for the boys, who'd been wanting to go to the water park forever. It was a full day trip, though, and she worked every day. Granted, she closed the shop one day a week, on Wednesdays, in the winter because business was so slow, but never in the summer. Of course the waterpark itself was closed in the winter.

So along with her irritation at Kim, there'd been a hefty chunk of guilt that she, somehow, had failed them as a mother. The carnival had been a perfect antidote to that.

She had yet another thing to thank Noah for, it seemed. She'd watched all three of them as Noah had talked about disappointment, and she had been astounded at how simply he'd handled their anger, how he'd empowered them to come up with a solution. It was a hard lesson, the one they were learning, and while she hated that they had to learn it, she was happy he had been there to diffuse the disappointment. This day would have turned out very differently otherwise.

He was good at everything, wasn't he? Good with customers, fantastic with a spatula and great with the boys.

He was good with her too.

She knew he was interested in something more than friendship with her—he made it more than clear. But he didn't pressure her. Didn't push. He simply made himself present. Gave of himself to her and the boys. And he quietly respected her request to keep things on a business level while he was working at the bakery, which was a relief. Her life, at the moment, was full of stress. She spent her days juggling multiple priorities, just as she had for years, all by herself. She didn't have the capacity to manage a relationship right now. Did she?

One of the reasons she'd never dated after George died, despite her loneliness, had been that wad of stress over her responsibilities and the fact that time with the boys was something she didn't want to sacrifice. But another had been that she'd never really felt drawn to any of the men she met. No one had ever made her feel the way she wanted to feel about a partner—excited, but safe at the same time.

There was just something about the way Noah looked,

though, when he threw back his head and laughed with the boys as they came off one ride and then ran to another that made her heart ache a little. Made her want to play a little too.

Sometimes it was hard, always being an adult.

"Who's the hottie with the boys?"

Amy nearly jumped. "Candace!" She'd been so deep in thought she hadn't even seen her friend approach. "Are you here with Maya?"

"She's in the petting zoo." Candace waved vaguely in that direction. "So? Who's the hottie with the boys?"

"Ah. Yeah. Remember the customer I told you about?"

Candace's eyes went wide. "The one who asked you out, and you said no?"

"Mmm-hmm."

"You didn't say he was that hot."

"I said he was hot."

Her gaze went back to Noah, and she shook her head. "I can't believe you said no to *that*."

Yeah. Right. "Anyway, turns out he's a military buddy of Jax's. He was at Sunday supper and…he and the boys hit it off."

"The boys?"

Okay. Maybe not just *the boys.*

"He's yummy. What's he like?"

"He's…" *Great. He was great.* "Tall."

Candace gave a snort. "I can see that. What is he, six-three? Six-four?"

Amy shrugged. "I haven't measured him." And then, "He's a Pararescue jumper." It took a minute to explain what that was because Candace had no clue, but Amy wished she hadn't said anything when Candace's expression got even hungrier when she said the phrase "special forces."

"You're not dating, are you?" her friend asked.

"What?" She didn't often bleat like a goat, but the question caught her unprepared.

"You and Noah? You don't have a thing, do you?"

Amy's brain short circuited, just for a second. "What?"

"Are the two of you…going out? I mean, now that you know who he is?"

Something icky slithered through Amy's belly. "Why are you asking?"

"Ames, honey. Don't you know? I mean, the last thing I want to do is step on your toes. We're friends."

Step on my toes? "Candace…you're married." As if she didn't know.

Candace rolled her eyes. "Rolf doesn't even keep the other women a secret from me anymore."

Sadness swamped her as Amy took in the expression on her friend's face. She'd always known that Rolf and Candace had a lot of fights—Candace wasn't shy about sharing. But other than that, they seemed to have a perfect life. A beautiful daughter and a nice big house on the beach here in the Cove as well as another mansion in Seattle where they spent the winters… Heck, they *entertained*. It had always seemed like a sophisticated and privileged life, one that anyone would envy.

To learn that they had deeper problems—that he was unrepentantly unfaithful—made her sad, but for Candace to casually accept Rolf's infidelity and want to reciprocate? Really sad.

"Oh, come on." Candace nudged her with an elbow. "You never cheated on George?"

"Never!" It never crossed her mind.

"Well," she said with a smirk. "Military men always cheat. They're away for months, years. How could they not?"

"No." Just...no. George had not cheated on her. And even if he had—which he hadn't—she would not have cheated on him in return. That Candace was thinking about sleeping with Noah—or anyone, for that matter— just to get back at Rolf was...well, nauseating.

Ugh. She did *not* want to have this conversation with Candace. Not with that look in her eye. Amy'd seen that exact expression all day long from every female customer who'd walked in the store, and each time it had made the little hairs on her arms stand up. That said, Noah was a grown man. She had no claim on him. He could do what he wanted.

Somehow, that thought made her a little nauseous too.

The carnival was a blast. Noah hadn't expected to have that much fun but, just as he'd suspected, experiencing it with the boys made everything fun. Their enthusiasm was infectious. Exploring the rides and games with them didn't make him feel like a child again so much as it made him feel like the little kid he'd never been able to be. And he loved it.

Amy was talking to a friend when he and the boys got off the roller coaster—second time straight—and headed over to her. His belly was starting to rumble, so it was time to think about something a little more nourishing than cotton candy and kettle corn. He didn't have to hunt for her in the crowd because his attention just naturally homed in on her. Also, she hadn't wandered far.

He didn't notice much about her friend at first because Amy's smile, when she saw them coming, blinded him. But as they came closer, he couldn't help but notice how different they were. For one thing, Amy's friend wore dress slacks, a silk blouse and heels, while the rest of the crowd enjoying the fair had gone grunge casual. And then there was the way she held herself—as though she were royalty.

Indeed, as he approached, she presented her hand as though she expected him to kiss her ring. "So…are you the PJ?" she asked in a sultry purr.

"I'm Noah."

"I know." *If she knew, why did she ask?*

"Noah, this is my friend Candace." See? Amy had the manners to provide an introduction.

"Hi. Nice to meet you." He took her hand—because she kept it dangling there—and shook it firmly.

"Noah's been helping me in the bakery," Amy said. "Oh, did I mention that Eloise took off without any warning?"

"Oh?" Candace looked him up and down. Again. "You can bake?"

"He's really good." Amy answered for him, so he just shrugged.

"Where's Maya?" Georgie asked, just as Candace was about to say something else.

Candace looked down at him and gave a smile, though it was a tight one. "She's at the petting zoo. Why don't you boys run along and find her, and let the adults talk?"

"Why don't we all go?" Noah had to say it. He didn't

like the way she was talking to Georgie. Or the fact that she wanted to send the boys off in this crowd without an adult—he knew Amy wouldn't want that, either. Besides, was it wrong that he'd rather hang out with the boys than with Candace? He certainly didn't fancy having an *adult* conversation with her. He glanced at Amy, just to check her temperature on his suggestion, and was rewarded by her smile. So, he added, "The food court is near there, and it's coming up on suppertime. Anyone wanna get some grub?"

"Grub?" Amy said with a laugh. "Do you boys want some grub?" And of course, they were all in.

They found Maya, who was a classmate of Georgie's— a sweet little girl who was also overdressed, especially for the petting zoo. Her mother was not pleased that she had llama spit and hay on her expensive outfit, and she whisked her away, off home to get cleaned up. It was kind of sad because it was clear how much Maya loved the animals.

Still, Noah was glad when Candace left. When it was just them again. They all ordered food from different vendors, sat down at an open table of the make-shift food court and had a feast—family style. Which, Amy explained, meant you got to eat each other's food as well as your own. So that night, they had Mexican, Chinese, Thai and mac and cheese. The mac and cheese had been John J.'s pick. Oh, and funnel cake for dessert.

Though it had sounded revolting, it was actually delicious, and the meal was loads of fun, especially when Amy suggested everyone eat with chopsticks. For everything. The result was hilarious.

Once they'd been fed, the boys slowed down a bit,

and the four of them did the Ferris wheel—for Amy—
and then wandered over to the carnival games for a
while. Though he was hardly a pro at darts, Noah was
able to win a stuffed T. Rex for John J. at the balloon
pop, and then he tossed quarters onto plates until he
won a kazoo for Georgie. At another game, shooting
water into a clown's mouth, he gave Georgie pointers
on how to aim, and he won a teddy bear, which the boy
then gave to his mom. She looked so cute cuddling it,
Noah had to smother the desire to pull her into his arms
and hug her.

As they walked to the parking lot just after that,
Noah put his hand on Georgie's shoulder. "It was nice
of you to give your prize to your mother," he said. Not
a lot of kids would do that. "Very mature."

The boy blushed a little and shrugged. "Well, I am
the man of the family, you know."

Noah nodded and smiled, even though the thought
broke his heart a little. It reminded him once again that
these boys had been through tough times, just like he
had. Oh, the circumstances were different, no doubt
about that, but the similarities were there too.

Maybe that was why he'd bonded with them so
quickly. Maybe that was why it felt so good spending time with them. It felt natural, their relationship.
It felt right.

Jax was still working at the studio when Amy pulled
up to drop off Noah, so of course the boys had to run
in to see him, chattering about their afternoon at the
carnival, but she didn't let them linger.

"Come on, boys—we have an early morning," she
said, rounding them back up. She shot a glance at Noah.

"I'll see you tomorrow," she said. "Bright and early." Turning to Jax, she added, "Bakery hours—you know."

"Yes, ma'am." Jax grinned and waved as they tromped out to the car. Noah waved as well, but it was hard to watch them go. It had been a great day, and he didn't want it to end.

Chapter Six

After Amy and the boys left, Noah and Jax went back inside. Jax started cleaning up the wood chips around his current work in progress. He was sculpting the head of a dragon from a fat chunk of cedar. "So, how's it going at the bakery?" he asked as he swept.

"Great. I'm really enjoying it. I hope you don't mind. I did come here to spend time with you after all."

Jax shook his head. "Man, I'm just glad to see you again. We'll get some time before the wedding, I'm sure. And I'm very thankful that you're able to help Amy out. I can't believe her pâtissier quit." He rolled his eyes. "It wasn't the first time."

"She told me." Apparently the last guy had decided that Coho Cove was too provincial and he'd moved his butt back to Seattle.

"I'm just blown away that you know how to bake… I mean, all that fancy stuff."

Well, maybe not *all* the fancy stuff. "Right? It's been a while, but it's all coming back."

Jax chuckled. "Dude, if someone had told me when we met that you knew how to make a croquembouche, I would have told them they were insane."

"Yeah." Noah huffed a laugh. "I kept that kind of stuff to myself. Can you imagine how much the guys in the bivouac would have razzed me if they knew?"

"Forget the razzing. They would have made you bake."

They both laughed because they knew damn well how much guys on active duty could shovel away. But when you were burning ten thousand calories before noon, you had to keep the machine fed. That had been one of the hardest transitions for Noah after leaving the service, other than trying to figure out what he wanted to do with the rest of his life—learning how to keep his physique without constant physical training. He'd found a balance, but he'd ached after the first day at the bakery. He knew he'd adjust to that, but working around Amy was clearly going to be a challenge. In more ways than one.

"So…" Jax went to the fridge and grabbed a couple beers, which made Noah happy because it meant he wasn't in a rush to leave. They popped the cans open and sat on the sofa. "What do you think of Amy?"

"Aw, man. I think she's great."

"Really? 'Zat it? Because I saw the way you were looking at her…"

"What do you mean?" Noah stilled and glanced at his friend—just to make sure his expression wasn't as ominous as his words. Thankfully it wasn't, and he relaxed a little.

Jax chuckled. "You know what I mean."

Noah had to laugh as well. "Okay. Yeah. I think she's…gorgeous. But…"

"But what?"

He didn't want to go into detail just now—hell, he wasn't even sure how to explain it if he did—so he stuck with old faithful. "It's complicated."

Jax barked a laugh. "It's Amy. It's always complicated."

"Well, I am working at her bakery…"

"She's pretty serious about the bakery."

"Yeah. Aside from that, she was George Tolliver's wife. That throws a new wrinkle into it for sure." Buddies didn't mess with each other's wives. It was an unspoken rule of the brotherhood.

"Oh." Jax's eyes widened. "I didn't realize you knew George."

"I did. We weren't close friends, but I respected the hell out of him." Everyone had.

"Yeah. He was a pretty hard-core soldier."

Noah nodded. George had been born into it. The military had been his world. Had he lived, he would have become a lifer for sure. "Yeah. I knew George. We met originally in Ramstein," a busy military base in Germany, "and then we ran into each other a couple of times in Bagram." The military world was a tangle of friendships that connected and separated and connected again and again. It was a small world, but there were a lot of moving pieces. No small wonder that the three of them had never been stationed together. Noah cleared his throat. "I, ah, was on the team that evaced George the night he died."

Jax swallowed. Hard. "Oh, hell."

"Yeah."

They were both silent for a moment, thinking of George, and all the other soldiers who hadn't made it back home. Everyone knew someone.

"So," Noah added, "that complicates things with Amy too."

"Well, if it matters at all, I knew George well, and I know he would want Amy to move on. I'm sure he'd want her to find someone who would care about her and the boys. Someone like you." He paused and then added, "You know, if it goes that way."

"You think so?"

"I know it."

That was really good to hear. Noah wasn't sure why it felt so good, but it did. Yeah, on the one hand, he found her wildly attractive, but on the other, his logical mind was able to come up with lots of reasons to keep himself firmly in the friendzone. But, damn, he was drawn to her. "Well," he said, "it's early on. And we agreed there would be no flirting at work, so—"

"What?" Jax squawked, and Noah cringed. Maybe he shouldn't have mentioned that because now he had to explain.

"Ah, well, the first time we met, I kind of asked her out. I didn't know who she was, of course—"

"Wait, you didn't meet for the first time at Pearl's?"

"Nope."

"You dog." He said this with a sly smile.

Noah grinned sheepishly. "I didn't mention it that night because she didn't."

"So, you asked her out right away?"

"Yeah." He huffed a laugh. "I've never done that before. Something about her...well, I mean, I just knew I wanted to get to know her better." He shrugged. "She turned me down flat."

Jax grinned. "I'm not surprised. She hasn't shown any interest in dating since George. And trust me, her sisters nag her about it."

"Also, some rando comes into your bakery and asks you out? Now that I know her better, I'm kind of glad she said no." He didn't like the idea of some other dude sweeping in on her, not at all.

"And..." Jax shot him an assessing glance. "Now that you do know her better, what do you think?"

He paused. Took a breath. Oh, he knew how he felt, but putting it into words, well, that was harder. Since he'd never felt like this about a woman, it was tough to put a label on it. After a minute, he tried. "I like the way she makes me feel. About myself. About the future. You know?"

Jax nodded. "I feel like that with Natalie. Like I'm home."

Exactly! Though Noah wasn't quite ready to say those words. The main difference being that Amy had made it clear that they were just friends.

"What do you think of the boys?"

"Aw, they're great. I love them." Damn. It just came out, but he couldn't deny the truth of it. When he thought about those boys, his heart got all warm and fuzzy and he smiled like a doofus.

"Yeah. They are great." Jax was quiet for a minute, then asked, "Have you ever thought about having kids of your own?"

"Nope." No hesitation. It had never crossed his mind, other than to remind himself he had no idea what it meant to be a dad because he'd never had one—other than a couple foster dads who'd had little to recommend them. He suspected he might be terrible at it because of that. But that didn't change the way he felt about *these* kids.

They chatted a little bit more about Natalie and Jax's work and an art show coming up that would feature them both, and then Jax left, leaving Noah alone with a half-drunk beer and the scent of cut wood and linseed oil in the air. And thoughts. Lots of thoughts.

About Amy and the boys, his past, present and future, and the hopes he'd been building for his life. One thing was clear to him: He didn't want to leave this place just yet. He didn't want to leave her. When he thought about it, a nasty panic slithered through his bowels.

He liked what he felt with her, and he knew if he didn't hang around and at least make the effort to explore it, to get to know her a little better—even if it was just as friends—he'd regret it for the rest of his life.

But it wasn't just Amy that drew him, was it? It was this place. The trees, the feelings, the people…even the air here stirred his soul. As he got ready for bed, he dug down deeper, exploring the whys of these unexpected emotions. What was it about this place that called to him? In the past, he'd been happy to experience places and people and adventures and then move on. He'd easily walked away looking forward to new explorations. It had been a simple thing for him to close a chapter and to start fresh somewhere else. It had been fun.

But now he wanted to settle. He'd been wanting to settle for a while, hence his long journey across the country...looking. He hadn't found it though, that nebulous thing to fill the hole in his soul. It didn't help that he'd never been sure precisely what he'd been searching for to begin with. But today, at the carnival with the boys, it had come into view and, unexpectedly, had left him a little shaken.

He'd been searching for family. A place of his own. A sense of...belonging.

He wasn't sure why he hadn't realized that earlier—it seemed obvious now, as he reflected. And he wasn't sure why he felt it so profoundly with Amy and the boys, but he did. For the first time in his life, he was experiencing something he didn't want to walk away from. A chapter he didn't want to close.

He'd been happy to keep things friendly with Amy because that had just been another experience, exploring someone who fascinated him. But now something had changed. Now a deeper yearning had been kindled. Now he wanted more. With her.

Hell, he wanted everything.

All he had to do was figure out what to do about it.

Something was different when Amy picked Noah up the next morning. She couldn't quite put her finger on it. It was something in his expression, perhaps? Or the energy humming between them. Or maybe she was imagining it. Maybe it was the fact that she'd been thinking about him, more than she should have, in ways that she shouldn't have.

She was the one who'd put the brakes on anything

romantic between them after all, but her surety was weakening. The better she got to know him, the more her attraction to him grew. And along with that, her fear. What if she opened up herself, and her life, to him and he let her down? It wasn't just her heart that would be broken. The boys would be crushed as well. An expectation could be a terrible thing.

On the other hand, he wasn't going to be here for long. If she was going to explore this—whatever it was—with him, there wasn't much time. She had to figure out a way to ignore her fears and insecurities and just act on her instincts. Trouble was she had no idea how to do that.

All she knew for sure was that she wanted more from him, more with him, and he seemed to be interested in the same.

But other than a whispered good-morning—the boys were snoozing in the back seat—the two of them didn't talk. Even after she dropped the kids off at the sitter's, they didn't really talk until they were at the bakery, prepping for the day.

He broke the silence. "I really had fun yesterday," he said. "I can't remember ever having that much fun."

"The carnival?"

He barked a laugh. "All of it, but the carnival especially. I really loved hanging out with the boys."

"Aww. That warms my heart."

"They're great."

"I think so." They were the center of her world. She couldn't imagine life without them.

They worked in silence for a while, her cranking out the apple tarts she was planning to offer as the daily special and him whipping up a batch of eclairs.

"Noah, can I ask you something?" she asked after a while.

"How do I make such light and fluffy choux pastry?" He grinned as he added the last half of the eggs and beat his batter.

She made a face at him, even though his little jokes lifted her heart. "Do military men always cheat?"

He stopped stirring—even though it was the absolute worst time to stop stirring choux—and he gaped at her. "What? Where on earth did you get that idea?"

She took the bowl and spoon from him, simply because her sensibilities would not allow the eggs to clot. "Something Candace said."

His nose wrinkled. "Candace?" Not a question. Not really.

"She said George probably cheated on me because all military men cheat."

He barked a laugh, but when she frowned at him, he sobered. "Well, first of all, *all* military men don't do *anything*. You know as well as I do that there are always different sorts." He shot her a look. "Did you ever worry about that with him?"

"No. Of course not. But, well, I am naive in the ways of men."

"The ways of men?" He grinned again.

"Candace told me I was being naive." And then, "I think she's interested in you."

His eyes widened. "Thanks for the warning."

"What?" She couldn't hold back a laugh.

"She's not my type."

"She's pretty." Oh, why was she goading him? She

didn't know, other than the fact that she liked his responses.

"How did this conversation come up?"

"That she's interested in you? She told me last night."

"Uh… Didn't she mention her husband last night? Isn't she married?"

"I guess that's not a problem for her."

She loved that he whirled around and harrumphed. "Well, it's a problem for me. I happen to think promises should be kept. And marriage is a promise."

"Me too."

"That Candace is something." He took the bowl from her because she'd forgotten the task and was overmixing. He scooped out the dough, filled a pastry bag and began extruding the eclairs in nice, neat little blocks. "Did you ever worry that George was unfaithful?"

"No." Not for a second.

He nodded at her. "Well, there you go. That's all you need to know," he said. "It's always funny…"

He didn't finish because he was focusing on the eclairs, but she was curious, so she prompted him with a "What?"

"Hmm?"

"You said it's always funny, but you didn't finish the sentence."

"Oh, right. It's always funny when people try to frame your life based on their own standards or experiences. If you're open to being unfaithful, then everyone is. A way to justify it, I expect." He paused and stretched, then bent back to his work. "All I know is I wouldn't want to be in a relationship without trust."

"Neither would I."

The funny thing was in the short time she'd known Noah, she'd come to trust him implicitly, simply because in each and every interaction, he had been consistent: honest and true. She knew it to her bones.

They finished their prep quickly that day—mostly because their teamwork was so efficient, but also because Thursdays in Coho Cove were notoriously slow, so Amy usually didn't make as many batches. As a result, there was time to have a coffee and a chat before opening. It was one of Amy's favorite times of the day because the streets outside were still quiet and the scent of freshly baked goodies hung in the air. The sense of satisfaction, too, was palpable.

They sat side by side in the rocking chairs by the window and sipped the heady brew and nibbled on a pastry, just reveling in the glow of work well done. However, Amy had something on her mind. It had been there for a while, but she had been loath to bring the topic up to him again, and honestly, there hadn't been an appropriate moment. Also, it was a heavy topic. She glanced at him and debated shattering the calm quiet they were both enjoying.

He must have felt her attention because he turned and caught her eye. "What is it?" he asked.

"You remember when you told me to ask you if I had, you know, any questions about George?"

He turned to her fully then, his attention fixed. "Did you want to talk about it?"

She sighed heavily. "Yes. I think I'm ready." It was time for closure she'd decided. Time to release her grief. Time to let George go. With great love and gratitude for what they'd shared…but it was time. This was the one last wound to face.

"Okay" he said. "Go ahead. Ask."

She drew in a deep breath and tried to organize her thoughts. "Okay. Well, I know the basics." She knew what the military had told her, but they were notoriously vague on matters like this. She'd debated with herself about asking because she wasn't sure she wanted to know more, but in the end, she'd decided she wanted to know, needed to, if she was ever to fully heal. "I know he was out on a mission, and there was an exchange of fire. And that he was shot, and he died."

He sighed. "Those are the facts."

"But it's never that simple, is it?" Nothing ever was. "What more can you tell me?"

"Are you sure you want to know?"

"Ha." She barked something like a laugh, but it wasn't one. "Yes. I need to." Most importantly, "Was he in pain when he died?"

"No." She loved how quickly he answered, the surety of his tone. "We started him on an IV right away. It's standard for…well, that type of injury. It's important to compensate for blood loss and, of course, for pain management. I pushed the meds myself. I can guarantee he was not in pain."

"Was he scared?"

His smile soothed her. "From what I knew of George, he was never afraid of an adventure." True. George had been fearless and brave. Too brave sometimes. "He was actually making jokes in the helo while we were patching him and his buddies up."

She blew out a laugh. "He did that." Sometimes at the

most inappropriate times. Often, the best times. Gosh, he'd been so young. One might even argue he'd been immature. She hadn't realized it at the time because she'd been so young too. She hadn't had years of maturity forced upon her yet. She hadn't had to grow up yet. Those early years with George had been fun and exciting and a wild ride. Maybe that was one of the reasons she looked back on it with such nostalgia and fondness.

Everything hadn't been perfect at the time—they'd fought and struggled early in their marriage, mostly because they'd been young and broke. It had been really hard for her being alone after their honeymoon—which hadn't been much of one, because he'd gone straight to basic. And then he'd been deployed, leaving her pregnant and alone and far from home.

No, it certainly hadn't been the dream marriage her eighteen-year-old self had imagined; those early days had been rough. Things had gotten better as they'd both adjusted to their new life, and great joys had grown from the struggle. Now when she thought of George, she thought of the good times—the travel and the laughter and the boys. It seemed wrong to remember unflattering things about a dead man, so she tried not to think about the rough patches. Over the years, she'd polished that patina to a fine shine. As a result, she'd rewritten their story into a fairy-tale romance when it really had been a very normal—if not typical—experience of young love.

"So it was blood loss then?" she had to ask.

Noah glanced away. She hesitated to urge him to continue; she could see the stress on his face as he relived that dark night. After a long moment, he shrugged. "Yeah. In the end it was too much stress for his body to compensate and his heart stopped. We did everything we could, Amy. CPR, defibrillation... But he just slipped away. We couldn't get him back. I'm...so sorry."

Oh, his grief cut through her like a knife. She swallowed hard. Strange that her sympathy, now, was for Noah. Then again, George was old trauma, revisited again and again. That pain had dulled.

She reached out and took his hand. "Thanks for being there with him. I'm just glad to know he wasn't alone. And he wasn't in pain."

He nodded. "I'm glad we were able to give him that at least."

"And thank you for telling me all this. I know it was hard."

"Well, if it helped you to hear it, it was worth it."

"You know, I realized the other day, the fourth anniversary of his death is coming. He'll have been gone longer than we were married." She knew she sounded wistful and maudlin, but she also knew he wouldn't judge her for it, and she appreciated that. Sometimes she felt like she couldn't talk about George to her friends and family like this, honestly, because it was so important to her to keep up the appearance of being strong and in charge. It was what they expected of her. But what she really wanted, sometimes, was just to unload emotionally. Noah was someone she could do that with. It was a gift.

"That must be a tough realization," he said.

She glanced at him and nodded. Yeah. He understood. "It's funny, my life's goal was to marry the man of my dreams. Check. Then have two beautiful children. Check. Check. Then open an award-winning bakery..."

Only a bit of a wobble there. "Check." Tears pricked at her eyes.

"So, your dreams all came true."

"Yes." Definite tear there.

"That's something a lot of people never get, you know."

"Yeah." She blew out a breath. "I know I've been lucky. I am so lucky…"

"So, what's bothering you?"

She blew out a damp laugh. "I checked off everything on my list… Now I don't know what comes next." Had she really said that? Out loud? She'd never told anyone that secret, that now, she was just marking time.

It was a heavy thought, but Noah just laughed and said, "You compose a new list, I guess."

She stared at him as the simplicity of his solution filtered through her grief and regret and frustration, clearing a path for hope. "A new list?" What a wonderful idea. What a wonderful lightness. As though a weight had been lifted. He was right. Absolutely right. George had died, but she hadn't. She was still here and alive and had a full life ahead of her, if she dared to grasp it. "So, what's on your list, Noah?"

"My list?" She loved the way his eyes crinkled when he smiled. "Well, when I was a kid, they moved me around a lot, from house to house, family to family. All I ever wanted was a place to call home, a family to call my own. I think that framed every decision I made. And then, when I got older, especially when Ma came into my life, I realized I wanted to do something that made the world a better place. In some way, you know. It didn't have to be earth shaking change."

"So, you chose saving lives?"

He chuckled. "I did."

"That's pretty earth shaking…for the people you save."

"I suppose. But I did it because it made me feel… powerful." He fell silent, reflective.

"You miss it."

"I do."

"Hmm. Sounds like you need a new list too."

He barked a laugh. "I'm working on it."

"You could still do work like that. Celeste mentioned the town council is looking for a paramedic…"

"Mmm-hmm." He nodded. "I do have the skills. But I'd need to be recertified."

"What else would be on this new list? Do you want kids?" She nearly winced when the question slipped out. It needed to be asked—she had kids, and if things… progressed with them, if they decided they wanted to be together long term, the kids kind of came along. Package deal.

He shrugged. "I like kids, but I've never thought about having them. I mean, I don't even know what good parenting looks like."

"Good parenting is just loving your kids more than yourself, that's all. Putting them first. Being present."

"You and I both know it's more complicated than that."

Yeah. It was. And again, it wasn't.

They fell silent for a minute, and then she huffed a laugh. "You know, I can't believe I'm talking to you like this."

He shot her a crooked grin. "Like what?"

She stared at him for a minute. "Honestly. I mean,

really honestly. I'm so used to keeping up appearances, I forget how much I lie to myself just to keep things on an even keel. It's nice to…"

"Unload?"

"Yeah." He *got* her. He understood.

"Well," he said with a dimpled smile. "You can always unload on me. I can take it."

She wasn't sure why that made her feel so…free, but it did.

Amy shot him a wicked grin, shifting the mood of their conversation to something lighter, more playful. "You may regret making that offer," she said.

"I doubt it." He would carry the weight of the world for her if he could.

Her sigh was dramatic. "I dunno. I have a lot of baggage."

"We all do." And then, after another long moment of quiet, he asked, "So, how did you and George meet?" because, all of a sudden, he wanted to know.

Her grin was adorable. He had to remind himself not to be jealous of the man who inspired it. "He pulled my pigtail."

"What?" he snorted coffee through his nose. He hadn't been expecting that.

"Yeah." She crumpled her napkin. "We were in the third grade, and he had the seat behind me in Miss Deveney's class."

"Wow. Love at first tug?"

"Hardly. I thought he was horrible. But then, years later, when I was in junior high, Dad was transferred to Pattonville in Stuttgart, and so was his dad. We met again there."

"I take it he'd developed a better game by then?"

She snorted a laugh. "Somewhat better. He was still young, you remember. But yeah. I thought he was terribly romantic." She chuckled again. "I was young then too." He watched as the light in her eyes faded. "I was devastated when Dad died unexpectedly."

"What happened?"

"Heart attack."

"That's rough."

"It was. I mean, losing a parent is always tough, but for us, it meant losing our way of life as well. Everything changed. We packed up and moved here to live with Momma's parents. Even living off base was a huge change."

"But you and George?" he prompted when she paused reflectively for too long.

"Well, we stayed in touch, of course. Gosh, I was so in love with him. By then we both were certain we were meant to be together forever. But it was hard because we were both so young and so far apart. Anyway, when his family rotated back to the States, he drove across the country that summer to see me."

"Romantic."

"Totally." She grinned. "Momma and Grandma didn't approve because we were so young, but that didn't stop us. As soon as I turned eighteen, we eloped." She sighed. "Then he went off to basic, and I enrolled in culinary school. I didn't finish." She glanced at him; mischief danced in her eyes. "Georgie was born eight months later. I had to finish my studies online."

"I bet George was over the moon to have a son."

"He threw up in the delivery room." They both laughed. "He was pretty proud though." She sighed. "He was deployed when John J. was born."

"So, you were alone? That must have been tough."

She straightened her spine. "Military wives are often alone. But really, I wasn't alone. As soon as George got orders, I moved back to Coho Cove to live with Momma and Celeste. Nat had already moved away. Nate was gone by then."

"Nate?"

"Our brother." She sighed. "Shortly after we moved here, he passed. Anaphylactic shock."

Two family tragedies so close together? That must have been hard. "I'm sorry." Sadly, all he could offer. Which was worse? Never having a family, or having them and losing them? He wasn't really sure.

She glanced at the clock then and sighed. "Well, this has been nice, but we should get back to work."

"Yeah." They still had to fill the cases. They both stood, cleaned up the crumbs they'd left and headed back to the kitchen.

"Gosh, you're so easy to talk to," she said as she started loading the rack with pastry-filled trays. "Why are you so easy to talk to?"

He shrugged. He wasn't sure why either, other than the fact that they had some kind of unnamable connection, one he'd felt from the first time they'd met. But he knew he felt just the same way.

"Oh. I know," she said, out of the blue. "It's probably because you're a temp."

He snorted a laugh. "A temp?" *Really?*

"Yeah. You're only here till the wedding, right?" Her eyes sparkled with amusement…and something else. Maybe a question? "And then you'll hop on that hog and off you'll go. North to Alaska. Right?"

He shoved his hands into his front pockets and shrugged. "That's the plan." At least it had been. He was starting to rethink it.

"So maybe that's why…"

She paused so long, he glanced at her and said, "What?"

"I don't know. I just feel…free with you. No expectations. No worries about the future. Just two people hanging out together enjoying each other's company for a moment, just…" She trailed off and something in her expression shifted. It was a softness, a wanting, a hunger in her eyes that something inside of him recognized because he'd been aching for it too. The energy in the small, fragrant room changed, warmed, sending a sizzle through him. The hairs on his neck prickled.

She stepped closer, and he leaned back. He thought he knew what these signs might mean, but he didn't want to assume. He needed to know. "Amy, what are you trying to say?"

She went red, all the way to her ears, and twined her fingers together the way she did when she was nervous. "Noah, I have a confession to make."

A slurry sloshed in his gut at her words and her expression and…everything. "Okay."

"I, ah, find you attractive."

He nearly laughed because he thought the fact that they were attracted to each other was pretty clear. Thank goodness he didn't laugh, though, because that might have gone over poorly with her at the moment. Instead, he said, "I'm attracted to you too." What he'd really like was to show her. Like, now. But he sensed she had some other point to make, so he didn't grab her and plant one on her right then and there. Even though he wanted to.

He was glad he waited when she cleared her throat and then blurted, "I'd really like to…kiss you. Is that… weird?"

Weird? He wanted to kiss her all the time. But somehow, he managed a strangled, "Not at all." But his heart kicked into gear.

"On the one hand, it seems perfectly natural thing to want to do when you're attracted to someone."

He nodded. It was.

"On the other hand, I'm the one who made a big stink about just being friends while we worked together. And now here I am, wondering what it's like to kiss you all day long."

"All day long?" He grinned, hoping it would release the tension.

She frowned at him. "You know what I mean. It's distracting, thinking about it and wondering… Anyway, I was thinking if we kissed, just once, then I would know what it was like, and we would know and could focus on work."

"Okay."

Her eyes bugged out. "What?"

"Let's just kiss and get it over with."

"Are you sure?"

Oh, he was sure. Granted, she'd made him promise that there would be no hanky-panky in the bakery, but he sure as shootin' wasn't going to bring that up now. Instead, he opened his arms to her, and she came into them, and damn, she felt good against him. She fit.

Without saying a word, he lowered his head and kissed her. And man, it was nice. She tasted like coffee and sugar, with a hint of cinnamon—and Amy—and she was delicious. Her mouth was soft and pliant and giving. When she made a little noise at the back of her throat, the heat, the hunger for her kicked in. He pulled her closer and cupped her cheek and tipped his head to deepen the kiss. She opened to it, to him, and wrapped her arms around his neck and clung as they feasted.

He'd intended it to be a gentle and polite first kiss, but whenever you started a fire, there was always a chance it might rage out of control. This—this kiss—was that.

As his passion rose, hers did too. They were both dizzy with it. So dizzy, it took a moment for him to realize the thudding in his ears wasn't just his pounding heartbeat.

Someone was knocking on the door.

What the hell *am I doing?!*

He pulled away and sucked in a breath, trying to steady himself against the delirium and desire. She frowned at him. "Noah?" Something wistful, something wounded.

"Customer," he rasped, scrabbling for sanity. He couldn't look at her, or he'd probably yank her into his arms again. "There's a customer."

"Damn it." He nearly laughed because he'd never heard her cuss before. "Damn it. Damn it. Damn it." She raked her fingers through her hair, hastily donned a pink apron from the peg and then grabbed the rolling rack which they had—thankfully—filled earlier, and she tromped out into the storefront, leaving him alone and cold. Hard.

And oddly lonely, without her in his arms.

Chapter Seven

Amy could barely function as she headed for the door, pretending to be surprised to see Marilee Hart waiting for her to open. Marilee ran the B and B down the road and was a frequent customer. It took all her concentration to turn the key in the lock and open the door. "Morning Marilee," she said as chirpily as she could. Hopefully she didn't look just-ravaged. Because she had been. Her pulse was still thudding, and there were little beads of sweat on her brow.

"Morning, Amy. I'm so sorry—I thought you opened at seven."

"No problem. I'm running a little late. What can I get you?"

"Oh." Marilee rolled her eyes. "We had an unexpected influx of customers last night, so I need to grab some extra pastries for breakfast. Anything, really."

"Sure. Let me set the trays in the case, and then you

can order whatever you want." It only took a minute or so to get the trays in place and build up a box for the order. Then, as Marilee pointed, Amy added the items to the box. It was a large order, but Amy had done this for her so many times, it was like autopilot.

Thank goodness because her brain had short circuited.

Oh. God. That kiss... It had floored her. Completely and utterly. She hadn't expected to be swept away like that. Her first kiss with George had been nothing like that. It had been awkward and a little sloppy, and they'd both been nervous, and there had been teeth. Oh, and she'd been fourteen. Yeah. Real different. Granted, she hadn't really understood where kissing led back then. She certainly hadn't experienced the joy of sex with a man she loved.

She'd asked Noah for a kiss to see what it felt like, to see if she might want to pursue the feelings she was having for him. And yes, he was attractive. Yes, she had a hard time focusing when he was around—it had helped to set those ground rules, for herself, mostly— but she'd never expected one little kiss to sweep her away like a raging flood. Now... Now all she could think about was getting rid of Marilee and going back to the kitchen for more. More Noah.

He was addictive.

"Do you have any apple fritters?"

Amy blinked. She glanced at the rack. It was empty. Surely they had made the fritters...

"Here they are." A shiver shot through her as Noah's deep voice rumbled around her. She stepped aside so he could slide the tray into place. Still, she could feel his body heat. Lord love a duck, he was warm.

"Two please."

Noah grabbed a pair of tongs and added them to the box before Amy could move. "Anything else?" he asked. Then he totaled the order, added the discount Amy gave other local businesses and finished the sale. And all Amy could do was stand there and smell his aftershave. Was it even more alluring than before?

When the door closed behind Marilee, he turned to her. He was close. So close. Heat rose, swirled in her. She couldn't look at him.

"Are you okay?" he asked softly.

"Mmm-hmm." She turned away in an attempt to regain her composure.

He caught her arm. "Amy." He waited until she met his gaze. "Are you okay?"

This time, she couldn't look away. "Yes. I... I just didn't expect...*that*."

He chuckled. *Chuckled.*

Seriously?

"Neither did I. Well, I knew it would be fantastic, kissing you, but—"

"Wait. You've thought about it? Kissing me?"

He laughed again, and she scowled at him. He ignored the scowl. "Um, yeah." He cocked his head to the side. "Haven't you thought about kissing me?"

She had. But never in her wildest dreams had she expected that...tumult. She raked back her hair with trembling fingers.

When she didn't answer, he stepped closer with an unmistakable glint in his eye. Panic flared, and instinctively, she stopped him with a hand to his chest and gently pushed him away. "Noah. We can't." One more kiss like that and she might lose all control.

And there was work to do. She needed to focus.

Damn it all anyway. Sometimes it downright sucked to be a responsible adult.

The expression on his face gutted her. Wistful and wounded. "You...didn't like the kiss?"

She barked a laugh, maybe harsher than she'd intended. "Are you serious? It was...fantastic." *Fantastic* wasn't even an adequate word. There were no words. All she wanted was to lean in for more. And that was the problem. Judging from his reaction to her putting a stop to it, she knew she needed to explain, but he had already turned away.

"Noah, please."

"No, it's okay, Amy. I—"

"Noah. Stop. Listen to me." She took him by the arm—trying to ignore the flexing of his powerful bicep below her palm—and turned him back to her. "Listen. Please."

"Okay." He settled his gaze on her face, but she could tell he wasn't engaged. Maybe it was just best to blurt the truth.

"I loved it. I want more. But..."

"But what?"

"We can't. At least not right now. I need to focus. I mean, do you know how distracting you are?"

She knew she'd reached him when he grinned. "Am I?"

She blew out a breath. "You are totally distracting, and I need to focus on business. I cannot afford to be distracted."

"Okay." He threaded his fingers together, as though he needed to—to keep his hands off her or something. "And when the work is over?"

She met his eye. "Then we reassess. Okay?"

He grinned. "Okay."

"But for now…"

He held up his hands, palms out. "For now…"

"Right." But seriously. How was she supposed to focus on her customers with that man in her line of sight? It was going to be a hell of a day.

Noah had a hard time concentrating on the customer's orders all morning. A couple of times, he had to ask people to repeat themselves. All he wanted to think about was the feel of Amy in his arms, her scent, the taste of her skin.

He'd known he would enjoy kissing her, but he hadn't been prepared for the reality. If he'd known, he would never have kissed her for the first time right before the bakery opened. It was torture, not kissing her again. But the excitement, the anticipation of future kisses was a delicious torment. More than once, in passing, their gazes clashed and clung. And then she'd grin or he would, and the excitement would rise in him again.

But she was right. They needed to focus on the customers and the specialty orders and other tasks that kept them busy when the shop was empty. By unspoken agreement, neither of them brought up the subject of the kiss again. Probably because they both knew if they did, they might end up in a heated clinch and miss another customer.

In fact, she kept herself mostly in the kitchen, and

he stayed in the shop, which worked just fine until the stream of customers thinned out. Then he had nothing to think about but kissing her. And more.

Tight leash, he kept reminding himself. *Tight leash*. But it was hard.

Real hard.

Natalie and Jax came in around lunchtime, which was a relief because he needed the distraction.

"Hey, Noah," Nat said cheerily.

Amy was in the walk-in, rearranging slabs of butter, possibly in an attempt to avoid talking to him, or maybe to cool down from the heat of their clinch, but she came right out when she heard her sister's voice. "Nat! What brings you into town?" she asked in a bright tone. Maybe she was thankful for the distraction as well.

Nat blew out a sigh. "We had to bring some more paintings over to Angel's gallery for the show on Sunday."

Jax grinned. "Thought we'd stop by and see how things are going."

"Great," Amy said in a cheery voice. "Just great."

"Very busy," Noah added, and then they both nodded.

"Very." She took a pair of tongs and handed Jax the last apple fritter.

"Well, that's good. Hey Amy," Natalie said, waving off a mute offer for a pastry, "I just wanted to say how much I enjoyed watching the boys the other day."

"Aw," Amy said. "They loved it too."

"Oh, good. Well, Jax and I were wondering if…" She paused and glanced at Jax, who nodded for her to continue. She sighed and then said, "We were wondering if we could watch them again sometime?" And when Amy didn't answer quickly enough, she added, "I know you have a sitter and everything, but we'd really love to spend more time with them."

Jax draped his arm around Nat's shoulder and tugged her close. "Now that we've got everything delivered for the art show this weekend, we've got tons of time."

"The boys would love that," Amy said. "Actually, so would I. I'm not very happy with my current sitter at the moment." She made a face. That was an understatement. She was still very unhappy that Kim and lied to her about Dylan being sick. "From what the boys tell me, she sits them in front of the television most of the day."

"Really?" Nat's eyes went wide. "Don't tell Momma that."

"Right?" Amy turned to Noah to explain. "Our parents were very strict with screen time when we were growing up."

"We played outside," Nat added. "We had a blast."

Noah had to grin because of the nostalgia on their faces was sweet. "Kids need to run off that extra energy."

"Actually…" Amy glanced at Noah, and his heart gave a thud because he knew what she was thinking. Hell, he was thinking the same thing. "Would you be willing to watch them tonight?"

Nat's expression brightened. "Oh, I'd love that." She whirled on Jax. "We could have a spaghetti party and set up that Frisbee-golf course on the lawn."

"Sounds like fun. Yeah." Jax glanced at Noah. "Do you have plans?"

Noah had no idea why he asked *him*. Or maybe he did, given the conversation they'd had the other day.

Still, Amy answered. "Just a night off," she said in a blasé tone. "You know. A *mom-cation*."

"Sure thing." Jax nodded somberly, but Noah knew he was biting back a grin. He hadn't thought this sizzle of energy between himself and Amy was obvious to others, but maybe he was wrong. Whatever. He didn't care.

"What time can we pick them up?" Nat asked. She was clearly excited.

"Oh, whenever works for you." Amy glanced at the clock. "I mean, I usually pick them up from Kim's around three thirty—"

"So, four?"

Amy laughed. "Actually, I was going to say you can pick them up now if you want."

"Could we? Oh. Could we?"

"Of course. I'll call Kim and tell her to expect you."

Natalie squealed and came around the pastry cases to hug her sister. "This is going to be great." After Amy gave her Kim's address, she practically danced out the door.

But Jax held back, just long enough grin knowingly at them and murmur, "Have fun, kids," before following Nat out.

When they were gone, Amy turned to Noah and said, "Feel like having a date night?"

He grinned and responded with a quick, "Yes, ma'am." He couldn't wait for the day to be over so that they could be alone again.

Amy got more and more nervous as three o'clock approached. There was excitement twined in there and anticipation, but fear was rampant. She hadn't been on a date in... Well, she couldn't remember.

When they'd been kids, she and George hadn't really dated—other than hanging out with friends, and the date nights they'd had after they'd been married hardly counted, did they? It was kind of stunning for her to realize that she hadn't really had an honest to God first date with a man. Hence the nerves.

She had to admit, though, she'd been afraid of her attraction to Noah from the moment she'd laid eyes on him, in that sexy set of black leathers. She'd known, even then, that a man like that, like him, had the power to upend her life.

Now, after that kiss—the one still swirling in her mind, filling her with an unfamiliar but exhilarating desire—she had to explore this...*thing* with him. She needed it. She needed to finally move on from George, to release the past to where it belonged. But there was more to it than that.

She also wanted this. Wanted him.

However, she knew herself. She wasn't ready to just leap into bed with him. She needed to know him a little better first. Part of her hesitation was totally logical—she was a mother and she owed it to her boys not to make mistakes. But part of her hesitation came from cold hard fear.

Her fears were rational. She was scared of giving him too much of herself and then getting hurt—but didn't everyone embarking on a relationship, testing the waters of trust, have that fear? She'd survived the worst thing that could happen to love. Surely she could survive again, if she needed to.

And then there was the worry that when things got really intimate—and they would, she hoped—how would he react to her mom bod? She wasn't an eighteen-year-old girl anymore; she'd given birth to two children, for pity's sake.

Aside from that, she was a mom. She'd lived her life in that reality for six years. Was it possible after all that time to be sexy again? Not in the physical sense so much as mentally and emotionally?

When the thought flashed through her mind, she had to grin because that had not been a concern when she'd been in the throes of his kiss. Nothing had been a concern in the throes of that kiss, other than one simple urge. *More.*

Still, she had to acknowledge that things might be awkward at first.

Heck, things were awkward now. But still, it was a tantalizing kind of awkward.

At three, Amy flipped the sign and they shifted into final-cleanup mode. Neither one of them spoke about their impending date but kept all conversation on the topics pertaining to work. It wasn't until they had finished everything and hung their aprons back on the pegs that he turned to her and lifted a brow.

"So…" The deep rumble of his voice resonated through her. "What now?"

She huffed a laugh. Even though she'd been thinking about it all afternoon, she was torn. Her lust-driven brain wanted to continue the kiss where they'd left off, maybe right here, maybe right now. But her mom brain told her they needed to take it slow, they needed to be cautious, that they needed to talk about this and discuss parameters and set boundaries. She hoped, maybe, there was something somewhere in the middle, where they could both feel safe and still enjoy the bliss of being together. But for that, given how hungry she was for him and how leery she was at making this monumental leap with him, a public place would be necessary.

"I was serious about having a date." She tried to be as stern as she could, but when he grinned, she wanted to grin back. Instead, she scowled. "I'm serious."

"I know." His dimple popped. "You're just cute when you're bossy."

Heat walked up her cheeks. Because he thought she was cute. Still, it was important to clarify. "I'm not being bossy. I'm speaking my truth."

He sobered then, nodded and said "Okay."

"This is all very new to me, Noah. This whole..." She waved a hand toward the spot where they'd kissed. "Thing. I don't want to move too fast and miss something important. Also..." She had to turn away from his too-intent gaze. "It's...well, it's been a while for me. Can you understand that?"

He reached out and cupped her cheek, so gently. "I do understand. And I respect it."

"So, you don't mind taking it slow?"

"No. Of course not. We're still exploring each other, right? Let's take whatever time we need." He flashed her a grin. "So, what kind of date do you have in mind?"

Oh, what a relief. Still, at the same time, his kindness, his understanding made her want to throw herself into his arms here and now. Though, if she was being brutally honest with herself, she'd wanted that anyway all day long. Somehow she made the effort not to leap into his arms and answered his question instead. "I thought maybe we could walk over to Bootleggers and have something to eat. I know it's early, but—"

"I could eat. That's sounds great. I was planning to check that place out. Natalie told me they have a great coconut shrimp appetizer."

"Oooh. They do. It's yummy."

"All right, then. Shall we?" He held out his arm, and she took it. Even though it felt silly, it made her happy. Not just the old-fashioned, gentlemanly gesture, but the fact that he was willing to give her the time and consideration she'd asked for. That alone told her a lot about him.

There were so many thoughts churning in her mind as Vic Walton, the owner of Bootleggers, seated them in a booth in the back. It was early, even for the happy-hour crowd, so the restaurant was quiet, but back here they were as private as they could be. And yeah, there was a second or two, after Vic had taken their order and left, when panic consumed her—*what on earth was she doing?*—but all she had to do was look at Noah, gazing at her from across the table, and her trepidation faded away.

"So." He folded his hands on the table and fixed his attention on her. "What do you want to talk about?"

Amy blew out a breath. What did people usually talk about on dates? She hadn't a clue. The truth was she knew what she wanted to share with him and what she wanted to know, but she wasn't sure how to broach the topic. "Us, I guess."

"Okay."

"Um, have you dated a lot of women?" She nearly

cringed. It was a horrible way to start the conversation, but at least it was a start.

He shrugged. "Not a lot. But a few. Nothing serious though. Not yet." He shot her a piercing glance. "But I've never met anyone like you before."

Heat slithered through her. He had that effect, she'd noticed, making her hot. "What do you mean, *like me*?"

He shrugged. "I'm not sure. It's just something I felt when we first met. A…familiarity? I felt as though I recognized you, you know?"

She nodded, even though she hadn't had that experience with him. Her reaction had mainly been a confusing slurry of excitement, lust and fear.

"And now, now that we've had time to get to know each other, I just want more. This—" he waved his hand between them "—just feels…right."

Yeah. It did. She couldn't explain it either.

The conversation paused as Vic brought them their drinks. He'd ordered a soda, and she'd asked for tea. She took a minute to doctor it up the way she liked it and then said, "You are so direct." It was not a complaint.

"I learned to be clear about what I wanted early on, or I never got it. If I was clear and specific, sometimes I did."

"Mmm. Tell me more about your childhood."

He barked a laugh. "That's a story." He didn't elaborate, and she didn't push, and after a moment of crushing ice with his straw, he said, "I think the hardest thing about growing up in foster care was the uncertainty. I mean, at any time, the social services people could show up and tell you to pack your things."

"So, a lot of moving around." She had to smile.

"Army brat. I can totally relate to that." But in her child-hood, only the places had changed. The people, her fam-ily had always been there. He hadn't had that. "How many families did you live with?"

He shrugged. "Seven? No, eight." He started jabbing his ice again. "Some places were better than others. Some were total chaos. So yeah, I learned to keep my nose out of trouble but be prepared to defend myself if I needed to."

She hated that as a child, he'd had to defend himself. She couldn't help but imagine her boys in that situation, and it was heartbreaking.

"Did you have any favorites?"

Oh, the grin transformed his face. "Ma, for sure." She had to smile too. His emotion was infectious. "She was the one who taught me to bake. I was about fifteen when I landed with her. She was older than most of my foster parents. All her kids were grown and out of the house. I think she decided to take in foster kids because she honestly wanted to make a difference. Some people do it for the money, you know."

"Did she? Make a difference? For you?"

He blew out a breath. "She did. I was heading for trouble about then, angry and impatient and making bad decisions."

"What did she do?"

"She put me to work. Gave me a clear vision of the world and how to survive. No, how to succeed. She taught me serving others could be just as important as being able to fight."

"You were lucky to have her."

"I know."

"So, are you still in touch?"

A shadow flickered over his handsome face. "No. She passed."

"I'm sorry."

"Me too. But I still carry her with me. Here." He tapped his chest. "The things she taught me, the care she gave. Everyone should have someone like that in their lives. I guess what I learned the most from her is that it only takes one person to give a damn, to make a change in someone's life. Just one person."

It broke her heart that he felt only one person had cared for him. It wasn't really true. It couldn't be. How could people have been so utterly ignorant of the layers and depths of his soul?

"Anyway, same as George, as soon as I turned eighteen, I went to the Air Force recruiter. Thanks to Ma and her nagging at me to get my grades up, I made the cut. They took me. And man…" He shook his head, the pride shining from his eyes. "I felt like a man that day. I felt…accepted. Everything changed after that, of course. I felt like I'd finally found my place."

"That's a wonderful feeling."

"Right? And I was good at what I did. I fit in. I excelled. Then a commander of mine saw my potential and recommended me for the pipeline."

"What is the pipeline?"

He chuckled. "It is the torturous path to the maroon beret." When she wrinkled her brow, he elaborated. "It's a series of courses you need to pass to become a PJ. Everything from Special Warfare Prep School to Combat Diver School to Airborne and Freefall Schools. Then SERE training—"

"What is SERE?"

"Survival, Evasion, Resistance, Escape. Basically, how to survive behind enemy lines."

"Fun."

He tried not to grimace but failed. "It was damn hard. Every minute of it. But it really got fun when we got into the medical stuff. I loved that. First, the EMT course where I had to learn the names of all the bones and muscles as well as triage and critical care, and then paramedic school where I learned advanced care like IVs, intubation, pushing meds and how to read ECGs. Stuff like that. Then they sent us on paramedic practicals, which was really cool—I did ride alongs in Philadelphia as well as actual hospital rotations. I got to do a lot of the stuff I'd learned."

"Sounds like a lot."

He shrugged. "I left a bunch out. Like the course on dirt medicine, where we learned how to do advanced medical procedures without all the fancy gear, just whatever you have in your ruck. Sometimes things happen out in the field. PJs need to be ready for any eventuality."

"What a lot of work."

"It took me nearly three years just to get through the courses. But it was worth it. Graduation day was one of the proudest days of my life."

"So why did you leave the Air Force?"

He made a face. "I had a bad jump. Got all banged up. And the doctor told me he wouldn't clear me to jump anymore. They wanted to give me a desk job. Seriously? A desk job?" He shrugged. "I figured it was time to find a spot and settle down. You know, the way grown-ups are supposed to do?"

She laughed. "It sucks being a grown-up."

They both leaned back when Vic brought in the coconut shrimp. Amy moaned as she caught a whiff. They both dug in, and indeed, it was delicious. What a treat. Not just the yummy food, but the conversation, the ambiance and the company as well.

"This is so good," she said as she wiped her hands on a napkin.

"Mmm," he responded because his mouth was full.

After they'd both had a bit to eat, she turned back to the conversation. "So, you left the Air Force with the intention of finding a spot to settle. Why not Virginia?"

He lifted a shoulder. "A lot of bad memories, I guess. And Ma was gone by then. Plus, I'd always wanted to see the country. It made sense to buy a Harley—I'd always loved bikes—and travel a bit. I visited friends and went to famous places—"

"Like where?"

"You know. Mount Rushmore, the Florida Keys, the Alamo…"

"Nice."

"I rode a mountain bike down a volcano in Hawaii, I learned to surf in California—or at least I *tried* to surf." He gave a little laugh. "Skied in Aspen—I was terrible at that too. But hey, it's all about the experience. Right?"

"Right."

"But all the while, what I was really looking for was a place to call home." He sighed. "Sometimes I feel like I've spent my entire life looking for my place."

Amy's heart clenched. While she could relate to both

his wanderlust and his hunger to find a place to call home, she knew at the same time she really had no clue what he'd been through, what he'd overcome to become the man he was today.

What she did know was that she wanted only one thing: To know him better.

Noah glanced across the table at Amy. Her expression, the warmth and understanding in it, moved him; it healed something broken within him. It was as though she truly *saw* him. Saw through the gruff, powerful exterior he'd worked so hard to build…to protect himself. She saw through all that to the wounded soul within, and she accepted him, embraced him as he was.

He was thankful, all of a sudden, that he'd reined in his heat, his desire to have her physically, to agree to this date rather than taking her straight to bed…because this exchange was something potent and deep.

After a moment of thought, she glanced up at him with a smile. One that shot sunshine clear through the lurking desolation in his heart. "Maybe it's not the place so much as the people we find there that makes it home," she said, so simply revealing the truth it had taken him nearly three decades to decode.

"I think, perhaps, you're right."

"So…what do you think about Coho Cove?" It was a leading question, but he didn't mind being led.

"I love it. I mean, I haven't seen too much of it, other than the bakery…" She laughed at his joke. Always a good sign. "But it feels…homey."

"It's a nice place," she said. Then she leaned in and added, "And I've been to Paris, *France*."

"Paris is nice."

"Gorgeous. I just don't think I'm a big-city person." She wrinkled her nose, which was cute. "I can't live in the country either. But a small town feels just right."

"It doesn't hurt that your family is here too."

"Totally."

They took a moment to eat a little more, even though the shrimp wasn't near as delicious now that it had cooled a bit. Amy was the one who broke the silence with a great gusted sigh. "So, Noah," she said.

"Mmm-hmm?" Her tone had changed, so he expected the topic would as well. He was right.

"Can we talk about that kiss?"

Something within him perked up. "Sure."

"I…" She seemed to find it difficult to come up with words, but he decided not to try to fill in the blanks. He took a slurp of his drink while she worked it out. After a minute, she blurted, "I was not expecting that."

Okay. "Not expecting what?" He thought he knew, he hoped he knew, but it was better if she explained the subtext.

She stared at him for a second, then blew out another sigh. "I… It… Well, it blew me away."

It was hard not to grin. "It blew me away too. I mean, I knew I'd enjoy kissing you. But—" He didn't want to say that he'd nearly lost all control, but he had. Hell, if Marilee hadn't come a knocking, things would have come to a head—so to speak—right there on the kitchen floor. Or against the wall. Or in the office. Maybe all three.

And while that would have been amazing—and it would have been—it might also have damaged what they were building, simply because he suspected she hadn't been ready to take that step. He wasn't sure why he felt that way, but he was certain it was true.

"I'll be honest," she said. "It kind of scared me, the way I…"

"Lost control?"

She paled. Nodded. But it was a tiny nod. Then she added in an equally tiny voice, "I'm a mom. Moms don't lose control."

He reached out and covered her hand with his. "You're also a woman. A beautiful, passionate woman."

"Passionate." She spat out the word like it tasted bad. "I mean, for me, the problem is that, well…" He could tell she was struggling, getting this out, whatever it was, but he let her struggle. She needed to get it out. And he wanted to know what it was. Especially if it was a barrier between them.

At long last, she sucked in a deep breath. Then she raked back her hair and blurted, "You see, before you, George was the only man I've ever kissed. Or, well, slept with. I'm…practically a virgin."

He stared at her, stunned. It was hard to believe, as pretty as she was, as vibrant and sexy. Then again, there was an innocence around her most mothers of two had long since shed.

But then, she'd told him, hadn't she? She and George had married at eighteen. Since his death she'd been busy raising the boys and running a business and trying to keep her family's world afloat.

When he didn't respond—because he was flabbergasted and processing—her expression collapsed in on itself. "Oh. You think I'm a weirdo now."

He caught her hand when she tried to pull away. "Not at all." He met her gaze and said, as sincerely as he could, "I think it's sweet. But why is that a problem? You know, in terms of, well, being with me?" Best to get back to the salient point of this conversation, right?

She made a face. "First of all, I'm not sure I even remember what to do." She snorted a laugh, so he suspected she was joking about that…maybe.

He tightened his hold on her hand. "It's okay, Amy. It's okay." But the knowledge kind of changed everything. Didn't it? Even though he'd known in his heart she wasn't the kind of woman who had casual sex, he'd figured she'd had at least one boyfriend in the years since George had passed.

At the same time, the knowledge that she hadn't… Well, it warmed him to his core. Because *he* was the one she'd chosen. Or at the very least, he was the one she was considering.

And if he was to be the one, he wanted to do it right. She didn't need a quick tumble. She needed a long, slow, gentle seduction. She deserved one.

He intertwined their fingers and stroked her hand with a thumb until she peeped up at him. "Yeah," he said. "I can see how it's a little scary after so long—"

"A little?"

"But we're taking it slow, right?" He waited until she nodded, waited until she met his gaze. "Okay, then. I promise nothing is going to happen between us that you're not ready for. Nothing."

"Nothing?"

"We're just exploring this connection between us, right?"

"Right." Oh, how he loved the way he could see her confidence grow. Loved, especially, her grin.

"There's no rush for anything, Amy," he said soothingly. "No rush at all."

And he meant it.

Chapter Eight

As they walked back to the bakery, Amy was floating on air. Excitement and anticipation simmered in the air around her. Noah had soothed the worst of her fears and assured her she was safe with him, and she believed him. With all that aside, all she could think about was tasting him again. And she didn't particularly want to wait.

So, she lured him inside the bakery with the excuse that she wanted to make sure they'd turned everything off—even though she knew that they had—and once she had him alone in the office, she set her hands on his shoulders, went up on her toes and kissed him.

It was a quick kiss, maybe a little shy, but it made him smile.

It made her smile too. "Thank you for the date," she said.

"Oh?" He locked his hands behind her back and

pulled her closer when she would have pulled away. "Is the date over?"

She shrugged. "I'm assuming. I'm hardly an expert."

"Me either," he said with a chuckle, but then he lowered his head and kissed her again and proved that he, at least, was an expert at that. And oh, it was nice. Slow, languorous and sensual. She could tell he was holding back. But then, so was she. They had agreed, hadn't they, to take this slowly?

All that nonsense went out the window when he shifted position and nibbled his way across her cheek and nestled in the crook of her neck—where the skin was so sensitive, where the nerves leaped to life. She groaned because the pleasure was so sweet, so unbearable. And because it was nearly impossible not to, she arched against him.

The knowledge that he was hard—hard for her—was shocking, stunning. She didn't know why she was surprised because she knew how such things worked. She'd felt a man's arousal before. But this was new. Raw. Electrifying.

She gusted a moan and pulled back to look him in the eye, and his expression stole her breath. It was hard, hot, hungry. It melted something within her—which might have been her resolve. "Noah." A plea.

"Amy." The passion took them both then, and he pushed her back against the wall and devoured her. And she devoured him. As they kissed, madly, savagely, he caressed her, stroked, explored. His thumb over her hard nipple made her shudder. His caress over her nape made her melt. The pressure of his length against her pelvis made her wild.

When he pressed against her there, between her legs, in the tender spot where her nerves were alive and aching, she seized and bliss rained through her. God, it felt so good. It had been so long. Too long.

Had she really thought she might not remember what to do? *Ha!* Her body remembered.

With trembling fingers, she scrabbled for the button of his jeans. He sucked in a breath and stiffened when they missed their mark and brushed against his hardness instead.

"Amy..." A warning tone.

He started to say something about taking it slow, but she couldn't hear clearly through the thudding in her ears. Or she ignored the words. Her arousal had consumed her reason. She reached for him again and found him, cupped him fully with her palm. And ah...he was hard. And hot. And ready. Her knees locked. Her hunger raged. She stroked him. Explored. And she took great pleasure in making him moan her name once again.

"Amy, we—"

She silenced him with another hungry, demanding kiss.

She hadn't intended to seduce him here in the office when she'd kissed him—at least, if she had, she hadn't realized it. She'd simply wanted another kiss. But intention hardly mattered at a moment like this.

Like teenagers, they fumbled and tugged and madly worked to bare what needed to be bared. She yanked his underwear down, and he got one leg free from her jeans. So close. So close.

But then, he froze. "Shit."

Her heart stopped. "What is it?"

His expression was contrite. "I almost forgot." He bent down, went through his jeans, pulled out his wallet and then riffled madly through it. "Oh, thank God," he said in a gust. "I have one."

"One what?" she asked. Her brain really must have been on the fritz, because when he triumphantly held up a familiar foil packet, she could only let out a sigh of relief.

Thank God he'd remembered. She hadn't. She hadn't even thought about it.

But she forgot all about it again after he slipped the condom on, and lifted her up—as though she were light as a feather—and he was in her.

That alone, that one thrust, brought her to bliss once more. But he wasn't finished. *They* weren't finished. Not by a long shot. He took her then, against the wall in the office of the bakery that had formed the foundations of her dreams. It was hard and fast and utterly out of control.

And so, so delicious.

She came again and again, practically with every plunge, and still she begged for more.

He gave it to her in long, powerful strokes and tiny nibbles and maddening draws on her hard, aching nipples—mind bending even through the fabric of her bra. He gave her everything until, with one massive drive and a soul-wrenching groan…he gave her his all.

They collapsed together, against the wall, his weight holding her in place, and Noah dropped his head onto Amy's shoulder, gasping for breath. Oh yeah. That had been amazing.

He couldn't process much more than that *oh yeah—*

and thank God he didn't need to. He just held her there and reveled in the sensations, in her warmth, the scent of her arousal and his, the delight that danced along every nerve.

He'd known it would be like that with her—the connection so organic, the joining so...right.

After a little while—or an eternity, whatever—he eased out, being careful to support her as he did. Then he pulled her closer and held her. Stroked her hair, nuzzled her hairline. It felt amazing to hold her in his arms as she recovered.

When she stirred, he glanced down at her. "Are you okay?" he asked softly. He'd promised to be patient. He'd promised to take his time. And he hadn't. Granted, she hadn't let him, but that didn't change the fact that he'd promised.

But when she grinned up at him, a blazing grin, his trepidation washed away, and he grinned back.

"Well," she said in a chipper tone. "That was unexpected."

"It always seems a little unexpected with us," he said, reaching out to loop a curl behind her ear. God, she was beautiful like this. He wanted to always remember her like this. He zipped up his jeans, then helped her fix her clothes. Once they were both somewhat decent again and fully back in the world, he kissed her. "Thank you."

She laughed, "Thank *you*."

"That was incredible."

"It was."

He caught her eye because she'd gone all shy again and dropped her gaze. "Are you...okay?"

"Oh," she said with a sigh. "I'm great. That was great."

"Good." He didn't want to ruin the mood, not at the moment, because it was still all magical and stuff, but at some point, he reminded himself that in the future, if—when—they did this again, he was going to need more protection. Thank God he'd had that old condom tucked away in his wallet. She'd kind of taken him by storm just now, and he had been utterly unprepared.

It felt a little awkward showing up at Nat and Jax's house with Noah to pick up the boys, still tingling with delight, but Amy reminded herself that no one *knew* what had just happened in the bakery. And they weren't going to hear it from her. But still, it felt weird, pretending that nothing had changed. It had.

The boys grabbed Noah as soon as they saw him step out of the car and dragged him straight over to the side yard to check out the obstacle course they'd built. But Amy headed inside.

"Hey," she called as she stepped into Nat and Jax's cozy cottage. "We're here."

"In the kitchen," Nat called, so Amy headed that way. "Hey, sis," she said when Amy rounded the corner. Jax, whose mouth was full of chocolate chip cookies, waved.

"Hey, guys. Thanks for watching the boys."

Nat grinned. "No thanks necessary. We had a blast." Without asking, she picked up a streaming teapot and poured Amy a cup.

"Mmm," Amy lifted it and drew in the subtle aroma. "Ginger? Yum."

"Cookie?" Nat offered her the plate, and Amy chose one.

"Thanks." She didn't usually eat cookies before dinner, but this, she figured, was a special occasion. Also, she probably needed to refill her energy stores. From all the moaning and thrashing. Probably. "Good cookie," she said through a mouthful.

"The boys made them," Jax said with a grin. Good. She liked that Nat and Jax had kept them busy rather than dumping them in front of a screen.

"So," Nat said in an amused tone. "How was your afternoon?"

Jax huffed a laugh. "Let's call it what it was—a date."

Amy frowned at him. Had she really thought no one would notice? She should have known better, especially with Jax. He knew her far too well. "Hush. I don't want the boys to know there was a date."

Nat lifted a brow. "You don't want them to know?"

"It's early on." Not all that early on actually, considering what had happened today, but whatever. "I don't want them confused. Let's keep it on the down low for now, okay?"

Jax glanced at Natalie and then nodded. "Sure. Yeah."

"And it's early on. Have I mentioned it's early on?"

Jax grinned. "You have."

"Besides…" She sighed. "I don't want them to think I'm being unfaithful to their father. That's a bad message. Isn't it?"

"Oh, Amy." Nat gave her a hug. "You're not being unfaithful to George."

"You've been very faithful to his memory," Jax added.

Nat nodded. "It's time for you to move on. Way past time."

"Besides," Jax said, "George would approve of Noah."

Amy sent him a sharp look. "You think so?"

"I know he wouldn't want you to be alone, and he'd want a good man for the boys. And Noah's one of the good guys. So, yeah."

Well, that made her feel better, a little less guilty at least.

"I like him," Nat said, gazing out the bay windows at Noah and the boys doing sprints on the lawn. "I like him a lot."

"Hey!" Jax grumbled, but it was clear he was teasing.

Nat ignored him. "He's handsome and kind." She gave Amy an assessing glance. "And he's got that military mindset. I know, I know. It shouldn't matter, but it does. There's a familiarity. Common ground. An understanding of the way things are done."

Amy glanced out at the lawn again and watched as Georgie tackled Noah and he pretended to fall helplessly. A smile tweaked her lips. Yeah. Maybe Noah's military bearing had something to do with the fact that they'd slipped so easily into a friendship. But the rest of it—the trust, the attraction, the affection—that had been all him.

"You're smiling," Nat said. "You like him."

"Oh, yes. I do. He makes things…easy."

"That's a good sign," Jax said.

"Of course, we both understand he may only stay till the wedding."

Jax gave a shrug. "Well, whatever happens, Amy, you know we love you and we're here for you."

"We are." Nat gave her another hug.

"Um… Thanks." Amy gave her sister a look. Not that it made her suspicious, but two hugs in one day? Nat wasn't a hugger. She also wasn't a crier, but the hint of tears glinted in her eyes. Something, some intuition made her ask, "So…what's going on with you two?"

It was supposed to be a casual question, a general query, but Nat's wide-eyed response was a little too quick. Her abrupt "Nothing" sealed the deal. Something was definitely up.

Amy narrowed her gaze—the way moms did when they *knew* something was up, crossed her arms and said, "Really?" Just that. Just, *Really*? It was all it took.

Natalie flushed. She glanced at Jax, who shrugged. "Go on. Tell her."

Aha! Moms *always* knew. "Just tell me what?"

"We didn't plan to tell anyone until after the wedding, but—we're pregnant." A whisper.

"What? You're *pregnant*?!"

Natalie's nostrils flared. "Shh! Hush. I don't want the boys to hear. They can't keep a secret, and we don't plan to make an announcement yet. You know." She set her hand on her belly. "It's early."

"Don't worry, Nat. I won't say a word. But I'm thrilled for you." She was. She could see the joy in Nat's expression and the pride in Jax's. Even though they'd already hugged today—twice—Amy hugged her again, but this one was long and warm and very, very nice. Their relationship hadn't always been easy, but now it was good. And soon, it would be better because they had something very precious in common. They'd be moms together.

"Hey. No hug for me?" Jax asked. "I did all the work."

Nat laughed and slapped him with a tea towel, but Amy did hug him too. "I'm glad you two found each other," she said, just in case she hadn't mentioned it. Because she was.

"Yeah," Jax said with a grin. "She's okay."

And Nat smacked him with the tea towel again.

Amy suspected it happened a lot. They were so cute together, and it made her happy to see them happy because she loved them both so much. Jax had been her savior, her lifeline, her sanity after George died. He'd treated his friend's boys as his own. It was because of him, and his willingness to support her as he had, that her bakery even existed. As a single mom of two and freshly minted widow, with all that entailed, she'd been tapped out. Utterly devastated and lost. But he'd been there for her.

Oh, her family had been there too—Momma and Celeste especially, as Nat had been living a thousand miles away in California—but it was Jax who had saved her. He'd been so good with the boys. And now… Joy filled her at the knowledge that now he could have a little one of his own.

"So, how are things going with the wedding planning?" She had to ask. The clock was ticking.

Jax grinned. "Great."

Nat glowered at him, but it was a playful glower. "I'm the one doing it all."

His grin widened. "She is."

"Fortunately, we both agreed it's not going to be fancy."

"Just family and friends."

"Ben has agreed to host the wedding and the reception at the hotel," Nat said.

Amy widened her eyes. "The Sherrod is beautiful."

She couldn't think of a prettier place for a wedding. "Am I making your wedding cake?" It wasn't really a question. More of a demand.

Nat's eyes teared up. "I wouldn't want it any other way."

But at the same time, Jax said, "How much do you charge?" When she quoted the commercial rate, he grabbed his belly as though she'd shot him. "But I guess I could give you the family discount." Of course, she would never charge them. It would be a true honor to make that cake. "Let me know what flavors you like."

"Flavors for what?"

Amy's heart jumped as Noah's voice surrounded her, and she turned toward him...and her thudding heart skipped a beat. He was grinning and gorgeous. His skin had a glow; sweat beaded his brow and darkened his T-shirt. Clearly the boys had given him a workout, but it was more than that. There was an aura around him. He looked...happy. It made her smile because she was happy too.

Granted, she'd just gotten laid for the first time in, well, way too long. But it wasn't just that rush of hormones that buoyed her. It was him. His presence.

The thought scared her a little, that she was intertwining her happiness with his presence. But somehow it was easier now to see that—even though it was scary—the risk was worth the joy.

It was an important lesson to learn.

Amy's smile was blinding. It caught Noah's attention—and his heart, and he couldn't look away. Hell, he could stare at her all day and never tire of it. Her smile ignited his. It also wiped his brain clean, apparently, because when Natalie said, "The wedding cake," he had trouble computing what she meant.

"Pardon?" he had to ask. It was hard to rip his attention from Amy to her sister, even for a second.

It was Jax who responded then, with something of a smirk—as though he understood the cause of Noah's distraction. "We're talking about flavors for the wedding cake."

Oh. Right. The wedding. It was the reason he was still here. Or it had been. He turned to Amy again, and a tingle shivered through him. She was the reason he was staying now. Well, her and the boys.

They followed him in—an explosion of energy—and of course, all attention shifted to them. He didn't mind at all because as Jax and Natalie engaged in an animated conversation with them, he and Amy were free to engage in their—nonverbal—interchange. Sometimes they had this unique ability to communicate without words, and now was one of those times.

The trouble was now, after that wild skirmish in the bakery, he could think of little else beyond having her again. And if he thought about it too much, his body would react. Which, in the presence of Natalie, Jax and the boys, would be awkward. So, he had to look away. He had to force himself to try and focus on the conversation they were having which, apparently, was about dinner.

Since he and Amy had eaten a delicious appetizer just a while ago, he wasn't particularly hungry, but when Natalie asked them if they wanted to stay, and the boys cried "Hurrah!" because they loved spaghetti and meat-balls, he and Amy agreed.

It was a raucous meal, full of laughter and jokes. They were mostly five-and six-year-old jokes, but that made them even funnier. It was somewhere during that meal, sitting around the table with Amy and her family, that the epiphany truly hit him, the truth, the rightness of her words.

Sometimes it was the people that made a place a home.

And this, so clearly, was that.

The warmth in his soul, the lightness in his heart—because of them, because of their presence—*that* was what home was. And he felt it. Here and now.

This was what he'd been searching for. This was what he hadn't found anywhere else on his long journey home.

And by God, he wasn't going to let it go.

It was a tremendous revelation and also a relief because he'd begun to suspect that his inability to find this feeling, this belonging, was because there was something deeply broken in him.

But maybe, just maybe, he wasn't broken after all.

That feeling stayed with Noah even after dinner was over, even as they piled into Amy's car and headed home. It wasn't even dimmed when Amy pulled up to the studio to drop him off. He wanted to stay with her, with them, but he had a very special errand to run.

As he unhooked his seat belt, John J. said, in a pout from the back seat, "Why can't Noah come home with us?"

Noah tried not to laugh. The last thing he wanted to do was leave them. "Well, my bed is here at the studio."

Georgie snorted. "You could just sleep in Jax's room."

Uh, what? He glanced at Amy, who rushed in to say, "Jax stayed with the boys back when I was training Eloise. Momma's housekeeper, who was also their sitter, broke her leg, and then Momma had a stroke and I hadn't found Kim yet, so Jax stayed over so someone was with the boys when they woke up. And well, he was such a help." And then, she added, "He slept in the downstairs bedroom."

"You should sleep there," Georgie pronounced.

He and Amy exchanged a look. They both knew that if he stayed the night in her house, he would not be in the downstairs bedroom for long. They hadn't talked about it yet, but he had the sense that she wouldn't be comfortable having him stay over *that way* because of the message it might give to the boys.

He wasn't sure how to answer appropriately, but Amy did. She was good at that. "Honey, sometimes grownups need me time."

"Like when you're in the bathroom for a long time?" John J. asked.

"Yes." Amy tried to stifle a laugh, but she failed. "Exactly like that."

"Will we see you tomorrow?" John J. asked. The tremble in his voice sent a pang through Noah's heart.

"Of course."

"You'll see him in the morning, silly," Amy said. And then to Noah, "Same time?"

"Yep." He tried to be as cheerful as he could, but it was hard because he didn't want to go. He didn't want to be alone in that empty studio filled with wooden statues. The hardest part was that it didn't feel right to get out of the car without kissing Amy good-night, but he knew he couldn't do that. And it really sucked watching her taillights depart.

He didn't even bother going inside. He went straight over to his bike. Since he needed to get those condoms and fill up his tank, he decided to head for the gas station over on Main Street. It was close, a quick run, so it only took a few minutes. He tried to focus on the joy he felt whenever he rode but found himself thinking about a completely different ride he'd had that day.

Yeah, Amy was distracting. She always had been, he'd found, but even more so now that they'd taken this monumental step in their relationship. He couldn't help thinking that being intimate with her had changed everything. Or at the very least, had shifted the foundation of his thinking. He hoped she felt the same.

He pulled into the gas station, put the nozzle into his gas tank and then headed into the store to grab a box of condoms while the tank filled up. He hadn't bought them in a while—had it been two years?—and there were too many options, so he just grabbed a box that looked familiar and headed over to check out the beer case. He wasn't much of a drinker, but he thought a beer or two might help quiet his mind and let him sleep.

When he came around the corner, heading for the checkout, a woman coming the other way bumped into him, and he dropped the box of condoms.

"I'm so sorry," she said as she bent to pick up the box. As she handed it to him, he realized, with a sudden flash of heat, that he knew her. It took a second to place the face because he'd only met her once—at Sunday dinner. And at the time, he'd been pretty obsessed with the cute baker across the table from him.

She was, in fact, Amy's sister. Her other sister.

She recognized him at the same moment, and her smile brightened. "Noah?"

"Celeste, right?"

"Yes. How are you?"

"Great." A totally automatic response. He was preternaturally aware of one thing—she was still holding on to the condoms. The ones he was buying. To have wild and crazy sex. With her baby sister.

Awkward.

Indeed, she glanced down at the box and her cheeks went pink when she realized what it was. She shoved it toward him. "Here. You dropped this."

"Thanks."

He was about to say something else, maybe ask how she was, but all of a sudden, she threw up her hands and said, "Oh, my goodness. I have to run. It was nice seeing you again, Noah," and she hurried out of the store.

He was still grinning about the interaction when he got back to the studio, cracked a beer and started checking his phone. When he saw a missed call from Amy, he called her right back.

"Hey, you," she said when she picked up. "I've been thinking about you."

His grin widened. "Same. Sorry I missed your call. I took a ride after you dropped me off."

"Fun."

"Yeah." He chuckled. "I ran into your sister Celeste

while I was buying a box of condoms. I can only imagine what she thinks about me now."

"You bought some condoms?" Her voice was bemused.

"Um, yeah. I only had the one. I figured I should take care of that…just in case."

"Just in case we do that again?" He could tell from her tone that she was making a joke.

"Yeah."

"Oh, my God. Thank you. I can't believe I didn't think about it! It's…just been so long since I even thought about stuff like that."

"I get it. No worries," he said. "I have a whole box now."

"Gosh. I guess we have to do that again, then," she said dryly.

"I guess so."

"It was superhot, though, wasn't it?"

He settled deeper into the sofa. "So hot." He'd lost his mind with her. It had been fantastic. She'd been fantastic. Even hearing her breathe over the phone made him stir.

"I wish you were here," she said in a sex-kitten voice.

"Me too. What are you wearing?"

"Umm." Her moan sent a sizzle of heat through his gut. "I'm wearing a very sexy… T-shirt and sweats."

"Wow. That sounds hot."

She laughed. "I'm doing laundry, Noah."

"So hot. Tell me everything."

He loved that he could make her laugh. Loved that they could play like this. He wouldn't have minded a little sex talk, but this was good too, listening to her describe in lurid detail how she was separating out the colors from the whites and presoaking one of John J.'s shirts that was stained with spaghetti sauce. At one point, Georgie came in to ask her for a glass of milk before bed, and Noah stayed on the line while she got it for him.

No one had ever made him warm milk to help him sleep—it had never occurred to him to want it, and he wasn't sure if he would even have liked it. But it was so nice to sit there and listen as she did it for her son. They were lucky kids to have a mom like her. Any kid would be blessed to have a mom like her.

Somehow, it helped ease the lurking pain in his soul, just knowing those boys, her boys, didn't have to go through what he had. Just knowing that such love existed…somewhere.

She had to go then, she said, because the boys wanted her to read to them. So, after asking her to tell them good-night for him, he signed off. He should probably go to bed too because 4:00 a.m. came early, but he sat there for a while longer with his eyes closed, just enjoying the moment, and thinking of her.

Chapter Nine

When Amy pulled in to pick up Noah the next morning, her heart caught. Just at the sight of him. Of course, she'd thought about him, about them, long past when she should have been asleep. And she'd dreamed about him. It had been a glorious dream, though she couldn't remember the details, just how it had made her feel.

Yesterday had been a big day for them—but then, so much had happened in a short period of time. In less than a week they'd gone from being complete strangers to knowing each other intimately. It happened, she supposed. Lots of people did it—tumbled precipitously into bed. But it felt different for her and Noah. The intimacy felt real and solid and right.

"Good morning," she chirped when he got into the car. She wanted to kiss him, and she could see in his eyes he wanted to kiss her, but the boys were in the back seat and watching. The boys were always watching.

"Morning," he said. "Hey, guys." He waved to the peanut gallery.

All the way to Kim's house, the boys chattered about this and that, and Amy and Noah joined in, answering their questions and remarking on their observations. But all the while Amy was aware of one thing—Noah by her side, and the fact that he'd surreptitiously taken her hand.

It was such a simple gesture, but it meant so, so much.

It also started a fire in her belly. She hadn't expected it to happen like that, so simply, so easily, first thing in the morning before she'd even had something to eat. But his touch set her alight. That and his grin when their gazes clashed during the short dark drive to Kim's.

Was it wrong that after dropping the boys off, they made love again in the bakery office? It was just as wild and just as frenetic and wonderful as it had been the day before, except it was more comfortable on her desk.

"I'm going to have to think about putting a cot in here," she joked as he held her in the aftermath—and they both laughed. There was no room for a cot. It was a tight fit as it was.

Gosh, there was just something about making love before work that set the day off on a happy note. Amy didn't remember it being this glorious before…but George had been a long time ago. At least, it seemed like a long time ago. A lifetime, maybe.

She didn't feel like that young girl anymore, not at all. But that wasn't a bad thing. She'd matured, ripened if you will. She knew the ropes, and she was at a stage where she could fully appreciate a gift like this—even though she was nervous about what people might think of a single mother having a wild affair in the back room of her bakery.

But you know what they say. What happens in the back room of the bakery...

They whipped through prep, which was usually a slog, and had bright smiles on their faces all morning long. In the rare moments when the shop was empty of customers, they cuddled and kissed in the back and devised nefarious plots to be able to spend more private time together.

There was a little guilt because she was a mom and her boys were her top priority, but they weren't babies anymore, and there were people she trusted who would be more than happy to spend time with them if Amy and Noah needed, ahem, *grown-up time*. Nat and Jax popped into mind, but they were hardly the only ones who had been asking for more time with John J. and Georgie.

Amy realized now that she might have been a little selfish of her time with the boys before. Understandable. They'd been all she had, or so it sometimes had seemed. She hadn't been willing to give them up during the hours she didn't need to be at work. Now, somehow, it felt easier to share them more. That said, she felt it was important that Noah spend quality time with them as well. Thankfully, that wasn't a problem because he enjoyed their company—and how wonderful was that? She could never be with a man who didn't like children, especially her own children.

At any rate, she felt confident they could find the time they needed to be alone together, if they made it a priority.

That was the heart of parenting though, wasn't it? Balance?

Amy was up front helping a customer and Noah was in the back prepping for the weekend—which was always busier than weekdays—when her sister Celeste strolled in. Amy couldn't hold back her smile. It was rare that Celeste stopped by because she had a busy schedule as a nurse at the local retirement home-slash-community center. She also took care of Momma, since they lived together in Grandma's old place.

Things had become a little easier for Celeste since they'd been able to find a really good day nurse to take care of Momma while she was at work. Still, Amy rarely saw her outside of work or home, so this was a treat. She hadn't seen Celeste since Sunday and—oh, dear. Had it only been five days? It felt like so much longer.

"Hey there, stranger," she said, coming around to give Celeste a hug once her customer had left. "What brings you to our humble establishment on this very fine day today?"

Celeste shot her a curious look. Okay. She was in a good mood. A *very* good mood. "I just wanted to check in. How are things?"

"Great. Wonderful."

"When's that TV crew coming again?"

"Not for weeks, but I'm excited. Hey, can I get you anything?"

"Not for me, but Momma likes that lemon cake. Do you have any today?"

Amy glanced at the cases and frowned when she realized that spot was empty, other than a few crumbs. "Hey, Noah," she called. "Are there any lemon cakes in the freezer?" It was one of the items she made ahead and thawed each morning.

"Yeah. Let me grab some," he called from the back.

She turned back to her sister with a smile. It faded when she noticed that Celeste had gone pale. She went a little paler when Noah came out with a couple pre-bagged slices. He looked adorable in that pink apron, with his dark hair flopping on his brow.

"Here you go." He handed them to Amy over the counter. "Hi, Celeste," he said with a cheery smile.

He might not have noticed Celeste's stiff demeanor, but Amy did. "Thanks," she said, and he headed back to work.

She handed the goodies to Celeste, who took them and tucked them into her purse. She waited until Noah had disappeared before she leaned in and whispered, "What's *he* doing here?"

"He's working here now." Celeste's tight expression didn't relax. "Didn't you hear that Eloise quit? Noah's filling in until I can find someone." Though, she hadn't really tried to find someone yet, had she? Oh well.

Celeste drew in a deep breath and tipped up her nose, a gesture Amy recognized right off the bat. Celeste had been her older sister her entire life. She was very familiar with that look. "No, I didn't know," she said in a wounded tone. "No one tells me anything."

"Oh. I'm sorry. It's been so busy, and everything happened so fast..." Celeste didn't respond, so Amy continued. "He's working out great. Did you know his first job was working in a bakery for one of his foster mothers?"

"No." She didn't say it aloud, but her expression said

it clearly. *How could I know when no one tells me anything.* But she did lean in again and say, "Amy, what do you know about him?"

She blinked. What did she know? A lot. At least, it felt that way. But Celeste had no idea what had taken place between her and Noah since Sunday. How could she? Amy wasn't even quite sure how to explain things to herself. "Well, he's amazing in the kitchen."

"Amy…" Celeste was whispering again and keeping a sharp eye on the door between the kitchen and the shop. "He's a complete stranger."

"Jax knows him." *She* knew him. Like, in the biblical sense, even. But she couldn't say that to Celeste. As the eldest, Celeste had taken on the role of protector to her younger siblings, almost a secondary mother sometimes. At least it seemed that way. While she couldn't change that about her older sister, she could do her best to explain away her overprotective concerns. "Listen, I desperately needed help, and he offered. And he's really good at what he does." Amy shot her a soothing smile. "I'm enjoying having him here all day. I hadn't realized how much I missed having conversations with an adult."

Her sister made a face. "I'm an adult."

"You know what I mean."

"I do."

"An adult of the *male* persuasion." Just to clarify.

Unfortunately, the clarification didn't help. In fact, it seemed to disturb her even more. She took Amy's arm and tugged her farther from the kitchen door. "Amy, I ran into him last night. *Buying condoms.*" The way she said made it sound worse than robbing a bank or oversalting your caramel. "He just got into town and already he's sleeping around. I know it sounds prissy to say that, in this day and age, but you should know, since he's working here."

It was hard for Amy to hold back her laugh. First of all, because Noah had told her about that encounter and how mortifying it had been for him. And second of all, "The condoms were for *us*, Celeste."

Her sister boggled. "*What?*"

Well, hell. See what she got for not informing her family of her every sexual interlude? "Look, I'm sorry I didn't tell you. It's just—"

"But you *just* met! You *just met* on *Sunday*!"

Technically, they met on Saturday… And yes, it had been a short amount of time, but it didn't *feel* that way. She felt like she'd known him, well, forever. It probably didn't help that Amy grinned, but she couldn't help it. "Like I said, things have moved quickly."

"I'll say."

Noah poked his head out to check on her, and Amy waved him back.

"Celeste, I just haven't had a chance to tell you yet. In fact, I think it's still too early to be telling people."

Her sister stared at her. "But not too early to sleep with him?"

Amy frowned at her. Her sex life was her business. Still, she made another attempt to end this line of questioning. "Look. I'm happy, Celeste. It took me a long time to get here, but I am. Can't you let me be happy?"

"But the boys—"

"The boys adore him. And he adores them. Besides, aren't *you* the one always urging me to start dating again?"

"That's...different."

"Is it?"

"Well..." Celeste gave a huff. "I don't know what to say."

Amy set her hands on her sister's shoulders and looked her in the eye. "Celeste, I really like Noah. He's a good guy. And... I need this."

It might have been the hint of loneliness and loss in her tone that captured Celeste's attention because she thought about it for a minute and then nodded. "You're right. I'm sorry if I overreacted. Maybe I just need a little time to...adjust to the idea. Truly, Amy, all I want is for you to be happy."

"I appreciate that. And—" because Amy felt she needed something "—thank you." She pulled her into a hug. "Thanks for always looking out for me."

Tears did appear then in Celeste's eyes, but she didn't let them fall. "You're welcome. Well... I should probably go. Momma's caregiver is off duty soon."

"Okay. Tell her hi for me."

"Mmm-hmm. Shall I tell her hi from Noah too?"

It was something of a sardonic question, but Amy decided to take it at face value. "If you like." And then, just to bring the point home, "It might be good to remind her about him." She was becoming forgetful lately. "Noah is going to be around for a while."

Celeste took the point and flung it right back with a quipped, "Till the wedding at least." And before Amy replied—if she even could—Celeste sailed through the door.

Amy shook her head as she watched her sister climb into her car and drive away. She was used to having difficult conversations with Natalie, not Celeste. They'd always gotten along. Today, however, something had been off. Something was definitely bothering her—something other than her concern that Noah was a philanderer. Amy wished she knew what it was. But Celeste, being Celeste, would probably never tell.

She had always been the rock of the family. Especially after George's death, and then again after Momma's stroke. Clearly, something else was going on with her, which seeing Noah buy condoms and then learning they were for Amy, had triggered.

"Is she gone?" Noah came out, wiping his hands on a towel.

"Yes." Amy shot him a grim look. "I had to tell her." They'd agreed not to share the news of their relationship with the family just yet—other than Nat and Jax—because they wanted to figure out how to handle it with the boys first, and the fewer people who knew, the less likely it was that the news would leak.

Noah made a face. "Was it the condoms?"

"Yes. It was."

"Rats. I should have bought them somewhere else."

Amy had to laugh. "Noah, you realize this is Coho Cove, right? Nothing's going to stay secret here for long." Nothing ever did.

The shop was kind of slow for the rest of the morning, so Amy and Noah spent the time doing the weekend prep. When they finished that, they moved on to doing inventory. It was usually a boring task, but it didn't feel that way with Noah by her side. They were just finishing up when Nat and Jax came by right before lunch.

Amy popped out of the office when she heard the bell ring and grinned at the sight of them. "Hey, guys," she said. "Back in town again already?" Since the two of them had gotten engaged, they'd been nesting, spending most of their time together either at the studio or the new house on the bluff north of town that they were still fixing up. It was a surprise to see them again so soon, but not an unwelcome one.

Nat grinned. "Jax has a lunch date with Ben, and we had some things to arrange at Angel's gallery. Plus, I wanted to come see you."

"I'm glad you did. Celeste came by just a little while ago too. It's like a sister twofer!"

"How is Celeste?" Jax asked.

"Oh, fine. We had a nice chat." No need for condom details. Not really.

"Well," Nat said, "I hope we're not interrupting."

"Interrupt away." Amy made a face. "Noah and I are doing inventory. Blech." She turned to the back and called, "Hey, Noah, Nat and Jax are here."

He poked his head around the doorjamb and grinned. "Hi, guys." He grabbed a cloth and wiped off his hands and came into the shop. "Nat." He gave her a quick hug. "Hey, Jax." They did some caveman-handshake men did.

Jax turned to her and shot her an entreating smile. She recognized it right away because she knew him well. "What do you want?" she asked in a sing-song voice.

He made a face. "What makes you think I want something?"

She didn't answer other than to tip her head to the side and stare at him, which made Natalie laugh. "Just ask," she said, nudging him with an elbow.

"Well…" Jax fixed her with his pleading-puppy-dog look. "I was wondering if I could borrow Noah for a while." He turned to Noah. "I'd like to introduce you to my friend Ben. I think you'll like him." And then, like a Ping-Pong ball, he turned back to Amy. "If you can spare him, of course."

Amy forced a cheery smile and said, "Sure." As much as she liked having Noah here, the morning had been abnormally slow and it was unlikely to pick up too much in the afternoon. Besides, she'd been feeling a little guilty about hogging all his time when he'd come to town to see Jax.

"I can stay and help you do inventory," Nat said.

"You don't need to do that," Amy was quick to assure her. "I think we're about done. But stay. We can catch up." It had been a while since they'd had a chat, just the two of them. She and Natalie didn't get much time with each other, mostly because of Amy's schedule, so it would be nice to hang out.

"You sure you don't mind?" Noah asked, even as he untied his apron.

"Go. Have fun. Ben is awesome."

Nat nodded. "He really is."

After the guys left, heading down to Bootleggers to meet Ben, Amy served up two slices of the lemon tart that Noah had made today, along with some decaf coffee. Then they sat at one of the parlor tables looking out on the street and relaxed. It was unusual for Amy to get to relax during the day, so it was nice.

"Mmm," Nat said as she took her first bite. "This is delicious."

Amy grinned. "Noah made it. It's one of his foster mother's recipes."

"So good," she moaned, wolfing it down. Yep. She was definitely pregnant. Normal Natalie would never have wolfed anything down.

"Uh, do you want another?" Amy asked, sliding her plate over.

"I shouldn't," Nat said, but she took the plate anyway. "So," she said, once she'd finished that one too and blotted up the crumbs with a licked finger. "How are things going with you and Noah?"

"Fine."

"Fine?" Nat narrowed her eyes. "Amy, I'm your sister. I see the way you look at him."

"Okay. Very fine, then?"

"Excellent. You deserve to be happy."

"I am."

Nat drummed her fingernails in a tattoo on the table. "So, what's bothering you?"

"Nothing."

Natalie laughed. "I know you better than that."

Amy huffed a breath. Sometimes having someone know you so well was annoying. She shrugged. Not that she didn't want to talk about Noah and her feelings for Noah, but she kind of didn't. Her emotions were a mess—ranging from elation to worry—and she just couldn't afford any messes right now. There was too much at stake.

She'd spent a lot of time thinking how they would manage this affair—which it was, at the moment, she supposed—especially while juggling two small boys and a business. In the end, she'd decided to let the affair manage itself. She wanted to explore whatever this was with Noah, and they didn't need any unnecessary barriers. And oh, how the thought of exploring things with Noah excited her. For the first time in a long while, she felt alive again.

She wasn't sure when she'd stopped feeling vibrant and excited about living. She hadn't even realized it had happened, not really. But Noah had opened her eyes.

The only problems were that nag of guilt and, of course, the fear she sometimes felt when her emotions overwhelmed her. Those things never happened when she was with him, of course.

"So?" Natalie asked again, when Amy didn't respond quickly enough. Nat could be relentless. "What are you worried about?"

Amy spurt a little laugh. "Because it's scary?"

"What are you scared of?"

Amy had to think about it, really think about it, for a minute. "I don't know." But she did. "Getting hurt. Getting the boys hurt. Replacing George—" She stopped short. Yeah. That was there too, wasn't it? Guilt. It was always there.

"Amy." Nat shook her head. "It's been four years."

"Three and eleven-twelfths."

"Puh-lease." Her sister rolled her eyes. "Well, whatever. The two of you are cute together."

Amy nearly choked on her decaf. "What?"

"I'm just saying. You're a good fit."

"Well…" Amy huffed a sigh. "He's not staying." She'd been thinking about that a lot lately.

Nat's eyes widened. "Did he tell you that?"

"It's not a secret that he's heading to Alaska after the wedding."

"I know. But he's also told Jax he's been looking for a place to settle and that he really likes it here. He seems to fit in so nicely. He could stay. He might."

Amy hated the way her heart lifted at that. The way hope seeped in. Yeah, when she thought about Noah leaving, her chest ached. A flicker of…something burned in her gut.

Aside from that, she knew if she got too attached and then he left, it might destroy her. She had too many responsibilities to allow that to happen. She had to keep it together, for the boys. For herself too.

"Well," she said with an oh-so-casual shrug, "it's up to him." He was a grown-up. They had absolutely no hold on each other. He was free to go.

She had no idea why the thought of him packing up and leaving sent such a pall over a previously delightful day.

Actually, she did.

As much as Noah liked working at the bakery, even puttering around the storage room with Amy, it was nice to get out and spend some time with Jax. It was a pretty summer day, and the short walk to Bootleggers was pleasant.

Ben wasn't at the restaurant when they arrived, so they ordered beers and played pool while they waited.

"How are things going with Amy?" Jax asked just as Noah was taking a shot.

He nearly missed and sent his friend a glower. "Good."

"Any progress?"

Noah arched a brow. "Progress?"

Jax leaned on his pool cue. "I was under the impression you were wooing her."

"I'm getting to know her. Or I guess it's more accurate to say she's getting to know me. As far as that goes, things are great. We work well together."

"But no *progress*?"

Noah chuckled. Surely Jax wasn't asking for details? "Dude. It's only been a few days."

His buddy blew out a sigh. "I know, I know. But Nat and I have high hopes for the two of you."

"You and Nat have talked about this?"

Jax sent him a blank look, as though to say, *Why wouldn't we?* "We've been waiting a long time for Amy to get over George."

"Yeah, well, between you and me, I don't think she's over him yet."

"Maybe not completely. But since you've been here, she seems happier."

Noah shrugged. "Maybe she's less stressed about work."

"Hmm." Jax didn't seem as certain of that. "It's just nice to see her smile again." Noah shot his friend a glance, but forbore mentioning she seemed to smile a lot. "Well," Jax continued, "I wouldn't complain if you found a reason to stay."

"Thanks, bud," Noah said.

"Ah." Jax laid down his cue. "Here's Ben."

Noah turned to see a tall man with dark hair heading their way. He was surprised that Ben was wearing a suit, but only because Jax was so laid back and casual. On the surface, he wouldn't have thought these two had much in common.

"Ben!" Jax called. "Come meet Noah."

"Hey, Noah." Ben grinned and thrust out a hand. "Great to meet you. Jax says you were stationed together overseas."

"Yeah." They headed for a table and sat, and Ben signaled to the bartender for another beer. "How did you and Jax meet?" Noah asked.

Ben and Jax shared a glance and laughed. "Was it second grade?" Jax asked.

"Third," Ben told him.

"You sure?"

Ben barked a laugh. "Oh yeah." He turned to Noah. "My dad bought some property here and moved the whole family…right when I started third grade. It was also just before my parents divorced, so yeah. I remember pretty clearly."

Jax made a face. "When he says his dad 'bought some property,' he means half the town. And the peninsula."

"Oh," Noah said. "Where that hotel is?"

"That's Ben's hotel," Jax said. "The Sherrod."

"Wow." Noah leaned back. "You own a whole hotel?"

"More than one," Jax put in. "His company develops properties."

"But this one is my favorite," Ben said.

"He lives there." Jax again. "In the penthouse. It's nice."

"Yeah." Ben chuckled. "You should come by and check it out sometime. I'll give you a tour."

"He has some really awesome artwork there," Jax said with kind of a smug look.

Noah didn't really understand why they both laughed, until Ben added, "He's talking about *his* pieces."

Jax lifted his glass. "He's my best customer."

"Oh wow," Noah said with a grin. "I'll definitely come by and check those out."

Vic came over with Ben's drink and took their orders for lunch. While they waited for their food, Noah learned more about Ben. He was a widower with a young daughter. Of course, when Quinn came up, Ben had to pull out his phone and show Noah pictures. Lots of pictures. Way too many of them. But Noah appreciated the love he had for his daughter, which was on full display, both in the pictures and on his face.

"She's beautiful," he had to say, because it was true. In every picture, her eyes were filled with complete adoration for her father.

"Thanks," Ben said. "She got that from her mom." His smile dimmed for the flash of a second as he thought of his wife. "She was beautiful too."

Jax nodded. "Stunning. You're going to have your hands full when Quinn is old enough to date."

Ben grimaced. "Don't remind me."

The conversation moved on from there to Ben and Jax's favorite hobby. Both, apparently, were avid fishermen. They talked about it enthusiastically, and while Noah had nothing to add to the conversation, he enjoyed being present for it. He'd had close friends in the military, but he'd never been as close to someone as Jax and Ben seemed to be. But then, Noah didn't have friends from his childhood, friends who knew every dirty secret. It was fun to watch them razz each other.

At one point, Ben was teasing Jax about an enormous

salmon he'd lost on their last fishing trip. "You should come with us, next time we go," Ben said to Noah. "Do you like to fish?"

He shrugged. "I've never been fishing actually." Fishing was something a dad did with his kid—he supposed—and he hadn't had a dad. He could have taken himself out fishing at some point, but he simply hadn't had the desire.

Ben's eyes went wide. "Never?"

"Nope."

"Hoh!" Ben cried. "You don't know what you've been missing." He went off, insisting they should get a boat and go out together as soon as possible. His fervor was so catching, it almost made Noah want to give it a try.

"We could take Amy's boys too," Jax suggested.

"Oh? They like to fish?" Noah perked up at that.

Jax grinned. "They love it."

Well, if John J. and Georgie liked it, he had to try. Noah nodded. "Let's do that."

"So, Noah," Ben said after their food arrived and they'd all sated their initial hunger. "What was it like being a PJ?"

Wow. What a question. It took a while answering because Ben had so many questions and, at his prompting, Noah spoke at length about his tours and some of the missions he'd been on.

"So, why did you retire?" Ben asked.

"I got old?" He forced a laugh, but it had felt like that.

"I can relate," Jax said. "But your job was even more physically brutal than mine was."

"It had its moments. On my last jump, I blew out my knee. The team had to carry me out." It had been mortifying. "The docs told me I was done jumping and sent me back to the States."

"That really sucks." Jax knew how much he'd loved his job as a PJ.

"Yeah. But to be honest, I was kind of tired of war zones."

Jax nodded. "I know the feeling. It was really tough for me to get past some of the things we saw over there." Most people didn't understand, couldn't, and good for them. War wasn't something he would wish on his worst enemy.

Noah nodded. "I didn't realize how much my identity was wrapped up in being a PJ…until I wasn't one."

"I can imagine." Jax turned to Ben. "The PJs are one of the most elite special forces in the country. Just earning the beret is a major accomplishment."

."Best day of my life," Noah had to say. And it had been. His heart still thudded with elation when he thought of it. And he'd loved the work. He'd loved the team. He'd loved making a difference, a real difference. "But after that injury, they wouldn't let me jump anymore. They wanted to put me on a desk."

Jax snorted.

"Right? That would have killed me." He shrugged. "So, I retired. Went on a rideabout."

Ben's brow wrinkled. "What's a rideabout?"

Noah grinned. "You've heard of an Australian walkabout? Well, that's what I wanted to do…but on my bike. So, I called it my great rideabout."

"Jax mentioned you'd been all over the country, looking for a place to settle?"

"Pretty much."

"Found it yet?" Ah, that was the question, wasn't it?

Noah answered with a shrug and a grin. "I dunno," he said. "Coho Cove seems pretty nice."

Jax and Noah didn't return from Bootleggers until two. Amy didn't mind because she'd had Nat for company. But it did surprise her how much she missed him while he was gone. She hadn't realized how used to his presence she'd become, how many empty nooks and crannies of her life he'd eased in to fill. The day seemed hollow without him there. Should she be bothered by that, or not? She wasn't sure.

Aside from that, he looked happy—really happy—when they came through the door. She wasn't sure how to feel about that either.

"How was it?" she asked in as chipper a tone as she could manage.

"Great," he said.

Nat grinned. "So…what did you think of Ben?"

"Seemed like a nice guy."

"Ben liked Noah too." Jax waggled his brows. "We're probably going to take him fishing with us."

Nat rolled her eyes. "*Huge* surprise."

"Ben even invited him to join our poker game tonight at the VFF."

"Oh, how nice." Amy forced a smile even though her heart sank; she tried not to let it show. She'd been looking forward to spending time with Noah tonight. It was selfish of her, and she knew it—she got him during the day, every day—but that didn't make it easier to share him. And he'd come here to see Jax, for pity's sake.

It didn't help her mood when Jax added, "Noah, why

don't you come on back to the studio with us now. Save Amy a trip later?" And Noah agreed.

Of course, he sent her an apologetic glance, as though he, too, might have had plans for her after the bakery closed its doors, but what could she say or do other than smile and pretend she didn't care?

But gosh, the bakery felt empty when the three of them left.

She knew it was silly to feel abandoned, but she just couldn't help herself. She spent most of the days with him yet still wanted more. Granted, their relationship, whatever it was, was still new. She'd heard about that honeymoon phase where couples just couldn't get enough of each other. This was probably that.

It was interesting because she and George had not had a lot of time together, either before or after their wedding, just because of the circumstances and his job, which had snatched him away right after they'd said their vows. But their time together—what they'd had— had been intense and real. Even when her family—and his—had objected, rather strenuously, to their precipitous marriage, they'd both *known* they were meant to be together.

Her relationship with Noah was different. With Noah, there was a lot of conversation, a lot of collaboration and brief glorious moments of bliss. Yes, the sex between them was a huge part of the attraction—as it had been with George—but there was an even deeper connection there. She had to believe it was because the two of them had lived full lives, they had matured, they approached relationships differently than they had when they'd been younger.

But there was so much more to it than that. Noah was great with the kids. He was great with her. He was great with everything.

It just sucked that he came with a ticking clock.

And sure, he'd told Jax he was looking for a place to settle, and he liked it here, but she couldn't pin all her hopes on that. She certainly couldn't pin her future on that. Or her sons' happiness.

Aside from all that—and it was a lot—Amy knew she needed to start looking for someone to replace Eloise. And someone to help in the front of the shop as well, now that things would be even busier after the interview aired. It was one thing to spend every day of the week at work when you had someone like Noah around to make it fun and easy. But when he left, she wouldn't just be alone again in a spiritual sense, she'd be all alone in the bakery too. And that was not sustainable.

There had been a day—before Pierre had flaked and Eloise had run off with her boyfriend—when she'd been more of a manager. She really wanted to get back there, but sometimes, she felt like a salmon swimming upstream.

She definitely needed to make some changes.

Sometimes, once a person makes a decision, the universe just falls into place. And that was how Amy felt when Kara walked into her shop shortly after Nat, Jax and Noah left that afternoon.

"Hi," she said with a little wave after introducing herself. "My husband and I just moved to town."

Amy came around the counter to shake her hand. "I'm Amy Tolliver. Welcome." In the past year or so, there had been a lot of newcomers as more homes had gone up in the new developments on the outskirts of town. Most of them were summer houses for folks who lived in Seattle and wanted a getaway to somewhere less busy, but a lot of them were for new residents. Though it was slowly changing the little town, Amy didn't mind the expansion because it was good for business. It was good for the town too.

"I just love your bakery," Kara said as she surveyed the art and the pastry cases. "It smells divine in here."

"Right?" Amy grinned at her. "That was one of the reasons I fell in love with baking."

"Me too."

"Oh?" Her manager antenna flipped up. "Do you bake?"

"Some." Kara laughed. "I used to work at a bakery in Seattle. It's where I met my husband actually."

"Aw. That sounds romantic."

"It totally wasn't. I spilled a cappuccino on him." Kara rolled her eyes, and they both laughed.

"So, you worked the counter?"

Kara nodded. "Technically I was the chocolatier. But you know how it is in a small shop. You do whatever needs to be done."

Ohhh. What an awesome attitude…and she had such a bright energy. Amy liked her right off the bat. She would be great to work with. It was hard for her, working every day of the week, as she had been since Eloise left. And she'd also been feeling guilty about trapping Noah here every day simply because he'd offered to help. Besides, she needed help. So, it only made sense to say, "Well, I'm looking for help, if you want to bring in a resume."

Kara's eyes widened. "Really?"

"Really. My pastry chef ran off with her boyfriend last week."

"Oh, ugh. How frustrating."

"It's hard getting trained help way out here."

"Well, I love being married, but Daniel works full time and I miss being busy. But full disclosure, I'm not a trained pastry chef. Oh, I can do the basics. You know, choux and pastry and decoration. I just never could perfect the fancy French stuff."

Oh, good glory. She sounded perfect. Just the fact that she knew her way around a commercial bakery was a minor miracle. "That's okay. I'm looking for help in the front of the shop too." And honestly, the really fancy stuff really only sold well around Christmas.

"I will absolutely bring in a resume. Thanks." She was about to leave, but then she paused at the door and said, "I'm so glad I came in."

Amy barked a laugh because Kara no idea how glad she was as well.

Chapter Ten

That night—and not because she was feeling lonely without Noah—Amy decided she and the boys would take Momma and Celeste out to dinner at the Salmon Shack. She wanted to spend more time with her mother, but her busy schedule—and exhaustion—always seemed to interfere. Intention, however, was nothing without action, so she made the call.

Momma was excited at the idea of going out. The boys were excited too—the shack was one of their favorite restaurants because it was right on the water. But when they heard Noah wouldn't be joining them, they both pouted.

"Why isn't Noah coming?" John J. asked in something of a whine as Amy loaded them into the car.

"I told you. He's having dinner with Jax tonight," she said.

"But why?"

"Doesn't he like us anymore?" Georgie asked.

Amy sighed. "Hon, sometimes grown-ups like to spend time with other grown-ups. Remember, Noah came here to visit Jax, and they haven't had very much time together." She thought she'd done a good job of explaining it, but the boys weren't mollified. They grumbled all the way to the restaurant. It hadn't taken long for them to become used to seeing him every day. Maybe too used to it. It bothered her, because it was a harbinger of how hurt they would be when he left Coho Cove for good. She really didn't like thinking about that.

It would be hard for her too, but it would be much worse for them.

Momma, as usual, was thrilled to see the boys, pulling them into long hugs until they squirmed, and then grilling them on every aspect of their lives since she'd seen them last.

The restaurant was a little busy—it usually was during the summer—but there was a large table open by the window. The boys were excited about that, and turned around on their chairs to watch the boats floating in the distance and the seagulls hunting any scraps dropped by the guests seated on the patio. The sun hadn't set yet, but it had painted a beautiful orange-and-gold limning in the clouds.

"This is so pretty," Momma said with a sigh.

"It is." Amy gave her hand a squeeze.

"Why don't we do this more often?"

Celeste chuckled. "Momma. You never want to go out for supper." Momma was notoriously cautious with money—she always had been—and when they were growing up, dinners out had been a rare treat for the

Tuttle kids. But then, Momma had been such a good cook that Amy had never minded all that much.

The waitress came around and took their drink orders then left. Everyone was looking at the menu, though they pretty much knew it by heart, when John J. made a squeal and wriggled out of his seat before sprinting across the restaurant. Amy had been too distracted by the thought of shrimp scampi to catch him in time. Fortunately, he didn't knock anyone over on his dash to the front door.

The reason for his excitement was clear. Ben Sherrod and his daughter, Quinn, had just come in. John J. adored Quinn. The two were the same age and Amy's son was utterly enamored with her. Indeed, the two of them jumped around and hugged each other with the enthusiasm of long-lost friends...even though they saw each other pretty frequently.

Amy waved to Ben, who grinned and, with John J. and Quinn in tow, headed over. "Hey, Amy," he said, giving her a quick hug. "Pearl. Celeste." Momma got a hug as well. Celeste, a nod. Granted, Celeste was on the far side of the table, but Amy suspected Ben's reserve came from another place entirely.

Both Ben and Celeste were deeply involved with the town's local politics, serving on committees and engaging in development projects and town events. They didn't always see eye to eye on things. She knew this because Celeste wasn't shy with her opinions on the matter. It was funny that they were often at odds because, in Amy's estimation at least, the two had more in common than not.

Amy and Ben, however, had been close for a while,

only partly because John J. and Quinn loved to spend time together. She and Ben had been friends from high school, they both had children and they'd both lost a spouse. They'd commiserated over being single parents more than once. She shot him a grin. "Fancy meeting you here," she said.

He grinned back. "Right? Quinn and I don't get out much." Why would they? They lived in a penthouse on the top floor of the Sherrod and all he had to do was pick up the phone to order five-star room service.

"Slumming it?" she joked.

He chuckled. "I had a hankering for their lobster roll, and Quinn loves the brownie sundae, so…here we are."

"Why don't you join us?" Momma said. She'd always been fond of Ben too, and absolutely adored Quinn. Only Amy noticed Celeste's frown at the suggestion.

"You don't mind?" Ben asked, glancing around the table…probably at Celeste.

"Don't be ridiculous," Momma said. "This table is huge."

Quinn had already taken the empty seat next to John J. and the two of them were engaged in some private exchange. It was mostly John J. chattering away, because Quinn was nonverbal. She hadn't spoken a word since the accident that had killed her mother nearly a year ago. Sweet little Quinn had been in the car with her—heaven only knew what havoc a trauma like that could wreak. Ben had explored every avenue he could think of—anything to get his daughter to speak again— but so far no one had been able to figure out why she remained silent. Somehow, though, John J. seemed to understand her. When they were together, it was like the rest of the world faded away.

Since Quinn was next to John J., the only other available chair for Ben was next to Celeste. Was it wrong that her dismay at sitting beside him made Amy want to laugh? It was fun seeing Celeste—who was usually so buttoned-up—tipped off-center.

Amy really enjoyed the dinner. The food was wonderful, as was the company. Ben was a great conversationalist and Momma was bright and engaged. It was also kind of fun to watch Ben and Celeste interact, especially when he occasionally brushed against her…and her face went bright red. The only downside was that the boys kept mentioning Noah. And lamenting that he wasn't there with them.

Amy had made the conscious decision to explore her feelings for him, but it was wrong, wasn't it, to let the boys get so attached when she knew he would be leaving? She knew she needed to protect her boys from that ultimate heartbreak—because they really loved Noah—but how?

Noah had a great time with Jax and his buddies in the volunteer firefighter hall that night. There was a little poker, a lot of laughter, a couple raunchy jokes and a ton of fun. It was easy to understand why Jax was friends with them. They reminded Noah a lot of the buddies he'd had in the military. Also, these guys were volunteer firefighters, the kinds of guys who headed toward danger rather than away, very much like the PJs. He felt right at home.

There was only one annoying moment, and that was

when one of Jax's friends, a real estate agent named Luke Larson, asked him how Amy was doing. He went on, then, for a while about how pretty she was and how cute the boys were and did Jax think Luke should stop by the bakery and say hello?

Jax's answer was a cheery, "Sure," but if Luke had to ask Jax—in Noah's opinion, at least—the correct answer was no.

Aside from Luke and his obsession over Amy, the guys were all pretty cool. While he enjoyed the camaraderie and the jokes and even winning a little bit of money off of them, he still couldn't help thinking about Amy the whole evening. Granted, at this stage in their relationship, he supposed, it was normal to think about a woman you were interested in all the time.

Unfortunately, by the time Jax dropped him off at the studio, it was too late to call her. He ached to talk to her again, which was pretty amazing in and of itself since he couldn't recall ever feeling that way about a woman before. He found himself lying awake more than sleeping, frustrated that he had hours to go until morning, when she'd pick him up. When he'd be with her again for the day.

As soon as he slipped into the car, he sensed a change in her energy and shot her an assessing glance. For her part, she kept her gaze on the road, so it was tough to get a read. And with the boys in the car, he certainly didn't want to ask what had changed. Even though he wanted to know, he decided to let her bring up what was bothering her.

He didn't have long to wait. She was pulling out of the sitter's driveway after dropping off the kids when she said, "I'm glad you and Jax had some time together yesterday. Did you have fun?"

"It was nice."

"Good."

"His friends are nice, but…"

"But what?"

"I missed you. Is that weird? We're together all day long, but… I don't know. I missed you."

If he had hoped this revelation would put a smile on her face, he was deeply disappointed. She looked away. "I missed you too," she said softly. "And…the boys missed you."

"Did they?" He couldn't hold back his grin.

"Totally." She sighed.

Something in her expression was concerning, but he wasn't sure what it was, so he had to come out and ask, "Is that a problem?"

It took her a minute to answer. "I'm worried that they're getting…well, too attached to you."

"What?" His stomach plunged. That wasn't what he'd been expecting. And damn, he hated that she avoided his gaze.

"Well, you're only here till the wedding. Then you'll go."

Yeah, that had been the plan, but that certainly wasn't the plan now. "Nothing's written in stone. I mean, I can stay longer." Hell, he could stay as long as he wanted.

She didn't hear him. Or didn't want to.

"But you *are* leaving," she repeated, and then she cut him off when he opened his mouth to say something— anything—that might shift this conversation. "I'm not talking about *us*." She barreled on. "The *you and me* of this. *I* get it. *I* understand that you may leave at any time. And I am prepared to deal with it when it happens."

"*If.*"

"But the boys… Noah, they just won't understand. They can't. If they bond with you, they'll be hurt when you go."

"What are you suggesting?" He suspected he knew, but he hoped he was wrong.

"Maybe you shouldn't spend as much time with them?"

Well, crap. He wasn't sure which bothered him the most, the fact that she wanted him to spend less time with the boys or the fact that she was cool with him leaving. But then, he didn't like either point.

It didn't help that he also understood her need to protect her boys from being hurt, and he had to respect it.

Trouble was he wasn't so sure he wanted to leave anymore. Or at all.

Amy could feel Noah's confusion; she could see it on his face. Oh, it was so hard talking about these difficult things she didn't want to talk about. But they needed to have these conversations. The truth was she had begun to realize just how much the boys had come to love Noah. And while she loved that they loved him, knowing he would be leaving—way too soon—she had to help her sons prepare for that.

Heck, *she* had to start preparing for that, as hard as it was.

But that was hardly the only revelation weighing on her heart. Before he could react or before the conversation shifted and she lost her train of thought, she pushed forward with the other concern that had been bugging her. "Aside from that, I've realized that it's not fair to keep you at the bakery all the time, when you really came to see Jax."

"Hey, I don't—"

She held up a hand to stop him. She knew what he was going to say. That he enjoyed working in the bakery. She enjoyed having him there too, but that was not the point. "Anyway," she gusted, "the reason I bring it all up is because I've been thinking."

He made a face. "Really?"

Though they'd arrived at the bakery, she didn't open her door. It made sense to finish this conversation here and now. Instead, she shifted in her seat so she could face him. "Technically, I most need you there in the morning, when we prep." And that was only because he could help with the items that required his special skills to perfect. "After prep is done, I only need help in the shop if it's super busy."

Noah huffed a laugh. "It's been super busy all week."

"Right." It had been. "But let's be honest, I don't need someone with your skills to sell pastries."

He shot her a look. "Are you saying you don't want me there?"

"No." *God, no.* "All I'm saying is that, well, I feel guilty, hogging all your time, when maybe I could find someone who could help cover the afternoons and give you more time with Jax. That's all." But there was more, wasn't there? "When you do leave—"

"If."

"I'll need to hire some help. I should have started looking as soon as Eloise left. We both know that this—" she waggled her finger between the two of them "—isn't sustainable."

He nodded, but he had that look on his face, the one the boys got when she told them something they didn't want to hear.

Oh, how she hated that she had to have this conversation with him, but she did. The bottom line was, business was business. She couldn't handle it by herself, and he wouldn't be here forever. As much as she might want him to stay, she needed to make sure that if he chose to stay, he did it because he wanted to, not because he felt he had to.

"Anyway, I wanted to let you know that a woman came in the other day. She's got bakery experience, and she's looking for a job." She blew out a heavy sigh. "She's bringing in a resume, and well, if it looks good, I'd like to bring her on board."

"Okay." It was a hard word to get out. Not that Amy wasn't right. She did need more help. And it wasn't his plan to work in a bakery for the rest of his life. In fact, with his training, he expected he'd eventually get a job as a paramedic or something in search and rescue. Something that demanded the skills he'd honed as a PJ. Yeah, when he'd agreed to help her out at the bakery, they'd both expected it would be a stopgap measure to get her through a crisis.

Still, Noah didn't like what Amy was saying. He didn't like it at all. And it had nothing to do with the bakery or his working here.

It had to do with *them*.

Everything had been going so well. At least, he'd

thought it had been. But now she seemed to be asking for space...at the bakery *and* with the boys. It made his gut ache. It went against everything his heart was telling him. But as they headed into the bakery to begin prep for one of the busiest days of the week, he kept his own counsel, and as he worked, he thought about what she'd said and how he felt about it.

In many ways, she was right to ask him to step back—and that was what she was asking for, wasn't it? Their relationship had not been normal by any stretch of the imagination, and they had been moving extremely quickly. It had been a little scary to him too, when he'd first realized how he was starting to feel about her and the boys—that they might be what he'd been searching for all his life. He could understand where her concern was coming from. Aside from that, he knew she had a lot more to lose in this relationship. She carried the heavy weight of making sure her decisions were good— not just for the two of them, but for the boys as well.

And after all, she hadn't said she wanted to break it off. She'd merely asked him to be aware of the impact he was having on the boys...and she was trying to make accommodations for him to spend more time with his friend.

There was no reason for that flare of panic. He wasn't losing her. Even if it felt that way.

Though everything in him revolted against spending less time with the boys, the best thing he could do was to hear her. To respect her concerns and give her the time and the space she needed. He resolved to do so.

So, for now, at least, he put his head down and focused on the work.

It turned out to be a good decision because just as he was congratulating himself at how well he was adjusting to working at the bakery and how manageable it felt…the weekend rush hit. Friday hadn't been all that busy, but Saturday was insane.

Usually, their daily schedule was to prep and do the baking in the morning before opening, then deal with customers after that. Then, if there was time, they would tackle some of the specialty items people ordered. Not so on Saturday. On Saturday, there was such a steady stream of customers, they soon ran out of some of the more popular items. Noah started to understand why Amy had been so focused on prep for the weekend.

At the time, he'd just done as she'd told him—he had lots of experience with that thanks to the US Air Force—but he hadn't understood why she'd wanted the fridges full of trays ready to pop into the oven or why she'd wanted so many ready-to-thaw croissants in the freezer. But she had it down to a science, and on Saturday, she blew his mind.

When any given tray hit the halfway mark, she'd go back to the kitchen and pull another batch out of the fridge to warm up or proof, and then, about the time the tray in the shop hit the three-quarters-empty mark, she'd pop that new batch into the oven. She knew which items were likely to move more quickly and for which ones demand might peter out just when supply did.

There were some hiccups in her system—like when one customer might come in and buy a dozen of any given item—but overall, it worked pretty well, and they were able to keep up with demand.

Even if she hadn't effectively kiboshed the prospect

of backroom passion with the tough conversation they'd had in the car that morning, there was no time for any passionate clinches.

That didn't mean he didn't think about it. He did.

He suspected she was thinking about it too—judging on the times he caught her expression when they passed each other in a rush—but there simply wasn't time.

There wasn't time for more discussion after work either because Jax and Ben popped by that afternoon, just as they were mopping up, to kidnap Noah and take him for dinner at the Sherrod. He had a great time touring the stunning hotel—including Ben's apartment on the top floor, where he got to meet Quinn who, while exceedingly shy, was cute as a button. But the conversation he'd had with Amy lingered in his mind.

Jax dropped him off at the studio after nine in the evening—again, too late to call. She'd already be in bed because she'd have to be up before four to get the boys ready and get an early start at the bakery. Instead, he texted her that he didn't need a ride to the bakery the next morning because he planned to ride his motorcycle instead.

Everything in his soul rebelled.

Funny how, in such a short amount of time, that morning ritual, bonding with the boys—even during the quick ride to the sitter's—had come to mean a lot to him. He hadn't realized how much until now. How much he missed their little faces. The silly jokes. Their presence. It kind of felt like that hole in his soul, which had been filling in, had suddenly drained again, leaving him cold and alone.

But this was what Amy had asked of him. So, even though he didn't like it, he did it. However, it cost him.

Sunday morning felt all wrong.

Amy saw Noah's text as soon as she checked her phone that morning—and her mood plummeted. She hadn't realized until then how much she looked forward to picking him up at the studio and listening to the banter between him and the boys...and of course, his presence sitting next to her in the car.

But this was what she'd wanted. Wasn't it? To protect her boys from disappointment? From getting too close to a man who might not stay in their lives?

Judging from their expressions when she told them they wouldn't be seeing him this morning, she certainly failed at protecting them from disappointment. Georgie went into an immediate pout, which lasted all the way to Momma's house—because Celeste watched the boys on Sunday mornings—but that was nothing to John J.'s tears.

He didn't say anything. Didn't pitch a fit or howl. It was just quiet little tears glinting in his eyes.

The guilt gutted her.

It took everything in her to hold on to her resolve.

Noah was already at the bakery when she pulled up. And though he waved and said a cheery hello, the energy around them was stilted, as though each of them was carefully considering the impacts of every word, rather than flowing from one topic to the other as they had before. Even though she'd been the one to ask for the retreat—as it were—she didn't like it. She missed the way things had been, the easiness of their relationship.

As a result of the awkwardness, they didn't talk about anything other than work as they started baking for the day—Sunday was a short day but a very busy one, so there was plenty to do. And once they opened, it was a constant flow of customers.

It was so hard, working side by side, yet feeling a wall between them and having no time alone to talk things through. She figured maybe, after the bakery closed, they could take a few minutes and talk about the change. Some time alone together, too, wouldn't go awry. The thought lifted her heart.

But as soon as she flipped the sign, he pulled off his apron and gusted a sigh. "Hey, Amy," he said with a smile that didn't meet his eyes. "Do you mind if I leave a little early today? I want to pop in to Nat and Jax's art show, then a ride up to Ocean Shores."

Her heart dropped. So much for that chat. And how could she say no? He'd worked so hard all week, he'd been a rock, and having him here had saved her from the nightmare of doing it all on her own. "Of course, Noah." What else could she say? "Have fun." She'd been planning to stop by the gallery too, for moral support, but she had to finish closing first, and he'd be long gone by then, wouldn't he?

"Great." His smile got wider, but still wasn't reflected in his eyes. "Jax gave me a route, along with a list of things to see. I can't wait."

He left then. Got onto his bike and roared away leaving her alone. That flare of irritation at Jax was irrational, and she knew it.

The reason she wouldn't be spending a lovely Sunday afternoon with Noah was because she'd listened to her fear and ruined everything.

Noah tried to enjoy his ride on Sunday afternoon, but it was hard because everything felt off kilter. The views along the coast were stunning—and totally unlike the beaches on the east coast or the ones he'd visited in California or Hawaii. Here, the beaches were rocky and littered with driftwood and enormous boulders and gorgeous. He also loved exploring the towns along the way. When he stopped for lunch in Ocean Shores, he was flabbergasted by the sheer magnificence of the surf, disappearing into the mist, and the long, rugged sand beaches that went on and on as far as the eye could see.

As he rolled through the main drag of town, he couldn't help thinking how much fun it would be to bring the boys here for go-kart rides or the sand sculpture festival. They even had dune buggies and horses for rent on the beach.

He took pictures to show Amy, but he didn't call her. She'd asked for space. He was determined to give it to her. Still, that night was the loneliest he'd been in a while.

It was a relief to wake up the next morning and head to the bakery. All he could think about was seeing her again.

She was already getting things set up when he arrived, and even though he was excited to see her, he was nervous. Until he caught her expression, until he saw the way she smiled at him. The light, the warmth in her eyes.

"Noah," she said with a little sigh in her voice. "How was your ride?"

"Lonely." He nearly grimaced. He hadn't planned to complain. "I missed you."

Her expression brightened to a glow. "Did you? I missed you too."

"Did you?" Was it wrong that he liked that she'd missed him? Was it wrong that she smiled at him just so and he opened his arms and she walked into them and finally—finally—he was able to hold her again? It had been far too long.

He and Amy made love in the office again that morning long before the sun rose—slow and easy and sweet— and it was wonderful. It felt like coming home.

Though Amy was still torn about her decision to protect the boys from becoming too attached to Noah, making love with Noah that Monday morning made her feel much better. At least she hadn't ruined everything. It put her mind at rest, at least a little.

Later that morning Kara stopped in and brought her resume, and Amy was floored by her experience. After a quick little interview over coffee and croissants— followed by a glowing review from her previous employer—it only made sense to have her start right away. Kara was more than happy to start training the next day.

To Amy's delight, Kara was a fabulous addition to the team. She and Noah got along wonderfully, and she was a quick study and interested in learning everything. The first day flew by, and the next and the next.

While Amy was excited to have her on board, it definitely changed the dynamic in the mornings between her and Noah. There were no more wild trysts in the office, for one. *Damn it.* For another, she didn't really need Noah to stay after the baking was done because she and Kara could handle it without him, so she'd shooed him off.

It hadn't been easy, but it was the right thing to do. Oh, she missed having him around all day long—and she really missed the sex—but she was happy that he was able to spend time with Jax and Ben and the other friends he was making in town.

As hard as it was, she stuck to her guns to keep the boys out of the mix as much as she could. She did break down and invite Noah to John J.'s birthday party, which was coming up, because when she'd told her son Noah probably had other plans that day, he'd burst into tears.

So yes. It was hard. A tough balance. The boys missed Noah and Noah missed the boys. She felt like the big bad wolf, at times. She was used to making hard decisions because she was a mom, but that was hardly mollifying.

On the plus side, Amy was so pleased with Kara's progress, she was comfortable leaving her alone in the bakery for a little bit at a time. It was so fun to go out for lunch with friends or pop in and see the boys, though Amy made it a point to stay close, in case she needed help. She and Noah were even able to squeeze in a couple dates—just the two of them. By the end of the week, she felt that Kara was ready to cover afternoons all by herself—she'd even agreed to cover for John J.'s birthday party so Amy didn't have to close the shop.

And oh, it was wonderful to have that freedom because Amy was getting a little antsy…for one particular reason. Going through Noah withdrawal or something. Though they'd had a few dates, they'd all been in public. It had been days since they'd been truly alone together...and intimate.

So, Friday afternoon, after she and Kara finished decorating the cake for John J.'s birthday, which was the next day, she gave Noah a call.

"Hey, you," he said when he picked up.

"What are you doing?"

"Not much. I'm at Jax and Nat's. They are whipping my butt at Monopoly. Did you know Natalie makes up rules?"

"Yes. Yes, I do." Their family had all kinds of extra rules, most of them their brother, Nate, had made up, so they were practically canon.

"Everything okay at the bakery?"

"Mmm-hmm." She smiled as she said it. "Kara is rocking it. She's ready for her first solo run."

"Good for her."

"So, I was thinking...maybe you and I...could have some alone time together? I've...missed you."

"I'll be right over," he said quickly, as though he'd been just waiting for the invitation. From his tone, he understood exactly what she meant. The thought made her grin.

Amy's heart started to thrum when she heard the roar of his Harley coming close. Somehow, he got there in record time. The sight of him riding up made her breath catch.

When he parked and levered off his bike, she turned to Kara. "You sure you're good?"

She nodded and said, with a smile, "I'll be fine. But if I need anything, I promise, I'll call."

"Okay. I've got my phone right here." Even though

she kind of felt like a parent leaving her child at day care for the first time as she walked out the door, she knew Kara was doing great and honestly, Amy needed this. She hadn't realized just how much until now.

"Hey, you," he said as they met halfway.

"Hey." She wanted to kiss him, hug him maybe, but the sidewalk was way too public. Their gazes, however, clung.

"So…" he said. "Where do you want to go?"

"Home?" It was the most private place she could think of and what she really wanted was to be alone with him.

And indeed, at the suggestion, his expression shifted. His throat worked. Something glittered in his eyes. Those beautiful lips kicked up. "Well okay. Do you want to take my bike?"

"Do you have another helmet?"

"Uh, no."

"Then let's take my car. Okay?" It made sense since she'd have to come back to the bakery anyway.

"Great. Let's go. What are we waiting for?"

She liked that he seemed to be as excited as she was about having time together, but on the way there, Amy started to get a little nervous, which was silly. This was Noah. There was no need to be nervous. Then again, they hadn't had real alone time for quite a while. Somehow, just sitting next to him in this close space had her nerves pinging around like little rockets. His singular Noah scent, the heat of his body so close to hers, his presence… It all worked to send her thoughts skittering toward desire.

On the one hand she'd been thinking that the two of

them needed to have a conversation, just to touch base with each other on what they were feeling about their evolving relationship. But on the other hand, all she could think about was having his hands on her.

While they'd been together, intimately, many times, they'd never actually had time to…explore each other. Up until now—other than a couple light make out sessions in her living room after they boys had gone to bed—their intimacies had been in the bakery office. She'd never been comfortable with the idea of making love with him in her house while the boys were there, and while they were getting ready for the art show, Nat and Jax had always been at the studio. Where else was there to go?

Balancing work and her children and family—all the business of her life—was complicated. But now the boys were at the sitters and Amy had someone to cover the bakery. This would be the first time they would be able to be truly intimate. With leisure. So, yeah. It was a little scary.

"What are you thinking about?" he asked.

"Nothing."

He chuckled, and she shot him a glower. Then he gestured to the steering wheel. "You're white-knuckling it."

"Oh." She deliberately loosened her hold.

"Are you nervous?"

She glanced over, just for a second. "Are you?"

It irritated her that he laughed. But then he said, "I'm nervous as hell." And she felt better.

"You are?"

"Yes."

"Well, good."

He shifted toward her. "Why are you nervous?" She could almost feel the grin in his words.

"It's been a long time for me…" she said. "In a bed, I mean. You know. Where there's…"

"Intimacy?" This, he whispered.

She nearly drove off the road. Yes. That. Oh, there'd been intimacy between them before, but this was different. This felt different.

This time they would see each other totally bared.

"Maybe we should take it slow?" It was a ridiculous suggestion. She knew it even as the words slipped from her lips. How do you take it slow when you've already taken it very, very fast? They hadn't waded in. They'd jumped right into the deep end.

He took her hand. Squeezed. "Honey, we can go as slowly as you need." Gosh. The words were so simple, but they did the trick. At least for the moment her nerves were soothed.

Her panic flared up a little again when she parked in the garage and they walked together to the house, but the second they stepped into her kitchen he took her in his arms and shattered every lingering reservation. He tucked his fingers beneath her chin and tipped her gaze to his. "Amy," he said, "I've missed kissing you."

"Okay," she said because her brain was a muddle. "Then maybe you should."

So, he did.

And once he did, once his lips touched hers, everything good inside her melted and everything bad inside her melted away.

He lost all control too, and he took her then, there, in the kitchen, barely remembering to use the condom.

* * *

"We did it again," Amy said as she gazed up at him, all limp and languid.

Noah pulled her closer and chuckled. Yeah. They had. When he got close to her, he lost all reason. "We really should try it on a bed."

"We should." She wriggled from his hold and then held out a hand. Something twinkled in her eye. "Shall we?" She meant to lead him, inveigle him up the stairs. And he wanted to go…but something stopped him. She must have read it in his energy somehow, that resistance, because she stilled as well. "What is it?" she asked.

He glanced up the stairs. "I… Well, it's kind of weird, you know, in George's bed."

Her eyes widened, as though the thought had never occurred to her. Then she shook her head. "Noah, George never slept in this house. I bought it after he died."

"Oh." Well, that was a relief.

Well, hell. What was he waiting for, then?

Without a thought, he whipped her up into his arms— laughing as she was—and carried her up to the top of the staircase. Then he stopped, did a quick recon and turned into the room that was not filled with toys and race-car beds. He tossed her onto the bed—that was not George's bed and never had been—and he followed her down.

"Here we are," he said, gazing down at her, reveling in her beauty, in her amusement, in her arousal. It was a perfect combination.

"Here we are," she said.

He cupped her face and stroked her cheek, her lips with his thumb. "I want to kiss you again."

"Then do it." There was such hunger in her voice,

he didn't delay. He kissed her hard, and he kissed her deep and long. Even though they'd just made love, he couldn't get enough of her.

This was the first time he had time—time to taste her, time to explore, time to revel—and he intended to savor every single second. He loved the taste and the feel of her lips, but the crook of her neck, fragrant and sweet, called to him, so he kissed her there as well. Her reaction was immediate and hungry, just as he'd suspected it would be. She arched into him and groaned.

It inflamed both of them to more curiosity, and as he began to unbutton her top, she yanked his T-shirt from his jeans. He was aware of her hands on him as she bared his chest and his back but only in the periphery of his consciousness. His attention was laser-locked on her breasts, cupped as they were in her lacy front-clasp bra. He swallowed hard. Damn. He could see her nipples through the lace. Damn. Damn.

He unhooked the front clasp of her bra, but she stopped him before he could open in it up. "Wait."

He froze and met her gaze. Even though he was hard and breathless and aching to see her, to taste her, he'd promised to be patient. He'd promised to take it slow. "What is it?" he asked through barely gritted teeth.

"I... I've had two kids, Noah."

He didn't really understand what she was saying, but he knew whatever it was was important because of her expression, so he just said, "Mmm-hmm," hoping she'd elaborate.

"I'm not... My body isn't perfect anymore."

Suddenly it dawned on him. Suddenly he realized what she was scared of. His heart thudded. Hard. He shook his head. How could she not realize. How could she not know? He cupped her cheek again, waited until she met his gaze. "You're perfect to me, Amy. Just perfect. Just the way you are."

And he meant it.

Because she was.

It wasn't true, and she knew it. It wasn't even close to true, but she didn't care. All she needed was to hear it. All she needed was to see it in his eyes. And Noah, beautiful, generous Noah, gave her that. She didn't bother to correct him.

Instead, she opened her arms and welcomed him in. She let him remove her bra and worship her breasts, and then she allowed him to unzip her jeans and pull those off too. She insisted that he lose his jeans before she let him take off her underwear, but he was happy to comply.

Her breath caught at the sight of his arousal—even through his briefs. Good glory, he made her mouth water. But she forced herself to wait before she bared him there because there was so much more to see. So much she'd never seen before.

For the first time, she was able to explore him. Really explore his body with her fingers and her lips…and her eyes because he was gorgeous, hard and muscled and tatted. His scars—and he had quite a few—made him even sexier.

But as she explored him, he explored her and before long, those caresses and kisses and torments turned to passion.

He took her slowly this time, easing in and out with

excruciating precision and bringing her to climax again and again. Afterward, he held her, and she held him as they recuperated. And she liked that just as much.

She traced one of the scars on his chest. "Is this a battle scar?" she asked.

"In a way," he said with the huff of a laugh. "That one was from a fight."

She levered up and looked down at him. "You don't strike me as the kind of guy who gets into fights."

"Sometimes, in life, you have to fight." She hated the emptiness of the words.

Something in his tone sent a shiver through her. "Can tell me about it? This fight?"

"I was twelve." He shifted, repositioning himself with his hands under his head, so very subtly creating space between them. While she hated it, she figured he probably needed it. After a moment or two, he continued. "I was living in a group home with a bunch of other boys. Most of them were older..."

"What was the fight about?" she asked when he trailed off.

He stiffened up at the question but then took a breath and relaxed, "Well, you don't want to know. Let's just say someone wanted something that I wasn't willing to give."

Even though he didn't give the dark details, somehow, she knew. Prickles danced over her nape. Her heart ached for the vulnerable little boy he'd been all those years ago. She hated that he'd been subjected to that kind of situation, where he had to protect himself, his body, in a place that was supposed to be safe, a place that was supposed to be home. "I'm so sorry."

"Thanks." He closed his arms around her again, and she cuddled closer, hoping it was soothing to him. "But all that garbage helped make me who I am, I guess. And I like who I am."

"It's important to like yourself, of course. Still, I wish it hadn't been like that for you."

He didn't say anything, but she felt him kiss her hair.

She decided to try for a lighter subject. "So, tell me about the tattoos."

"Okay. Where do I start?" He had a few after all.

"This one." She pointed to the one on his big bicep. "It says, *These Things We Do…*"

"*That Other May Live*. That's the PJ motto. Yeah. Good one to start with. I got this one after I earned the maroon beret."

"Big moment?"

"Very big." His grin was a solace, chasing away the weight of the earlier topic.

"And the tiger?" She loved the way the tail whipped across his chest.

"That was my first tat. I got it after INDOC."

She gave a chuckle because she knew lots of soldiers celebrated passing their basic indoctrination in some way or another. Many chose a tattoo. George had, but his had been an American flag.

"Why a tiger?"

He huffed a laugh. "That was the name the guys called me—Tiger—probably because I was so gung ho. I kind of got it as a joke, but I still like it. That's a good sign."

It definitely was. She gave up her survey of his ink and settled back into his arms because it just felt so good to lie against him, skin to skin. She tried not to think of the time—she had to be back at the bakery by three to help close. And she tried not to think of the other ticking clock.

It was now, right now.

The future was far, far away.

Chapter Eleven

Noah loved having that time with Amy on Friday, but even though she hadn't asked him to stick around and have supper with the boys, she had invited him to attend John J.'s party, which was the next day. He knew it was still important to her to manage the boys' expectations about his presence in their lives—and he respected that, as hard as it was—but he was happy that she was letting him in a little more. It gave him hope.

Noah had never in his life been to a six-year-old's birthday party—not even his own, because the foster parents he'd had between ages four and seven didn't celebrate birthdays. He had no idea what to expect. But still, the sheer chaos he was faced with the next day when he, Nat and Jax stepped into the private party pavilion by the pool at Ben Sherrod's resort was terrifying. There were screaming children everywhere.

Jax clapped him on the back. "Be brave," he whispered.

"Very funny." A creature—possibly a little girl?—wearing a mask and a cape ran by, shrieking at the top of her lungs. He stepped out of her path, but barely in time. "Remind me why I'm here again?"

"John J. wanted you to come?" Natalie suggested.

Oh yeah. He was here for the guest of honor.

And his mother. But mostly for John J.

The party pavilion was festooned with lights and streamers and featured numerous picnic tables, all of which were covered with dinosaur-themed tablecloths. One of them was piled with gifts, but the party spread far beyond that, taking up most of what appeared to be a small water park with slides and tubes and multiple pools, all surrounded by lush greenery. Adults stood in little clusters near the pavilion, chatting away, while the children were everywhere. They jumped in a bouncy house over there and played in the shallow end of the pool over here. The braver ones were practicing dives in the deep end, and a few of them had even ventured to the top of the hill, waiting their turn on a big curving slide.

Way over on the far end of the pool plaza, he spotted some quiet cabanas, and he secretly yearned to escape to one of them to avoid the cacophony, if only for a minute. But hey, this was John J.'s party, not his.

"Noah!" Amy waved at him from across the distance, and all the chaos melted away. All it took was her smile. "Nat! Jax! You made it!" She wove her way through the crowd toward them, but it took a while because she had to stop and respond when people greeted her. At long last, she reached them. "I'm so glad you're here. John J. will be thrilled."

"Where is John J.?" he asked. Since many of the kids were in costume, it was hard to tell.

"He was in the wading pool with Quinn a minute ago." She glanced that way and frowned. When she saw Georgie at the top of the water slide, she called him over. It took a minute for him to get there because it was a long slide that curled around, over to a different pool. He landed with a splash and a laugh, then made his way out of the water. When he got to them, he was grinning from ear to ear and soaking wet. "Georgie," Amy said as he padded over. "Where's John J.? Noah's here."

Georgie grinned. "He's up on the slide. We're doing slide dares with Dylan."

Amy frowned. "You know I don't like you guys doing dares." She shot an aggravated glance at Noah. "Boys will do anything on a dare, and it's—"

"Mom! Noah!" They both turned then at John J.'s call. "Look at me!" And there he was, standing at the top of the slide, waving like mad. He looked so little and so far away. It hadn't seemed like such a tall slide when Noah had spotted Georgie up there. He reminded himself to relax. John J. was just having fun, like all the rest of the kids.

But then, to Noah's horror, the boy standing behind John J. pushed him onto the slide. He wasn't ready. He lost his balance and fell. He came down the serpentine slide like a rag doll, disappearing into the other pool.

He did not come back up.

The hair on Noah's nape prickled, his lungs locked, as he watched for John J. to reemerge, but even then,

Noah was on the move, sprinting across the deck. His heart stuttered, then went cold as he spotted the boy— his boy—still, on the bottom of the pool.

Shit.

He was in the water in a flash, ignoring the shock of going from the heat of the sun into the cold water. He'd done this before, a thousand times, but it had never been as scary as this.

He got hold of John J.'s limp body and, careful of his cervical-spine, lifted him out of the water and onto the cement. His heart clenched when he realized the boy wasn't breathing, and wasn't responding to stimuli. Somehow, he snapped right back into PJ mode. He told the crowd to move back, and take the little children away from the scene—emergencies like this could be traumatizing—and directed Ben to call 911. Then he aligned the boy's airway and administered two rescue breaths, while he checked for a heartbeat.

John J.'s skin was cold, but Noah was able to detect a slight thump in the boy's carotid artery. His guts nearly liquified with relief.

He'd saved people in his line of work and he'd lost them, but he'd never been as stricken with terror as he was at this moment.

Amy was utterly petrified.

She'd seen John J. up at the top of the slide, calling out to her—she'd even waved back. But when Dylan had pushed him and he'd tumbled down the slide and disappeared into the water, her heart had stopped.

She'd heard stories about mothers suddenly having super strength and lifting cars to save their children…

but her body had done the opposite. She'd frozen. Time had slowed. Her brain had switched off.

But Noah hadn't frozen. He'd been off like a shot. Almost before she'd realized what had happened. Now she moved, in some kind of fog, toward Noah and her lifeless son, barely aware of the people around her, the cries from the crowd, barely aware of anything. All she could do was watch, helplessly, as he tried to rouse her child.

Her heart thudded and her lungs locked as Noah gave John J. a breath and another. And another. All to no avail.

She clenched her hands together, felt her pulse beating through her nerveless fingers as she prayed. *Please, God. Please.* John J. looked so small and pale, lying here. And what could she do?

Nothing.

"Momma," Georgie said at her side. Oh God. He looked terrified too.

She knelt down so she could hold him, cling to him, as together they watched—for what seemed like an eternity—as Noah struggled to bring John J. back to them.

She nearly collapsed when, finally, his ministrations brought forth a spurt of water and John J. rolled over onto his side. Noah patted his back, telling him in a gentle voice that everything was going to be all right. "Just breathe," he said, even as John J. began to cough. "Good. That's good. Get it out."

He glanced at her then and nodded—his expression pallid and tense but tinged with relief. "He's okay," he said to the crowd, but mostly to her. "He's okay."

John J. seemed fine, once he'd recovered from the shock of nearly drowning. When he called for her, Amy had to go to him. All she wanted to do was scoop him up into her arms and hold him but she had to settle for holding his hand because Noah suggested they not move him yet. "Let's wait until the paramedics have a look," he said, "just to make sure he doesn't have a neck injury." Somehow, he talked John J. into lying quietly just a little while longer until the paramedics Ben had called could look him over.

As the paramedics checked John J.'s vitals, Noah explained what they were doing so the hovering parents—and Amy—could understand what was happening. When they gave her boy the all-clear, everyone cheered.

Except Amy, who was still shaking.

"Are you okay?" Noah asked.

"No." She glanced up at him. "I was so scared."

"I know." He put his arm around her. "I was scared too. Thank God he's okay."

She snorted a laugh that wasn't really was one. "Thank *you*. I can't imagine if you hadn't been there."

For some reason Noah shrugged. "I'm sure the lifeguards know CPR and rescue breathing."

She gave him a look. They probably did. They'd probably had classes. But he'd done it. Actually *done it* before. Aside from that, he'd realized at once that her boy was in trouble and had been off at a run before she'd even processed what was happening. Heck, he'd already had John J. out of the water receiving life-giving oxygen before the lifeguards had even noticed the kerfuffle. "I'm so glad you were there." Ha. *Glad* was hardly the word. But it was the only one her poor tired brain could come up with. "Thank you."

He grinned. "I'm glad I could help."

She went up onto her toes and kissed him. Right there in front of everyone. And she didn't care who saw. Maybe it was time for her to forget what other people thought and listen to her heart.

And what did her heart tell her?

Well, simply said, she wanted Noah. She wanted him beside her and around her and in her life. More than that, she loved him. After everything she'd been through, after loving George and losing him, after hurting so bad she thought she'd never heal, after grieving and breaking and putting herself back together again, she'd never thought she could love, like this again. But it was something she could not deny.

She loved him. With everything in her.

The revelation was something of a surprise. And at the same time, it felt as though it had always been.

That night, Noah came home with them. The party ended soon after John J.'s tumble. Even though the medics determined that he was physically okay—no concussion or neck trauma—everyone was a little shaken. Nat and Celeste had stayed to manage the guests and clean everything up, bless them.

John J. asked Noah to tuck him in that night, and even though Noah had never done such a thing before, he gave it the old Air Force try. It helped that John J. told him what to do.

It was nice, calming, reading the boys a story and talking to them about their day. And then after the boys were in bed, he and Amy walked downstairs and sat together on the sofa.

There might have been some kissing. Neither of them let it go too far because the boys were just upstairs. But that didn't mean he didn't want more. He did.

He hated getting up to leave, but he knew she had to get up early. Just because he wasn't on the schedule didn't mean it was fair to keep her up. "Will I see you tomorrow?" he asked. He knew her Sundays were pretty full with work and family.

"Will you come to Sunday supper tomorrow?"

He shot her a look. His feelings were a mishmash. While he was happy and relieved that she was including him again, he was confused. It hadn't been that long ago that she'd asked him to spend less time with the boys. He'd learned that straight-forward questions were the best approach in situations like this, so he said, "I would love to come, but the other day you said—"

She made a face. "I know what I said. I think I was just scared about…"

"About what?"

"I…" She blew out a breath. "Forget what I said. I was wrong. I was worried that if the boys bonded too strongly with you, they'd be hurt when you left. But now I see that was a mistake. I *want* you to bond with them. I want them to bond with *you*. I mean, if we're going to take this seriously—and we are, aren't we?" She glanced at him.

There was a hint of apprehension in her expression, so he quickly said, "I am."

"Good." She gusted a sigh. "Well, I am too. And if

we're going to take this seriously, we need to move forward as though it will work out. What do you think?"

"I think yes." And thank God she'd changed her mind. It had been hard not seeing the boys. "I'd love to come to Sunday supper tomorrow."

"Awesome." She went up onto her toes and kissed him, but then she kind of pushed him toward the door. "You'd better go," she said with a laugh.

He knew she was right. But damn, it was hard to leave.

Noah slept pretty well that night, which was a surprise because he'd expected to lie awake wanting her all night. Instead, he fell asleep thinking about the pleasure he'd had just hanging out with her and the boys... as a family.

There was even more a sense of family at supper the next day. There was a lot of laughter and interesting conversation and special moments with the boys and Amy and everyone. It only underscored the feelings that he'd been having about this place and these people. This was where he wanted to be. Forever.

Celeste pulled him aside at one point. He was a little nervous about what she had to say because the last time he'd talked to her, he'd been buying those condoms. He knew that had given her a bad opinion of him. He could hardly blame her considering how it must have looked to someone on the outside of the relationship, but the last thing he wanted was a confrontation with Amy's sister about sex.

Fortunately, she had something else entirely on her mind. "Noah, I just wanted to thank you," she said.

Thank me? Okay. He unclenched a little. Not what he'd been expecting. "For what?"

Her eyes went wide. "Um, hello? You saved John J.'s life yesterday?"

Oh. Yeah. "Hey, I'm just glad I was on hand."

"I'm glad too. Look, I know I was a little wound up that you and Amy were…" He nearly grimaced, preparing for the lecture, but she shook her head and started again. "I just want you to know that I think you and Amy are a good fit. And it's clear to see that the boys idolize you. So… I apologize if I was, you know, a little persnickety about things."

Persnickety? The word made him grin. "You're protecting the people you love," he said. "There's nothing wrong with that."

"So, you forgive me?"

"There's nothing to forgive." There really wasn't. But he appreciated it. He appreciated her hug too.

And then she proceeded to nag him—just a little—about going down to city hall and applying for the paramedic job. Pretty soon Pearl joined in, and then Jax and Nat as well.

And somehow, that nagging made him feel even more certain that he'd finally found his clan.

The next few weeks were so much fun for Amy. Thanks to Kara's amazing talents and the fact that Eloise had returned and was ready to work again—with the understanding that if she ever flaked again, she would be promptly fired—Amy actually got some days off. Full days.

She'd had days off before, but never with Noah

around. Days off before had been all about catching up with the laundry or taking the boys to the dentist or getting her stupid car fixed.

Now it was like a whole new world. A whole new life.

She and Noah and the boys had adventures. Sometimes with Nat and Jax—occasionally even Momma and Celeste came along. They went on picnics and hikes. They went to Seattle to visit the Woodland Park Zoo and to Pike Place Market to watch grown men throw massive fish and to the Pacific Science Center and Miner's Landing for a Ferris-wheel ride and a sourdough bread bowl full of clam chowder...all of which the boys loved. She did too.

Noah insisted on taking the boys to the water park in Auburn—the one Dylan had gone to without them. It was so touching to watch Noah work with John J. when he was nervous about going on a big slide again. They went down the first one together, but after that, John J. was raring for more, too excited and impatient to even wait for Noah to catch up.

Oh, and Amy started taking pictures again. It surprised her how much she loved that. Especially because most of the pictures were of Noah and the boys. She loved flicking through them on her phone. There was one of Noah and her boys hiking Mount Rainier—not the advanced trails, of course, the easy ones around Paradise. And there was one of Noah with John J. on his shoulders when John J. had gotten too tired on the path—both of them grinning. She really loved the one of Noah on the boat proudly holding up the steelhead he'd caught—his first catch!—with Georgie at his side.

He'd called her son over to be in the photo because Georgie had *helped him* reel it in.

She didn't get a shot of Noah barfing over the side of the boat, though he had.

Her favorite picture of all was Noah on the beach, teaching John J. how to fly a kite. *You have to run against the wind if you want your kite to soar*, he'd said. And it had.

Just like he had.

He'd run against the wind his whole life. And just look how he had soared.

There were a lot of other memories from those days as well, where photos weren't appropriate or, in general, appreciated. Because Noah and Amy were able to find lots of time to be alone together as well. She kept those images in her mind, and whenever one fluttered into view, she had to smile. He was a generous lover. He was funny. He was kind. He was honest and sincere with the boys—and her.

It was a good time. And Amy reveled in every second.

For Noah, it seemed as though everything his life was falling into place.

He loved it here—Jax and his friends, the vibe of the town, the weather…everything. He might have wanted to settle here even if he hadn't met Amy. But if he was being honest, she was the reason he'd stuck around long enough to fall in love with the place. He realized he'd begun to put down roots. Oh, they weren't big old tree roots. More like little baby shoots, but he felt the power of them. And he'd started to understand how the right place, the right people could feed the soul in a way he'd craved but never really understood.

He loved all the activities he and Amy and the boys had done—catching his first fish had been a highlight—and he loved that he and Jax had been able to go on some rides together. He really loved that he and Amy had more time to be together. But what he liked the best were the quiet times, at night, just the four of them. Playing card games or charades or even watching one of the nature shows Amy liked.

It sucked that he had to leave at the end of each evening, but he did. Every night he went back to the studio and slept alone. He knew it was the right thing to do. He and Amy had talked about it and agreed that it was important not to blur the line…for the boys. But it was hard to leave. Each and every night. He started thinking more and more about the conversation he needed to have with Amy about how he was feeling and what he was wanting.

He was sure now—absolutely sure—that he wanted to stay, that he wanted her. What held him back was that he wasn't sure if the time was right for her, for him to bring up a forever conversation. Last thing he wanted to do was scare her off by being all, *I know we just met, but marry me, please.*

He could bide his time. He was used to it. Half of military life had been *hurry up and wait.* Aside from that, he'd waited his entire life to find this. He could be patient. He had to be.

He was looking forward to next week when the boys went off to summer camp. Not that he wouldn't miss them, but at least he and Amy could have some nights together.

The Friday before camp, Amy invited her family over for a barbeque, and they had a blast. Then again, most meals with these characters were a blast.

"So, John J.," Natalie said as the boys dug into their ribs, "your mom says you have your very first sleepaway camp next week. Are you excited?"

John J. shook his head. "I changed my mind. I don't want to go."

"What?" Amy frowned at him. "But you were so excited."

Noah put his arm around John J.'s shoulder. "Why don't you want to go, kiddo?" he asked.

The little boy crossed his arms and put out his bottom lip. "I'd just rather stay home."

Natalie shook her head. "But sleepaway camp is the best. So much fun. Didn't you have fun at camp last year, Georgie?"

"Yes."

"And your mom and I used to go, didn't we, Amy?"

"I loved it," Amy said in a gusty voice. "I loved being in the woods."

"And toasting marshmallows," Celeste chimed in.

"And making arts-and-crafts projects." Nat again.

But no matter what they said or how they gilded the lily, John J.'s lip just came out further and further. "I don't want to go." A little tear shimmered in his eye.

"Oh no, hon," Amy said when she saw it. She came around and knelt by his side. "What's wrong?"

Georgie gave a little snort. "He's afraid."

"Am not."

Amy hugged him. "John J. There's nothing to be afraid of. I promise."

"He's afraid of the dark," Georgie said.

"I am not. I just don't want to go."

Georgie sniffed. "I wasn't scared when I went last year, and that was my first time."

"But you're older!" John J. wailed.

"Do you know what I think?" Noah broke in because this looked like a brewing row. The boys' heads swiveled. "I think we should do a practice campout."

Georgie did a funny little double take. "A what?"

"A practice campout?" John J. seemed a little leery.

"Sure." Noah cracked a huge grin. "We did practice runs all the time in the military. It's where you try something that's a little scary but in a safe environment. So you can work out all the kinks before the real thing."

"Really?" John J.'s expression eased, just a tiny bit.

Noah nodded. "Then when it comes time for the real thing, it's not scary because you've already done it. Heck, in the military, we did more practice runs than actuals."

Jax snorted a laugh. "Ain't that the truth."

The boys seemed to be listening, so he went on. "It'll be fun. We can set up some tents in the yard—"

"Why not do it at the studio?" Jax suggested. "Then we can have a bonfire."

"Oooh. And roast marshmallows," Celeste put in. That girl really needed to get her some marshmallows.

"That sounds like fun. We should all do it." Amy said, and Noah shot her a surprised glance. He hadn't expected she would want to sleep outdoors with the bugs. But judging from her grin, she was game.

* * *

Amy loved the idea of practice camp. She loved that Noah had suggested it—because it was brilliant. Once they started planning it, the boys became even more enthused. Noah and Jax sat down with them and wrote out a list of supplies, and then they had the boys plan the menus. Then Jax and Noah took them to buy what they needed.

It was stunning the way Noah so easily set them up for success. The way he folded life-skills lessons into a simple activity like planning for a campout. Amy didn't even have to pack for them because Noah was teaching them how to load a rucksack.

The next afternoon, they loaded up Amy's car with all their gear and food and extra wood for the campfire and headed over to Jax's studio.

Amy never expected practice camp to be so much fun, but it was. All the adults—with the boys trying to help—set up the tents in the yard, down by the water, and then built a fire in the firepit. For dinner they roasted hot dogs on sticks and cooked beans in a can. But the fun really started after the sun went down. They roasted marshmallows and told really bad jokes around the fire and laughed.

She loved it all. The woodsmoke, the hypnotic dance of the fire, the crash of waves in the distance, the blanket Noah brought over and put around her shoulders because she was feeling a little cold… It was nice.

At one point, the boys started asking for stories and Noah told them the tale of the very first Pararescue mission in history. The one that had started the PJs to begin with. It had happened during World War II, when an American plane had gone down in the wilds of the Burmese jungle. Twenty-one soldiers and a media team had been wounded and stranded behind enemy lines. Then Lieutenant Colonel Don Flickinger—Noah said his name in an awe-struck whisper—had led a team of medics on what had been considered a suicide mission, jumping out of an airplane into danger, to come to the rescue.

The boys were enraptured. They stared, mouths open and eyes wide, as Noah wove the thrilling tale of how these first rescue rangers parachuted into the jungle, rescued and treated the wounded and led them to safety. "It was the very first PJ mission," he said. "It was their bravery that started it all."

"Now thousands of people have been saved by the PJs," Jax added. "They're heroes."

"Noah," Georgie asked, after a moment of silence, "what made you want to be a PJ?"

He took a deep breath, thought about it for a minute, then said, "I think I was about seven the very first time I realized I wanted to be someone who could save other people, even though I didn't even know about PJs back then. I was living with a foster family at the time. They had three kids of their own, and a couple of us foster kids lived with them."

"Did you like it there?" John J. asked with a worried look.

"Very much. The boys were about my age, but they also had a little girl named Charlotte. Anyway, one Saturday in the summer it was really hot, so we all went to Virginia Beach. It was such a beautiful day. Everything was perfect. It was sunny and warm, and we were all playing on the beach. Charlotte was right at the water's edge when, all of a sudden, a big wave came along and swept her away."

The boys gasped.

"Yeah. It was really scary. But you know what?"

"What?" Oh, it was so sweet, the way they hung on his every word.

"We all stood there, not sure what to do, and then out of nowhere, a lifeguard came running along beach, and he jumped into the water and swam and swam. It seemed like he was in there forever, but when he came out, he had Charlotte in his arms."

"Was she okay?"

"No, John J.," he said solemnly. "She wasn't okay. She wasn't breathing." The boys gasped again.

"Like John J.?" Georgie asked in a small voice.

Noah nodded. "Exactly like John J. But the lifeguard knew what to do."

"Like you!" The boys chorused.

"Yes. He pulled Charlotte out of the water and gave her a breath. Like I did for John J. And then he checked for a pulse." He mimicked touching his neck. "Now, John J. had a pulse. So, all I had to do was adjust his airway and deliver a breath. But Charlotte didn't have a pulse. So, the lifeguard had to do CPR."

Georgie scooted a little closer. "What's CPR?"

"Well CPR stands for cardiopulmonary resuscitation—" He stopped when he saw their confused glances. "Okay. You know that in order to be alive, people need to have a pumping heart—which is cardio—delivering oxygen to the body through the lungs—which is pulmonary. Right?"

Georgie frowned. "Do zombies have a beating heart?"

"They gotta. They're still alive," John J. said.

"No." Georgie made a face. "They're not alive."

"They're walking around, so they gotta be alive."

"Well, we're talking about people, not zombies," Noah reminded them. Amy bit back a smile at his very patient response to their jagged segue. Indeed, it was an important distinction to make. "People need a beating heart and oxygen to live. The lifeguard knew that. He could tell that Charlotte couldn't breathe for herself, so her gave her a breath and then helped her heart beat, through chest compressions, to circulate the oxygen so her brain didn't starve. Basically, since he knew CPR, he was able to save her."

"So, she was okay?"

"In the end, yes, John J. She was okay because he knew how to save her. So, there I was, this young kid, watching this man breathe life into that little girl, and something just clicked. That's when I realized I wanted to be the kind of person who knew how to save somebody."

"That's amazing," Nat said, wiping something from her cheek.

Jax put his arm around her and pulled her close. "It is."

"What ever happened to that little girl?" John J. asked.

Noah shrugged. "She grew up, I suppose."

Georgie wrinkled his brows. "Don't you know?"

"No, I really don't. A little while later, I had to leave that house and go live somewhere else."

John J. tsked and shook his head. "If you liked it

there, why didn't you just stay?" His solemnity would have been funny if it weren't so tragic.

But Noah was stoic. He often was. "Foster kids don't always get to decide where they live. Of course—" he gave a depreciating chuckle "—back then I thought for sure one of the families I lived with would adopt me."

"Did they?" John J. asked plaintively.

"Well, no. They never did."

"I can't believe no one adopted you," Nat said.

Neither could Amy. He must have been a precious boy. It made her heart hurt when she thought of him fending for himself in a cold world all those years.

John J. got up from his stump, crawled into Noah's lap and patted his enormously strong shoulders. "Noah, we can adopt you if you want."

"Aww. Thanks, buddy." He glanced at her as he gave John J. a hug, and she caught a glint in his eye.

"We can." Georgie turned to her. "We can. Can't we, Mom?"

She had to smile. "Sure."

After a moment and a couple surreptitious sniffles, Natalie said, "I just think it's a credit to you, growing up all alone without a lot of stability, that you were able to accomplish what you have in your life. Good for you, Noah."

It was dark, other than the fire, but Amy knew Noah was blushing. "Well, thanks, Natalie, but I wasn't alone. Not really. There were a lot of people who helped me get where I was going."

"People like Ma?" Amy had to ask.

Their gazes tangled for a moment, and he smiled. "Yeah. Like Ma. And so many more. Social workers, foster families, all kinds of organizations, really good people…"

"Still…" Nat interjected. "A lot of people who go through tough childhoods choose to use it as an excuse to fail."

Noah nodded. "And there are a lot of people with every privilege who use that as an excuse to fail as well." He chuckled. "Ma always said, *It doesn't matter where you come from. It matters where you are.*"

"Well," Georgie said, standing, wiping the pine needles from his butt and heading over so sit next to Noah…who made room for him on the now-crowded log. "I'm glad you're here with us."

"I'm glad too," John J. said.

"Me too." Yeah. Everyone said it.

And now Noah was definitely blushing.

Amy sat back and took it in. It was something to see, Noah with the boys like that. Together, comforting each other. She took a mental picture of this moment so she could remember it forever. This was what mattered in life. This was what it was all about.

And this was worth fighting for.

This was worth everything.

Chapter Twelve

After practice camp, John J. was more than excited about real camp. There was no more talk about staying home. Amy was happy about that, but not just because she'd have extended time alone with Noah. It was important that John J. was facing his fears and trying new things. It was his first week away from her, which was a big thing—also hard for a mom—but it was an important step in every child's life.

And she knew this camp. She'd gone there herself one summer in high school. It was run by a local church that had a campground by a lake in the mountains on the north end of the Olympic Peninsula. The boys would be there for a week, but it was a couple hours away.

Though Noah had let the boys pack for themselves for practice camp, Amy did the packing for the real thing. Independence was important, but so was reality. She diligently packed seven pairs of white socks for each of the boys knowing that, just like last year, six pairs would come back pristine and still folded and one pair would be a nasty gray. But at least they would have the extra clean socks, there in the wilderness, should they be inclined to change them.

With Kara on board and managing things better than Amy could have imagined, it also meant that while the boys were gone, Amy and Noah could spend some real alone time together.

On Monday morning, she and Noah took the boys to the drop-off spot in the school parking lot where the camp bus and a collection of nervous parents had assembled.

As they got out of the car, John J. seemed a little skittish, but then Noah went down onto one knee and the two had a talk. After that, her son picked up his backpack, slung it over his shoulder and that was that. He walked with Noah over to the bus without so much as a *Bye, Mom.*

It was a good thing. Right?

The kids were quickly loaded onto the bus, but the parents hung around the lot as they waited for it to take off. Some of them stood near the bus, chatting with their kids through the windows. Noah was one of those. It was a great image, so Amy pulled out her phone and took the shot. She was lining up to take another when Candace sidled up to her. Amy had seen her earlier, dropping off Maya, and they'd shared a wave.

"Well," Candace said under her breath, "you could have told me you were *dating* him."

"What?"

"The hot guy. What's his name? Noel?"

"Noah."

"You could have *told* me you were dating him."

It was true. They hadn't talked in weeks—since the carnival, in fact. Amy hadn't called her because she'd been really busy at work and with Noah. But Candace hadn't called her either.

In fact, come to think of it, it was usually Amy who did the reaching out. Unless, of course, Candace wanted something.

Though she didn't feel she owed Candace any explanations, she said, "Well, you know."

Candace waggled her brows. "Oh, I do." *Ugh.* Her tone was so…lurid. Amy wasn't sure why that bugged her, but it did. But then Candace said, "So how is he?" in the same smarmy way, and she nearly barfed.

The last thing she wanted to talk about with Candace was Noah's prowess. Fortunately, she was saved by the sound of the bus engine starting up—and the cheers of the passengers. The parents all stepped away from the moving vehicle and waved madly as the bus—tooting its horn—rolled away.

In another universe, Amy might have been broken up, watching her babies leave her for an entire week, but she was so preoccupied with escaping that conversation with Candace, she completely forgot to be melodramatic.

When Candace turned to her again and opened her mouth like she wanted to ask something really intimate, Amy looked at her wrist—where her watch was supposed to go—and said, "Oh gosh. We have to scoot. See you soon, Candace." Then she quickly rounded up Noah and got into her car and left.

It was sad to realize, but she and Candace had nothing in common anymore. Maybe they never had.

After dropping off the boys, Amy drove straight home. There was a moment—when they stepped into her house and she realized they were completely alone—that Amy felt a shard of nervousness, but it melted away the moment he took her in his arms and kissed her. From then on, it was nothing but the delight of exploration and bliss. But the best part was...no ticking clock. No reason to leave each other at all.

Waking up with Noah was the best waking up Amy had experienced in a long time. He was warm and naked and ready. And so was she. But it was more than just the sex. It was being together, it was little moments, it was the intimacy.

Watching Noah shave, for example. She had forgotten how sexy it was to watch a handsome man shave. He did it the old-fashioned way, with lather and a razor blade, the way so many military men did. The way her father had. The way George had. As though it was a ritual, a gift to himself and his woman, rather than a chore. And his cheek, when he finished, was like satin.

And there were more intimate moments she savored, the kind of moments you only found when you were together day and night. Watching Noah work out was one of them. Was it wrong that she couldn't tear her eyes away? The flex of his muscles as he lifted jerry-rigged weights in the backyard, the contraction of his six-pack when he crunched. He made her mouth water.

Thank goodness for Kara and even Eloise because Amy only had to pop into the bakery every now and again. The rest of the time, it was just the two of them together at home. It was like a vacation. A honeymoon, almost.

There were occasions—very few—where they ventured out into the world. Apparently the world was continuing on. The day before the boys were coming home, Jax invited Noah to attend the monthly VFF training exercise, and even though she wanted him to herself, Amy could see how his eyes lit up at the idea. She knew how much he missed being a PJ and working with a team, and she knew how much he wanted to go, so of course, she insisted that he attend.

It only made sense that she spend that afternoon with Nat while the men were doing their firefighter training. They sat around the breakfast table in Nat's cute little nook, talking about the wedding plans, which were in full swing, but Natalie also had a lot of questions of Amy about her pregnancy. It was kind of nice, being the expert for once. That didn't happen a lot with older sisters.

Pregnancy was life changing, so Nat had a lot of questions. They chatted for quite a while about the weird things that were happening to her body and the even weirder things she could expect and the joy that came when it was all finished.

Then, at one point, Nat made a casual comment, one that tipped Amy's world on its axis. She said, "Isn't it weird, not having a period? I'm not complaining. Just saying..."

Amy laughed. "It's one of the benefits of being pregnant actually..." And then she stilled as a realization hit. Well, hell. How long had it been since she'd had her period? She did a quick calculation and... Her blood chilled for a second. Over a month. She'd been due for one about the time Noah had come, in fact. *Ye. Gods.*

"What's wrong?" Nat said.

Amy forced a smile. "Oh, nothing." But her mind was in a whirl. Oh, God. Could she handle that? Could she manage that? Work and the boys *and* a new baby? She barely managed as it was. Oh, she kept her chin up and pushed on through, no matter what, but really? Did she have enough gas in her tank for that? Granted, with Kara on board and Eloise back helping with prep, work wasn't as draining, but a new baby would change all that.

A new baby would change everything.

Even more terrifying, what would Noah say? What would Noah do? He loved the boys, but every time she'd asked him how he felt about having kids, he'd been a little reticent. The thought that he might leave because of *this*, petrified her.

"Amy." Her sister gave her *the look*. "I can tell something's wrong."

Normally, she was able to be stalwart and stoic. Normally, she could keep her worries to herself with no one the wiser…but the wave of emotion rocking her made it impossible.

She forced herself to draw in a deep breath and calm her whizzing mind. She was probably jumping the gun. She'd missed a period before, hadn't she? Though she couldn't recall it having happened, it was possible. Wasn't it?

"Amy, you don't look well." Her sister set a hand on her forehead. "Are you sure you're okay?"

"I… Ah… No," she said. "Now that you mention it, I

missed my period. I think I need to go get a pregnancy test."

Nat's jaw dropped. Her eyes lit up. "Really? Oh, my goodness, Amy. How fun would it be to be pregnant together?"

Amy gaped at her for a second. She really had no clue, did she? She and Jax were settled, but that wasn't the case for Amy and Noah. Yes, everything between them seemed wonderful, and it felt like they were heading for something permanent, but neither one of them had been inclined to talk about the future. So, they hadn't.

But this was all too much to share with Nat, and thinking about it was making Amy feel a little nauseous. She needed to know, and she needed to know now. "Can we go into town and get one?"

Nat grinned. "I think I have an extra upstairs."

"What?"

She laughed. "After my first one was positive, I bought a couple more just to be sure. Let me go see if I can find it."

That was how, fifteen minutes later, Amy stood in Nat's bathroom holding a stick that confirmed it…she and Noah had created a child together. At least, that was what the test said. She'd have to go to the doctor for a confirmation, and she would, but her heart told her the test was right.

One part of her was over the moon with joy. But another part of her was scared spitless.

Because, no matter what, her life was about to change forever.

Amy decided to tell Noah the news that night—the boys were coming home tomorrow, and they needed privacy to talk about something this big. There really was no reason to wait and her nerves wouldn't allow it. Besides, she had the big TV interview two days after that, and she didn't want the worry of how Noah would react hanging over her for that. It would be better to know. It was always better to know.

Still, she was nervous as all get out. She had no idea how he would react. Though he loved the boys, that didn't mean this would be good news for him. In fact, she knew damn well it might end everything between them.

None of that mattered though, because he deserved to know.

She waited until after they'd eaten dinner to tell him, and even then, she waited. She thought she'd done a good job of being cool and collected and patient and all, but she must have failed because he blew out a big sigh. "Amy," he said. "Why don't you just tell me what's bothering you?"

Heat walked up her cheeks. "Why do you think something is bothering me?"

He sent her a sardonic glance. "You haven't spoken all evening."

"I have." But when he looked at her again, like that, she knew she couldn't continue to protest. She had been preoccupied. "Okay." She folded her hands in her lap. "Noah…" Oh, how to blurt it out without blurting it out? "I…" Might as well just say it. "Noah, I'm late."

There.

She waited for a second, and when he didn't say anything, she glanced in his direction. There was a blank look on his face. "Late for what?"

She rolled her eyes. "I'm late. As in *late*."

He shook his head.

Oh, good grief. "Noah. I'm *pregnant*."

His expression went blank, his body still. Though she stared at him, watching, intently, for some kind of response, she couldn't tell what he was thinking. Would he stay? Would he run? He didn't give her a hint. As she waited for him to respond, for something, her heart thudded like a tin drum.

And then, after an excruciating moment, processing this life-changing news, he glanced at her and said, "Okay."

She stared at him. *Okay?* What kind of response was that?

Her frown became a glower. "Is that all you have to say? Noah, I'm *pregnant*."

He shrugged again. "That's not a problem." *Not a problem?* "We can just get married."

While part of her was relieved he hadn't just walked out the door, part of her was irritated by his blasé response as well. He didn't really realize what another child meant. She did. Besides, what kind of proposal was that? It was probably her annoyance that led her to snap, "People don't get married just because they're pregnant."

In response, he quirked a brow. "People get married because they're pregnant, like, literally all the time."

"Well, *I* don't." But she had. That was one of the main reasons she and George had eloped. They hadn't wanted anyone to know. That was, however, hardly the point. "Noah, I have two children to think about—and their very complicated daddy issues. I don't want to add to that by getting married to man just because he got me pregnant."

He looked hurt for some reason. "Are you saying you don't want to get married?"

"Not like that! Noah, when I get married, I want it to be…forever."

He literally cringed. "You don't think it would last?"

She gusted a heavy melodramatic sigh. "I didn't say that—"

"Do you *think* it?"

Did she think it wouldn't last? "No, of course not."

He took a step back and paled, and she realized how poorly she'd answered.

Quickly, she added, "I do not think it wouldn't last." And she cringed. Well hell. That hadn't come out right either. She sucked a deep breath, set her hands up on his shoulders and met his gaze. "I *know* we would last. I feel it in my heart."

"You do?" Her gut unclenched when his tight expression melted away.

"I really, really do. I just meant, well, I guess, that I wish we'd had a little more time to be sure about us before… Well, before we *had* to."

"Had to?" He stared at her, shook his head. "Amy. I don't have to marry you. I *want* to. I love you."

"You do?" He *loved* her? Oh, what a wonderful thing to hear.

"More than…" He paused, swallowing. When he spoke again, his voice was choked with emotion. "More than I ever thought I could."

"Oh, Noah. I love you too." It was wonderful to say. It was wonderful to feel. It was wonderful to experience.

She wanted to dance, she was so happy. "So, you *want to* spend your life with me…and the boys?"

"I do. God, I love them both so much. I'll be honest, I never really wanted children." Her heart fell at that, but he continued. "But I'd never spent any time with them, until Georgie and John J. Amy, they've taught me so much. I thought I'd be a terrible father because I hadn't had one, but that's not true. I know I can be a great father, because I know, for a fact, what a difference a great father can make. I gotta be honest…the thought of having a baby with you—a little boy or a girl with your adorable nose—makes me, well…" He didn't finish the sentence, but he didn't need to. The tears welling in his eyes spoke for him. He sniffled a bit and swallowed and then took her hands and said, "So yeah. I want to spend my life with you, and the boys, and any other critters that come along." He went a little red in the cheeks. "To be honest… I've been trying to figure out how to ask you to marry me for a while."

Really? Her heart gave a big ker-thump. "Oh, Noah."

"Do you…want to spend your life with me?"

"I do." It felt sacred, somehow, saying that, just now, just the two of them.

"Well…" He shrugged. "Okay, then."

"Okay, then. But seriously, Noah, are you okay? About this?" She set her hand on her belly. "You didn't seem happy when I told you."

"Only because I was surprised. Shocked, really. I wasn't expecting it."

"And now that you've had a little time to process?"

He stared at her for a moment before saying in a

small voice—which was strangely adorable coming from such a large man, "Honestly? I'm kind of scared."

She gave him a big grin. "Good. That means you're paying attention."

She liked that he laughed, that the trepidation washed from his face. She knew, then and there, that he was okay with it. That he would be.

And he would be a great dad.

He already was.

He was going to be a father.

Noah hadn't known how to react, what to say when Amy had told him. It had come right out of the blue, and he'd been gobsmacked at the prospect. Now that he'd had some time to take it in, he was excited.

Oh, scared to death, for sure, but thrilled.

Aside from that, he'd been looking for a way to let Amy know he was ready to settle down and that he wanted to settle here. With her.

In fact, this was everything he'd ever wanted. Everything on his list.

And even some things he'd never even considered putting on his list.

He was still spinning with the news of the baby and the fact that Amy had agreed to marry him when he met up with Jax at the studio the next morning for their ride up to visit their friends at JBLM.

"So?" Jax said in a leading tone as Noah came through the door. "Any news?"

Noah frowned at him. As if he didn't know. "What? Natalie didn't tell you?" Amy had told him that Natalie knew about the baby, and if Natalie knew, it was a sure thing that Jax did. He was just playing coy.

Indeed, he batted his lashes. "Tell me what?"

Oh, for pity's sake. It was all over his face. "Amy and I are getting married."

Jax blinked. Apparently, this wasn't precisely the news he'd been expecting, but his grin was huge. "Excellent!"

"I need to come up with a romantic proposal."

"Wait. Didn't she already say yes?"

"Well, we talked about getting married." Noah blew out a breath. "But I'd like to do something, I dunno, more formal?"

Jax nodded.

"Do you have a ring?"

Oh crap. A ring. He needed a ring. Definitely needed a ring. "Is there a jewelry store in town?"

Jax blew out a laugh. "Nope. But we can stop by a jeweler in Olympia on the way to JBLM."

"Okay. So that covers the ring…" That was the easy part. "Now I need some romantic gesture…" He shook his head. "I'm not very good at romantic gestures."

"Neither am I. But let's think about it… You could bake it into a pastry. She might like that."

Noah frowned. "I read story on the internet about a woman who choked on a wedding ring during a proposal like that."

"Okay. I was just thinking bakery. So…no food-related proposal. Did you want something splashy? Skywriting? Dinner cruise? I know a guy."

"She doesn't like splashy."

"No. You're right. She doesn't. What does she like?"

"The bakery," Noah said on a laugh. But then, all of a sudden, it wasn't funny. Not funny at all.

Because he'd thought of the perfect idea.

Amy was nervous the day of the TV interview. Who wouldn't be?

Even though the boys were back from camp and she and Noah had—kind of—talked things through and everything was—kind of—normal again, she was on edge.

Granted, this coverage of her bakery was huge. Nerves were normal. She wished Noah was here for her to cling to, but he and Jax had taken a ride up north to visit his buddies at JBLM and weren't due back until this afternoon.

To her delight, the interview went well. They'd done a quick camera tour of the kitchen and storefront for B-roll, then they'd filmed her icing a cake and doing some other baking tasks. Then they'd filmed her helping a customer. They even filmed she and Dani, the segment producer, sampling some of the most popular items. It was all a little unnerving because Amy wasn't used to being in front of the camera and every little gesture felt fake. But she did it. Because she loved her bakery.

After the B-roll shots, they closed the shop and arranged a tiny set in the corner of the bakery. Then she and Dani had a casual intimate chat between two bakery-loving friends and a full three-perspective camera crew and booms.

It was surreal.

But once the conversation got started and Amy forgot about the cameras, and they started talking about the bakery she loved… Well, that had been wonderful.

They were just finishing up, and the crew was starting to break down their gear when she heard the thrum of Noah's bike and her heart lifted. He'd only been gone overnight, but she'd missed him.

"Who is that?" Dani asked as she peered out the window at the hottie in the black leathers levering off his bike.

"That's Noah. My...boyfriend." He was a sight more than that. "He's been out of town." They watched as he reached into his saddlebags and pulled something out. And—*aw!*—he'd brought her flowers. How sweet.

He stopped short after he came through the door and saw the camera crew and shot her a look. "Hey, you. Am I interrupting?" he asked as he handed her the flowers.

"Hey, you," she said giving him a kiss, which he returned. The flowers were nice, but gosh, it was good to smell *him* again. "We're just finishing up. Noah, this is Dani. She's producing the segment. And this is her crew, Chris, Tom and Mike."

Noah shook Dani's hand and gave the crew a nod, because their hands were all full of gear. "So... How'd it go?" He asked Amy, but Dani answered.

"Fabulous. This bakery is adorable. And what a wonderful little town. I'm going to come back when I get some vacation time."

Noah nodded. "That's the way I felt when I first arrived. Then I just decided to stay." He shot a look at Amy that made her heart warm.

As much as she just wanted to sink into his presence, she couldn't—yet. Technically, she was still on the clock. "Dani, thank you again," she said, thrusting out her hand. "I can't tell you how much I appreciate your coverage."

"My pleasure. I assure you. Your goodies were delicious."

"Oh. That reminds me. I made up a sampler pack for you guys to take on the road." She headed behind the counter to pull out the large box.

Dani said, "Oh, how sweet. You didn't have to do that," but the crew gave a little cheer. It was a long drive back to Seattle, so Amy gave them all coffees for the road as well.

As she and Noah stood on the sidewalk and waved them off, Amy's heart was full. For all its awkwardness, it had been a really good experience and she was brimming with excitement for the future. The future of the bakery was only part of it.

With a sigh, she took Noah's hand, and they headed back inside. "Happy?" he asked.

"So happy." She pulled him into a big hug. "What a great day. And I'm so glad you're back. I missed you."

"I missed you too."

"Did you have fun with your friends?"

"It was great to see them, yeah. But I'm glad to be back."

"I'm glad you're back too." She shot him a quirky grin. "Just in time to help me clean up." She was only teasing, of course. She'd cleaned before the crew had arrived.

"Amy," he said. There was something in his tone, something that caught her attention and wiped the smile from her face. He sucked in a deep breath and raked his hair back and seemed, suddenly, ill at ease.

"Noah? What is it?"

"I, ah, have something I need to say."

Her heart stalled, just a little bit, but when he dropped

to one knee, it started pounding like a big bass drum. "Amy Tolliver—Oh, shoot." He paused and fished around in his pocket, pulled out a box, revealing a beautiful diamond ring, which he thrust in her direction, then continued. "You are the home I've been looking for my entire life and I would like nothing more than to spend my life in your arms. Will you marry me?"

As adorable as all that was, the cock of his head and the solemn, sincere look in his eyes sealed the deal. Gosh, she loved him. Loved him so, so much it made her chest hurt. It was all she could do not to kiss him right there. But he was waiting for a response, and she didn't want to be rude. "Oh, Noah," she said. "Yes. Yes. Of course, I will ma—"

But that was as far as she got because he leaped to his feet, whipped her into his arms and kissed her.

He kissed her long and hard.

"So…" he said when they finally came back down to earth. "How do we tell the boys?"

She set her palm on his cheek and sent him a smile. "Together."

Everything would be together, from here on out. And it was wonderful.

As a PJ, Noah had done some pretty scary things, but he'd never felt as much trepidation as this—sitting across the kitchen table from John J. and Georgie that evening, with Amy by his side—preparing to break the big news.

Man, he was sweating.

"So, boys," he said after clearing his throat several times. "Your mom and I have something to talk to you about." He glanced at her, and she nodded in encouragement. "You know that your mom and I are good friends, but she's also my girlfriend."

John J. fiddled with his toy airplane. "We know that."

"You do?"

Georgie shrugged. "She kissed you at John J.'s birthday party. Duh."

Noah and Amy glanced at each other and laughed. Yeah. She had. They hadn't realized the boys had noticed.

"Well…" Amy picked up the thread. "Noah and I have realized that we love each other. And we want to get married."

John J.'s brow wrinkled. "What does that mean?"

"Well, that means that Noah will live with us now."

"And forever." It bore mentioning.

"In Jax's room?" John J. asked.

"Um, no," Amy said. "He'll sleep in my room. With me."

Noah nodded. *Damn straight.*

Georgie thought about this for a minute and frowned. "Will you be our new dad?" he asked.

Well, hell. How could he answer that? "I, ah, don't want to replace your dad…"

John J. looked up at him with a woebegone expression. "Don't you *want* to be our dad?"

Noah swallowed. Hard. "I would. I would like that very much. But your dad will still be your dad. He'll always be your dad. I guess that's what I'm trying to say."

"So, you'll be like an extra kind of dad?" Leave it to Georgie to explain it with logic.

"Sure. If you're okay with that."

They boys exchanged a look and then, in tandem, nodded.

"Yes," Georgie said. "We'd like that."

John J. nodded solemnly and parroted, "We'd like that."

"There's more," Amy said. "When Noah and I get married, there may be brothers or sisters in the future. How do you feel about that?"

Both boys stilled and exchanged another glance and then Georgie said, "Well, I wouldn't mind a brother. But girls are kind of gross."

Noah barked a laugh. "We'll take that under advisement," he said.

But to be honest, he'd be happy with either one. Or both. Heck, he was just plain happy.

Though Amy had known that the boys loved Noah, she hadn't been sure how they would react to the idea of him joining the family. Their acceptance of the idea of having a new dad—and potential siblings—was a huge relief. There was still a lot to think about and a lot to do—including breaking the news of the engagement to her family—but the most important thing for Amy was that the boys were on board.

Since Nat and Jax had invited the whole family over for a barbeque at their place that afternoon, they were the first to find out—as though they didn't already expect it. All Amy had to do was flash the ring, and Natalie squealed.

After congratulations and lots of hugs, the guys went out to the yard and start up the barbeque. Naturally the boys—who loved fire—went with them.

After they left, Nat gusted a sigh. "Oh, my goodness, Amy. I am so happy for you! Look at that ring!" She gave Amy a hug another hug. "I am so excited for you."

Amy grinned. "Thanks."

"So," Nat said as they set about setting the table and laying out all the sides Nat had made. "What are you thinking about for a wedding?"

Amy shrugged. There wasn't a lot of time, and they both knew it. "Neither of us wants anything fancy. We'll probably just go to the county courthouse."

Nat reared back, a look of horror on her face. "You can't do that."

"It's what George and I did."

"That's my point. You deserve a real wedding."

"That is a real wedding."

"You know what I mean. The flowers and the dress and...family." And yeah. That was the thing, wasn't it? She and George had eloped. Their wedding had been witnessed by strangers. They hadn't cared—they'd been so into each other and so thrilled to be together and so young, they hadn't really thought about anything else. Or anyone else. They certainly hadn't realized how eloping would disappoint the family.

Natalie sighed. "Momma deserves to see you get married. And I think it would be important for the boys too."

She had a point. A ceremony would be a memory they would carry with them. It would be one of those great markers in their lives between a before and after. It would help inform their impressions of marriage and their own relationships in years to come. But... "Ugh. It's so much work, and I'm so busy as it is."

Nat's eyes lit up. "Why don't you share my wedding?"

Amy gaped at her. "We're not doing that. This is your first wedding."

"My only wedding, hello."

"Sorry, yes. That's what I meant. It's *your* special day. Noah and I can go to the county courthouse."

Nat made a face. "Eww. No."

"I've already been married. It's not a big deal."

"It is a big deal, if not for you, then for Noah and the boys. It's a ceremony. A rite of passage—"

"Something *you* shouldn't have to share."

Natalie's eyes went soft, glinted. "I don't mind sharing it with you." Something in her tone, the sincerity, the wistfulness, made tears prick Amy's lids.

Amy softened at her sister's generosity. "I wouldn't mind sharing it with you either."

The guys walked in just then, and Nat said, "So Amy and I have been talking about the wedding plans, and I had a pretty brilliant idea."

"If you do say so yourself." Amy laughed.

"What?" Jax asked, a chunk of cornbread halfway to his mouth.

"She wants to do a double wedding," Amy gusted, investing her exasperation in every syllable, just so they would realize how ridiculous an idea it was.

The men, as usual, did not perform as expected. Jax and Noah shared a glance, and then, in tandem, they both shrugged.

"Sounds good to me," Jax said.

"Me too." Noah grabbed a slice of cornbread as well.

"Come on." Nat grabbed Amy's hand. "It'll be fun to do it together. It'll be a bonding experience."

Oh, that sounded nice. Really nice.

When the rest of the family arrived, they loved the idea. Momma was delighted—she'd always knew he was a fine young man, she said. And Celeste was in tears, but Amy could tell, they were happy tears. She hugged Noah and then hugged Amy and then hugged Noah again.

Oh, Amy thought as she sat back and watched her family embrace the man she loved, it had been a long hard road. She'd been through heartbreak and loss, but she'd grown through it and persevered and created a new form of herself, of her life, through the chaos.

She was happy. So much happier than she ever thought she could be again.

That happiness had come through hard work and perseverance, from collecting all the broken pieces and knitting them together again. With care and patience and a whole lot of love. It hadn't been easy. But it had been worth it.

The future now spread before her in a glorying array, seeded with hope and joy.

Noah came over, once everyone was done hugging him, and put his arm around her shoulders. "You okay?" he asked with a kiss to her brow.

"Okay?" She shot him a smile, one filled with all the delight and love she thought her heart could possibly hold. "I'm better than okay," she said, going up on her toes to kiss him. "I'm perfect."

He chuckled and tugged her closer. "Yeah," he said. "I know." Then he kissed her again. This time on the lips. Right there in front of everyone.

And yes, life was perfect indeed.

Epilogue

For Noah, his wedding day was like a dream, passing in a blur. It surprised him how quickly it all happened. And while the wedding vows didn't take long at all, the path to this place had taken him a lifetime.

But what he did remember, what he would always remember, was the look on Amy's face when she said *I do*. And her joy when he responded in kind. It was, by far, the most precious moment he'd ever experienced.

As the preacher said those magic words, *husband and wife*, something potent swelled in his heart. Because now, after everything he'd been through, after all his searching…he belonged. Finally, he had a family. To love and to cherish from this day forward.

He was a husband now and a dad—with two amazing young men to raise. It was a chance to flip the script and be the best damn father in the world. A chance to give them everything he hadn't had. Georgie and John J. and the new baby, when it came. They would get all of him.

Ma had been right. It didn't matter where you came from. It mattered where you were.

And he was here.

He was home.

* * * * *

Look for Celeste's story, the next installment in
New York Times *bestselling author Sabrina York's*
new miniseries for Harlequin Special Edition,
The Tuttle Sisters of Coho Cove.
On sale January 2024, wherever
Harlequin Books and ebooks are sold.

And catch up with Natalie and Jax's story,
The Soldier's Refuge
Available now!

Get 3 FREE REWARDS!

We'll send you 2 FREE Books <u>plus</u> a FREE Mystery Gift.

FREE
Value Over
$20

Both the **Harlequin® Special Edition** and **Harlequin® Heartwarming™** series feature compelling novels filled with stories of love and strength where the bonds of friendship, family and community unite.

YES! Please send me 2 FREE novels from the Harlequin Special Edition or Harlequin Heartwarming series and my FREE Gift (gift is worth about $10 retail). After receiving them, if I don't wish to receive any more books, I can return the shipping statement marked "cancel." If I don't cancel, I will receive 6 brand-new Harlequin Special Edition books every month and be billed just $5.49 each in the U.S. or $6.24 each in Canada, a savings of at least 12% off the cover price, or 4 brand-new Harlequin Heartwarming Larger-Print books every month and be billed just $6.24 each in the U.S. or $6.74 each in Canada, a savings of at least 19% off the cover price. It's quite a bargain! Shipping and handling is just 50¢ per book in the U.S. and $1.25 per book in Canada.* I understand that accepting the 2 free books and gift places me under no obligation to buy anything. I can always return a shipment and cancel at any time by calling the number below. The free books and gift are mine to keep no matter what I decide.

Choose one:
- ☐ **Harlequin Special Edition** (235/335 BPA GRMK)
- ☐ **Harlequin Heartwarming Larger-Print** (161/361 BPA GRMK)
- ☐ **Or Try Both!** (235/335 & 161/361 BPA GRPZ)

Name (please print)

Address   Apt. #

City   State/Province   Zip/Postal Code

Email: Please check this box ☐ if you would like to receive newsletters and promotional emails from Harlequin Enterprises ULC and its affiliates. You can unsubscribe anytime.

Mail to the **Harlequin Reader Service:**
IN U.S.A.: P.O. Box 1341, Buffalo, NY 14240-8531
IN CANADA: P.O. Box 603, Fort Erie, Ontario L2A 5X3

Want to try 2 free books from another series! Call 1-800-873-8635 or visit www.ReaderService.com.

HSEHW23